AMY J. HEART

LOVING L

DAMAGED SOULS GOLDEN HEARTS
BOOK ONE

Author's Note

Loving L starts with a glimpse of L at sixteen, hinting at the abuse that shaped him. It quickly moves to his last night on the streets at almost nineteen, before jumping four years forward to the heart of this gritty, love-heals-trauma story.

"It's beautifully and evocatively written. It feels personal and intimate. It might be difficult for some readers as it deals with dark and serious issues... With that said, this is a tale of hope, new beginnings, romance and love, with a glorious HEA." – **Amazon review**

"I want a Lightning Boy of my own! Sweet, horrifying, and touching, this story is one not to be missed. I highly recommend this book!" **– Amazon review**

Prologue

L

Yellow light spills through a crack in the doorway, the color pale and sickly, reminding me of the monster who creeps into my bedroom in its wake.

"Go away," I croak, dragging the covers higher around my shoulders.

I hum under my breath, trying to escape. The aim is to float away from my body, up to the ceiling, so I can look down at the blue covers that bind me to the mattress as firmly as rope or chains would. I need to see them from afar, not feel them pressing down, not be underneath them, bound and trapped like a trussed-up hog.

I squeeze my eyes shut and try harder to *leave*—to go somewhere else. Somewhere better. *Anywhere* will do as long as it's out of this room, this bed, this house. But preferably somewhere safer. Wherever Mom is would be perfect.

Wrapping my arms tightly around myself, I rock back and forth, the old bed frame squeaking. The sound is soothing. It really shouldn't be.

Why the hell did you have to go and die on me, Mom? Why?

"You're so skinny, my little lion," she used to say. "I need to fatten you up with treats. From now on, you can have dessert three times a day—buttery cannelés for breakfast, lunch, and dinner."

My fingers, cold and sweaty, fumble under the pillow searching for my most treasured possession, needing to feel its smooth texture, its familiar edges, lined with creases from carrying it around in my pocket all the time.

It's the sketch she did of me when I was ten, sitting by the creek, long hair almost touching my bare shoulders, a goofy grin on my dial aimed right at her. I remember every single second of that day like it was yesterday. Sunny and warm, the familiar drone of insects filling the air, and I was happy. Loved. Not alone.

Not like now.

The monster who's in my room now doesn't care about how skinny I am. Or whether I'm happy. All *he* ever says to me is, "Cut your hair, stupid. Are you a boy or what? Or *what*, I reckon." Then he laughs. Gravel on gravel, always grinding my bones to dust.

He thinks he's so funny.

But this guy is the opposite of a comedian. Yeah, he's the devil incarnate.

A floorboard creaks near the bed.

"Go away!" I yell in French as I choke on rising nausea.

"Speak English, you little shit. Your pretty French momma ain't here anymore. No one can understand that rubbish."

"I said get out!" I switch to English this time, my words echoing in the darkness. Loud. Then swallowed by the shadows. Nobody can hear me.

No one ever hears me.

"That's better. Now I can understand you." He does the gross evil-clown laugh again. "Do I look like some fancy Frenchman to you?"

"No. You look like an asshole," I mutter into my pillow, flinching as the sound of leather sliding through denim cuts the air. *Whoosh-crack!*

Shit. It's his belt. Will I ever learn to shut my mouth? Probably not. I might be scared, but I'm always gonna fight back.

"Don't say you didn't ask for it," he says, his voice rough with the promise of violence.

While I wait for the blows to rain down, I tense every muscle, clench my fists so hard they ache. Then it starts. The pain.

I won't cry. I won't scream. It isn't happening to me. I'm somewhere else. Somewhere far, far away. Safe.

I curl into a ball, become as small as I can. I think of my name, reduce myself down to a letter—just one. It's easier this way if I'm no longer a person. Just a letter.

A letter is nothing. Can't be hurt. Can't be damaged.

"Go away," I whisper. I bite my lip, liquid metal filling my mouth.

"You're only getting what you deserve. I see what a loser you are, boy. I know everything about you. Hear your every thought. See your every move."

Yeah? Well, here's something he doesn't know... Tomorrow I turn sixteen, and this year I've promised myself a special birthday present. Revenge.

It'll be an awesome gift for me and a great surprise for him. One he'll never see coming.

Because tomorrow, *he'll* finally get what *he* deserves. What all monsters should receive at some point in their lives.

A hole blown right through their guts.

Not long to wait now.

Not long at all.

I crack my eyes open, searching for the LED numbers that flash on the bedside clock—12:03.

Guess I'm sixteen already.

Chapter 1

L

"**O**h, hell, Lightning. Yeah."

I reach up in the dark, wrap my fingers around his neck, and squeeze. I want to make sure it hurts when he comes. His skinny hips buck erratically, his dick battering the back of my throat. Fingers bury deep in my hair, pulling and tearing. I crush his windpipe tighter and whack his hands away.

"Don't. Touch. Me," I say, slamming him against the restroom wall. He grunts and then makes gurgling sounds. Tasting the first salty drops of come on my tongue, I shove away from him and spit off to the side.

Fucking gross.

Scrubbing my mouth with the back of my hand, I stumble to my feet. The guy's moans and ragged breaths echo off the tiles, making me want to punch him. He looks so stupid, suit pants crumpled at his ankles, a hand rubbing his pudgy stomach in the afterglow.

The water from the faucet is cold as I rinse my mouth out. Spit. Gulp. Swallow. Repeat.

The creep speaks. "Well, you certainly live up to your name. No wonder you're notorious around the scene. That was damn fast and—"

"Shut up. Just give me the money."

I straighten and look down at him with my arms folded. The stance draws attention to the size of my biceps, my chest muscles, the tatts curling out of the sleeve of my T-shirt. It says *don't fuck with me.*

He doesn't. He's a lightweight. Small. Scrawny. Ugly. And by the sound of his cultured voice, rich as fuck. He paws his jacket and withdraws his wallet.

"It's fifty," I say, just in case he's forgotten.

Dark eyes roam my body. "Oh, I think you're worth significantly more than that." He pulls out two Benjamins, and my heart thuds one hard beat. Fuck. Yeah, he's loaded *and* stupid.

He waves the bills between us, then whips them away as I make a grab for them. "Wait on," he says.

Oh, great. Here we go. Looks like I'll have to smack him. But, nope, his hand delves back into his wallet, and he produces three more bills.

"Because I'm feeling extra generous tonight, here's five hundred. That absolutely blew my mind, and you're the most gorgeous thing I've ever seen. I wouldn't want you to starve out there and disappear forever."

I snarl at him as he puts the money in my palm.

"Tell you what, you swallow next time, and I'll double that."

Really? Fuck. This guy *is* an idiot.

Shaking my head, I give him my back and strut to the door.

"See you soon, Lightning," he sing-songs like I'm his pizza delivery guy.

Paint flakes off the door frame when I grip it and dig my fingernails in deep. "I hope not," I mutter. I glance over my shoulder and find him still slumped against the bricks. "You might wanna pull your pants up before you leave. You've got nothing to be proud of."

Shoving the money in my pocket, I walk into the crisp night air.

Hell. Just my luck. It's raining.

Chapter 2

L

Other than me, there's hardly anyone out hustling in the park. That's weird for a Friday night.

The rain falls harder, but I don't mind. Thanks to the rich idiot who's probably still in the restroom with his pants around his ankles, I'm smiling as I stride along the path in the dark.

My work for the night is done.

And if I use this money wisely, I might not have to look at another dick for at least a week. Rent sure is cheap when you sleep under a bridge.

A shiver runs over my skin. Man. It would be heaven to have a break from this hell. Even a short one.

But I'll need more money soon because I plan to blow tonight's earnings faster than I did that suit-guy. I haven't eaten anything since yesterday and stuffing myself full of fast food isn't gonna satisfy the aching hole in my gut. No way.

Tonight, I want something amazing. Like the French stuff Mom used to cook when I was a kid before she went and died on me.

Memories of the smell of hot butter and Mom's floral skin twist my gut into hard knots. I push away images, sounds, and every thought of her—just like I always do. Because remembering anything good about my mom leads to bad thoughts. And memories of *him.*

The wail of a distant siren saves me from spiraling black thoughts, dragging me back to the here and now. It's shitty, but it's my reality. I pat the pocket of my jeans to make sure the wad of cash hasn't disintegrated. By some miracle, it's still there.

Chunks of wet hair hang in my eyes. My T-shirt is soaked through, and the rain doesn't look like it'll let up anytime soon. But it smells clean and fresh. And normal. And I need some normal in my life.

It's what my gut burns for tonight.

Fuck it. I want *better* than normal. To taste something *incredible* instead of gross. Obliterate the foul tang of a stranger's come. Pretend that I'm exactly like everyone else. I want people to look me in the eye without disgust—like they can't wait to rush away and cleanse me off their retinas.

But those strangers are right. Being homeless is barely existing.

But, hey, I've got five hundred bucks getting damp in my jeans right now. I can afford anything I want. Even something special.

Leaves squish under my boots as I cross a barely lit path, taking a shortcut through grass and trees to exit the park fast and get into the restaurant district.

It must be around eight-thirty, so the streets are busy. I bump shoulders with Friday night revelers as I stride past Vietnamese cafes, seafood restaurants, strip joints, gin bars, dive bars. Whatever you want to shovel in or guzzle down—you name it—it's all here for your pleasure. I head east, pushing through crowds, until the clothes get fancier, the noses point higher.

Peering in restaurant windows, I try not to sneer at the diners who stare back at me, looking outraged over their wine glasses.

"Hey, look out!" a gangster-dude says, smacking into me. I stumble sideways because he's a little bigger than me, which is rare. I might be young, but I'm tall, and I spend a lot of time hanging off beams and tree branches to keep strong. Being homeless, it's best if your appearance says *fuck-with-me-idiot-and-you'll-be-sorry*. Mine blares that sentiment loud and clear.

When I glance up, I spy a gold sign swinging gently from an awning. The way it moves, glinting in the streetlights, is spellbinding.

L'Arbre. Means *The Tree* in French.

Such a stupid name for a restaurant. Swirling leaves and branches are embossed over the sign. They've entangled me, and I can't look away. I stare for ages as if this is all I need—me and the awesome patterns—nothing else.

But I *do* need something else. I need to see inside this joint.

With my hands stuffed into my pockets, I walk in a daze to the window. The bottom half is covered in gold paint or some weird fabric that keeps the tables, the layout, and the customers hidden. It's a French grill restaurant and going by what I can see of the ceiling—again covered in gold—it's swanky as fuck. Upscale. Out of my league. And I want inside so bad it hurts.

My mouth twisting, I inspect my clothes. The Nirvana T-shirt I stole yesterday is kind of clean. My jeans with the knees ripped out, not so much. I earned every tear in them, too, and not in a cool way. My black boots have gaffer-taped soles. Shit. I look exactly like what I am. A hobo.

My stomach groans loudly. I need to get inside this place and eat until I can think straight again. But I hesitate. They'll probably take one look at me and kick me back into the gutter.

What will I lose if I try? Only my dignity and that's long gone. If they call the cops, I can run fast. So, fuck it, I'm going in. I tuck my hair behind my ears, a futile attempt to look more respectable, and open the door.

I've stepped into a dream. One of those nightmares where you turn up to school dressed in chaps and a dumb hat, and it turns out wild-frontier day isn't until next week. Or you're completely naked at a funeral.

The cavernous space drips with gold and, fuck, it's loud. Classical music plays, but it's the good type. Full of warmth and life. There are suits everywhere, ladies in slinky dresses, and a sea of shiny up-dos floating above swanlike necks.

A beautiful blond girl slides out from behind a metallic desk, velvety, red dress shimmering over her thighs as she glides toward me. She's smiling, but it looks a little strained.

"Good evening, sir." She tips her head regally and glances down at her copper clipboard. Like the sign out the front, it has leaves and branches engraved in the metal. "May I have the name of your booking, please?"

My heart thuds so loudly that I'm amazed she doesn't start tapping her pen along with the beat. I clear my throat to drown out the noise. "Ah, a booking. I don't have one."

Smiling politely, she scans my body and then my face. "And the number in your party this evening?"

"What?" I say dumbly.

"How many people will be joining you?"

Shit. I should at least try to talk like my brain works. I can do a lot better than this. I don't spend days in libraries reading shit, trying to keep stuff in my head for nothing. I've been out of school now for thirteen months, and I miss it like hell.

"Uh, it's just me." *Man*, listen to me. No great improvement there.

"A table for one, then, sir. I'll confirm we can accommodate you. Please wait there." She slinks off behind a long bar tucked against the wall and consults with a man. He's Don Draper smooth, teeth so white they could blind you.

Don ducks his slick head around a metal column and checks me out while flashing those blinding whites. It's a smile I know well. It means trouble, and it makes me feel bad.

He gives the girl a nod, and she weaves her way through the surreal setting toward me. Feeling like I'm watching a movie, I hold my breath.

"We have a lovely table for you tonight, sir. I'm sure you'll be very pleased with it."

Yeah, I'm pretty fucking sure I will be, too.

I nod. "Great."

"Please follow me," she says, leading the way.

Thank fuck. I'm about to pass out from hunger. The food smells are pure torture.

I squelch my way through the restaurant, hoping my socks will dry out soon.

A long table flows down the center of the room, smaller ones scattered on either side. They're overflowing with flowers and food and surrounded by chattering, bored-looking rich folk. A massive mural adorns the back wall, biblical but somehow sexy. Gold drips like stalactites from the ceiling. I feel like I'm in an old European palace.

Sleek heads follow my bedraggled progress through the room. I must look hilarious, dressed for a rock concert while their attire is *A-Night-at-the-Opera* slick.

The girl stops at a table for two that has a perfect view of the whole joint. I'm amazed they aren't going to shove me out of sight.

The white linen is neat and clean with way too many utensils laid out in a complicated arrangement. I have no idea what to do with most of them.

"Will this be satisfactory?" she asks, patting her perfect hair.

I grin like a kid. I can't help myself. "Fuck, yeah… ah… I mean absolutely."

She giggles. Not something you normally hear from an ice queen. Guess I'm a funny guy.

"Where's the bathroom? On the way here, I came off my bike," I lie. "And now I need to, you know, freshen up a little."

She gives directions, and I enter the most amazing restroom I'm sure I'll ever live to see.

Man, these people love their gold. It's everywhere. The rest is black tiles and mirrors. Far too many mirrors. Everywhere I glance, I see my reflection staring back at me, and I really don't need reminding of what I look like. No thanks.

The central chandelier is about the size of a baby elephant. Rainbow prisms bounce off the wallpaper and my clothes, an improvement to my shitty appearance, but it makes me dizzy.

I take a piss and then, ignoring the mirrors, make friends with the soap. I splash water on my skin, comb wet fingers through my hair, and then scrub my face. Fluffy hand towels hang from copper rails. As I press a cream-colored towel against my cheek, longing seeps into my chest—for what, I'm not exactly sure.

While I dry off as best as I can, I sniff my armpits, then laugh. Shit, I smell like fucking soap.

After that, I stare at my reflection like an imbecile. I'm shocked. I don't recognize myself. The guy gazing back at me looks crazy, desperate, and as mean as all the other assholes I meet living rough out there on the streets.

Stares from diners burn holes through me as I trek back to the table. Fuck these people snickering and whispering to each other. I don't care what they think.

Cutlery clatters as I take a seat and grin at the girl who hands me a fancy, fabric-covered menu with one hand, while stifling a giggle with the other. She's probably laughing at my wet hair.

Biting my lip, I check out what's on offer. It's all in French. And, of course, I can understand it. Not everything, but quite a lot. It makes my chest ache and brings my mom to mind.

What? That's fucking ridiculous. Am I eleven years old or nearly nineteen? I push back memories. Sounds. Soft touches. Quiet words and French nursery rhymes. Shit, this place is bad for my health.

"Shall I suggest something, sir?"

"What? No, thanks. I can read it," I say, frowning.

Of all the posh places in the area, trust me to pick a French one. "I'll have the Côte de Bœuf Grillée," I say in a perfect Toulouse accent. Thanks, Mom, for that useless skill. Fuck, but it hurts to hear that sound, that language come out of my mouth. I slap the menu on the table so I can't see the words anymore.

Funny how the girl, whose name tag says *Sandrine*, has a proper smile for me now. As if speaking French automatically makes me a bad-boy billionaire. Potentially someone to date. She wouldn't be looking at me like that if she knew what I'd been doing on my knees an hour ago.

"And, hey, could I have a beer, please? Your choice."

She bats her eyelashes. "What attracts you in a beer?" The way she licks her red lips makes me suspect she's not talking about beverages.

"Something fresh. Clean tasting."

"Coming right up," she purrs, and swings her svelte hips away. She's pretty sexy. If I was normal. If I wasn't fucked up, I'd definitely want to sleep with her.

There's nothing to do while I wait for dinner other than listen to my stomach moan. I don't even have a cell I can pretend to scroll through texts on as though I have a life. Like I've got family or friends. Or anyone who gives a shit.

So I kick back and enjoy the insanely great food smells, eavesdropping on snippets of conversation. Then my beer arrives. This time, Don Draper serves me. Bubbly amber liquid gets poured into a glass, and the guy flirts his ass off while looking over his shoulder every few seconds at the girl behind the bar.

They've got some kind of game going on that involves me. Maybe they're trying to figure out the story of the weird street urchin who somehow made it through the velvet ropes. Or maybe they're just playing a cruel game for laughs, wondering which one of them I'd like to fuck against some dumpsters in the back alley. But whatever it is they're hoping for, I ain't biting. I'm polite, but

I want this guy to go away so I can enjoy my normal—no, my *special*—time in peace. Even if it's only for an hour.

Chapter 3

L

The beer gives me something to do with my hands. It's icy and goes straight to my head courtesy of my empty stomach. The buzz makes me careless, and as I check out an elegant older lady's meal, I accidentally lock eyes with her.

The plate sizes look decent. Thank fuck. I'd probably cry if they were bird sized.

This woman is interesting. Middle-aged, very classy, and I guess the best word to describe her face is handsome. She raises a regal eyebrow and one side of her scarlet lips at me. I give her a nod, ignoring the silver foxes in sharp suits at her side.

Better not look her way again. Don't wanna give her any ideas.

Shit, I can feel her staring as I drink my beer, play with my knife, and then a dessert spoon. I won't look. Nope, I won't look.

Finally, my meal arrives. Ribs. The juicy, fatty smell nearly knocks me out. The hot, spicy sizzle. Before the ice queen has even left the table, I'm hunkered over my plate, attacking the meat like an animal. I *am* an animal, and I don't give a shit if I look uncivilized.

All my senses narrow to the meat in front of me. I focus and just *feel* and *breathe* the meal down in greedy mouthfuls. It's unreal.

In under five minutes, I've used a whole basket of bread and soaked up every orgasmic drop on the white plate. I'm exhausted. This feels like some kind of transcendence, like good sex must for normal people. Transporting. Base, savage, and the best thing ever.

When I lean back, my chair creaks. I don't realize I've closed my eyes until I hear a raspy, cultured voice above me.

"You enjoyed that, darling?"

My eyes fly open. It's the attractive older woman standing in front of me. "Yes, *ma'am*, I sure did." I drag the title out in a sarcastic drawl.

I wonder how much dough she'll offer me to eat *her* out for dessert.

"Can I join you?" she asks.

Here we go.

"Sure. Why not."

She sinks into the chair, crossing her well-toned legs gracefully. "My dinner guests and I were watching you."

The two swish dudes lift their glasses at us.

"Yeah?" I smirk. "No kidding."

She plays with a sapphire pendant that sparkles between her breasts. Probably real. But I bet those breasts cost more than I could earn in a lifetime. She's so noble looking I can't even *think* the word tits when I'm sitting this close to her.

"You're an incredibly beautiful young man."

"Really? Huh. Thanks, I guess."

"I imagine you've heard that a lot."

I nod. I sure fucking have.

"Let me buy you a drink. What do you fancy? Top shelf whiskey? Or we could split a bottle of the most expensive champagne *L'Arbre* has to offer."

"You could afford that?" I ask.

"Yes, of course."

Man. "I'll just have another beer."

"You're young."

I nod.

"So, no more than twenty?" she guesses.

"I'm almost nineteen."

"That young. And what is your name?"

I don't want to tell her. No, maybe I do. It'll be fun to watch her expression change and grow scornful.

"Lightning," I say, lifting my chin.

She smiles but doesn't give me the satisfaction of looking shocked. "You have very, *very* blue eyes. And so beautifully shaped. Do you wear colored contacts?"

Jesus. I laugh. "No. They're my real eyes."

She calls the waitress over. Orders drinks in an arrogant manner.

Licking her glossy lips, she shakes her head at me. "Your face. The bone structure. Your body. It's all perfectly packaged raw sex appeal. A tattooed avenging angel. You are exactly what I need."

I'm sure I am. And she's right about the avenging part.

I lean in and give her a blast of the electric eyes she's so into. "You know, lady, this is getting boring. I reckon your friends over there must be missing you by now."

"I see this toughness you exude is no act." She smiles and reaches into a black and gold purse. It goes nicely with the decor. "But frankly, I think your bark is worse than your bite. Otherwise, I would not be so drawn to you." She pushes a card across the table. A business card? Who uses those anymore?

I check out both impressive sides of the card. Ariana Wilde. Surely not her real name.

"I'm an agent for one of the most prestigious modeling agencies in both Europe and America. I can procure you a tremendous amount of work." She pauses and pats my hand. "And I can make you very rich."

I choke a little, spluttering on my beer. That's not what I was expecting her to say. "Bullshit."

"I would not lie to you. It's the truth. So, tell me about yourself, Lightning. What do you currently do for a living?"

"Most people call me L."

"All right, then—L it is." Her smile grows. "The clients will love that. It suits you. Wonderfully direct and sexy. Are you a struggling artist? Perhaps a musician?"

"Wrong, but sort of close. I live under a bridge and suck dirtbags off just so I can buy a burger and fries every few days. And I try not to die of starvation. That's my main goal So, yeah, you were right. I'm a creative guy."

This time, her face *does* change, and her expression turns my blood piping hot.

I fucking hate pity. *Hate* it.

"So how much are you thinking of offering me to fuck you tonight? Got a car parked nearby? Because you probably wouldn't wanna take me back to your home. That'd be dangerous, you know? And I should mention that as a bonus, I give great head. In fact, I'm famous for it." I don't tell her that I have zero experience using these spectacular skills on a female. "That's how I got my name... you know, Lightning? Because I'm real quick at getting someone off."

She makes a shushing sound and puts a soft hand over mine. "L, stop. Just be quiet, and I will make a call to a friend. This man works for my agency, as I hope you soon will. We're going to help you."

I don't understand what she means. Help me? People don't do that for nothing.

"My friend can answer all your questions. Now relax. I promise you won't have to do those horrible things to survive ever again."

While she taps on her phone, I can't stop swallowing. There's a lump about the size of a packet of smokes in my throat that won't shift no matter what I do.

When she holds the cell up to her ear—it's gold, of course—a wide smile brightens her face, making her look trustworthy. "Angelo darling!" she says when someone answers. "Yes, of *course* it's me. How many other Arianas do you know? Oh, I see, three others!" She tinkles out a laugh.

As she speaks, she's still wearing her kind face. But I'm not stupid. No one's honest or dependable. Even when they smile nicely, they all want things from you. Bad things. Wrong things. And then they cry and shout and blame you for making them want that stuff in the first place.

"So, darling, how was Tokyo?" she says into her cell. "Oh, that sounds wonderful. I want to hear all about it, but for now I need to speak to you about a favor for a new friend. His name is Lightning—" She breaks off to laugh again. "Yes, *Lightning*, that's what I said, didn't I? I'm hoping he'll come to work for me, but he has nowhere to stay. Wait until you see him. He's the most beautiful waif you could ever imagine."

Light glints off her jewelry as she scans me from head to toe.

"Yes, he's my new project. Angelo, can you look after him until we get him on his feet? The two of you will be great friends. I just know it." She smiles and nods and trills like a fucking parakeet. "Thank you, darling. You truly are an angel. Love you." She makes kissy noises and ends the call.

She turns and beams at me.

"So," I say. "Who the hell was that?"

"My Angelo. You're going to love him."

Yeah, not in the way she's imagining, I bet.

"No, L, don't scowl at me." Her graceful hand shoots out. "Pass me your cell instead."

I don't move.

"No phone?" She sighs and tut tuts at me. "I'll send one over to you in the morning. You're going to need it."

"Over to where?" I ask.

"To Angelo's, of course." She pulls out a sparkling pen—probably diamond encrusted—and scrawls on a napkin. "Here. Go to his apartment and stay there. Be warm. Be safe. Have fun. And let me fix your life for you."

I frown. "So... you don't want me to fuck you tonight?"

Grinning, her gaze sweeps over me. "L, what I want and what I do day to day, or night to night in your case, are two very different things. I'm going to help you, not take advantage of you."

There's that word again. Help. Yeah, right.

She smiles like a banker. "And make us both lots of money while I do so."

Bingo. There it is. The truth.

She summons a waitress, demands a triple serving of crème brûlée in one bowl, and tries to extract information from me while I attack the sickly caramel goodness. In six seconds, I've inhaled the lot.

I give her zilch details about my past, zero information about my current situation, and, still, she pays for my food and gives me a hundred-dollar bill for travel expenses.

As I get to my feet, all eyes in the room shift my way. Fucking busybodies, every single person in this joint.

"You'll go straight to Angelo's apartment, L darling, won't you?"

I nod. "Sure."

"Because I wouldn't want to lose you. Not when I've only just found you."

I laugh as I stuff the money and the napkin with the address deep into my pocket. It's funny to have someone care about what I do—even if they *are* only pretending.

The lady's thin, gangly limbs shoot up, balancing on towering heels, and she steps around the table like a racehorse heading for the feed bin. "This is not a joke, L. It is real. I want you to think of me as your personal fairy godmother come to grant your every wish."

Okay, sure, I think. Whatever you say.

One side of my mouth hikes into a smile, but I don't tell her that I believe she's nothing more than a crazy woman who gets a kick out of pretending to be a savior.

Her jewel-covered fingers clutch my T-shirt, pulling me closer, and then her arms wrap around my neck. She's fucking hugging me! No one's tried to hug me since Mom died.

My hands hang limp, heart dancing against my ribs.

I want to drop to the floor. I want to push her away.

My palm lifts, then falls. Then lifts again until it's resting against her back. This is insane. I'm touching someone and, as far as I can tell, there's nothing at stake here. Nothing to sell. No sex-vibe. Nothing. It's sleaze-free, as if she only wants to comfort me.

Two light kisses tickle my face. Then she strokes my cheek and says, "Trust me."

Guess I'll give it a go. Like I said before, I've got nothing to lose.

Whispers swirl as I sway through the tables, heading for the exit. It's hard not to listen to the shit people splash around.

The popular opinion is that I'm an indie actor. Some diners even think I front a rock band and Ariana is my manager. That's kind of cool. A few people bravely snap pics as I pass. It's all very hilarious.

If I wasn't freaking out, I'd be doubled over laughing.

Chapter 4

L

I stagger out of the restaurant, holding my aching stomach. Overindulging hurts like hell. And it feels *fucking amazing*.

It's nearly eleven. I'm so tired and freaked out by the idea that I might be warm tonight, might sleep on something soft, that the pavement rolls like an earthquake beneath my boots. Shit, there's actually a chance that maybe for the first time in months, *or longer*, I'll be safe.

Months? No, that's wrong. If I include the period of my messed-up childhood, it's more like years since I've gone to sleep without fearing for my life. An age since I've drifted off in peace.

I should find a cab and head straight over to this Angelo guy's place, like Ariana suggested. But I can't. My head is too messed up, spinning with the unbelievable events of the last couple of hours. I need to wander downtown for a while and process the fuck out of it. Because, somehow, within a very short space of time, I went from kneeling in a stinking restroom to lounging back in princely luxury.

And that's fucking insane.

It started out the same as every other shitty night I spent cruising for money to stay alive for a few more days.

Head pounding. Tick. o

Gut nauseous. Yep.

Sucked a guy off. Check.

Hated myself for doing it. Yeah.

Contemplated walking in front of a speeding car to end the misery. Roger that.

And then...

I dined at a palace. Got ogled by an ice queen, Don Draper, and my fairy godmother all within the same hour.

Wait just a second... back the fuck up.

Maybe if I shake my head hard enough, I'll wake and find that I'm back under the bridge—home sweet fucking home—while old Nelson steals my rotting blanket, the prodding of his bony fingers conjuring dreams of classy older ladies and walls that drip with gold. It's a dream. The last couple of hours were just a dream.

I stop dead in my tracks, and a guy crashes into me. "Move!" he says, circling around.

"Sorry, man," I say.

Weaving unsteadily in his expensive suit, he looks over his drunk-as-fuck shoulder. Dark eyebrows jump, and he zips around, walking backward to check me out. His eyes sleaze their way down my body. I curl my lip at him and not in a friendly way. On any other night, I'd have forced a crooked smile and a head flick. The universal signal for *hey, if you've got the money, then I've got the time.*

The guy takes a step forward, and I growl like a freaking werewolf. Giving me the finger, he turns and disappears into the mob of people. There goes an easy fifty bucks.

But, tonight, thanks to Ariana's fairy godmother wand, I don't think I need to give any fucks at all.

What I do need—is to see that business card again, make sure I didn't imagine it.

"Come on. Come on," I mutter, fumbling in my front pocket. With my luck, it's probably slipped through a tear in the denim, never to be seen again. Wait. I remember shoving it in my back pocket. Yep. I can feel the cardboard. Thick and smooth. Expensive.

Finally, I tug it out. Thank fuck. It's as real as the pavement cracks that I've been tripping over, the letters raised and glossy under my fingers. I can't stop rubbing them, looking at them. Even under the streetlights, they shine gold. What a surprise.

I stare at her name glowing in the light of an amber neon sign.

Ariana Wilde.

Ariana Wilde.

That lady is the most elegant thing I've ever seen. So confident. And probably full of shit.

More than anything, I want this woman to be on the level, but given the way my clusterfuck of a life has gone so far, it's unlikely. But the only way to know for sure is to knock on this dude's door. And if he turns out to be any sicker than the restroom guys, I can always pummel the crap out of him.

I drag my numb fingers through my hair and frown at the crowds stumbling in and out of cafes and bars. These people have jobs. Friends. Normal lives. And somewhere warm to sleep every single night.

I try not to let jealousy crush me because it sure as hell won't do me any damn good.

The rain continues to piss down, wind tearing through my cotton T-shirt. Shivering, I realize I need to steal a coat soon because the weather's already turning brutal.

But maybe I won't need to if Angelo and his spare bed end up being real and Ariana can magic me up some paid work for...

For what, getting my photo taken?

Yeah, right.

With my luck, I'll be the star of a snuff film and get my limbs hacked off in some dingy basement. Shoving the card deep in my pocket, I study the street, musing on what I should do next. Back to the bridge to attempt some shut eye? Or off to the potential serial killer's pad?

I decide to head for the seedy part of town—where I belong—so I can remind myself of the garbage I might leave behind if only I have the balls to take a gamble on Ariana and her promises.

Who am I kidding? I want that warm place to sleep tonight more than I want to score. I'll be rolling the dice for sure.

Drugs. Now that's a fucked-up scene. I try not to buy too often, the streets are hard enough without an addiction to feed, but getting high blurs the edges nicely, makes everything butter soft for a few hours. And shuts off the nightmare voice inside my head.

It's a filthy way to live, like an animal really, but I'm as human as those rich fuckers back there in the ritzy district. I deserve a chance at a better life, don't I?

After ten minutes of walking in a stupor, I'm back among the grunge, the strip clubs, and hookers.

Standing on Jackson with my hair dripping water down my back, I stare at the drug dealers and shitty burger joints. The sight of Joe Junior's in particular churns my gut. After the last meal I ate there, I puked for two days straight. That was a fun time to be homeless.

The rain-drenched street is like a movie set—a glistening, weird sci-fi porno film or something. To kill time, I check the people out, casting them roles in the movie I'm making in my head.

The old guy over there huddling in the hardware store doorway, his trench coat ragged, is a mad scientist on the run from a genetics lab. A yard away from him stands a girl in a black dress. She's the love interest or...

Wait. What the fuck?

I do a double, then a triple take back to her.

"God."

Did I just say that out loud?

I'm pretty sure I've never even *thought* the word *god* before. Growing up under the same roof as a real-life demon, there's never been any point in appealing to a higher power. Or enthusing out loud like a sixteen-year-old about a pretty girl. Any second now, I might start bouncing on my toes and squealing like a cheerleader.

Worse. What the fuck is happening to my body? I feel hot, itchy. Turned on.

Who the hell is this girl? And why does my dick seem to care?

Okay, I tell myself. *Chill out.*

I need to calm down and look at her again. She's just a girl.

So, I gulp down some air and then look.

Everything around her warps, sliding into slow motion like that Munch painting—The Scream—I saw in an art book at the library a while ago. Colors stretch and go fuzzy. Street noises disappear. This must be a dream, most likely a nightmare, but it's too early to tell yet.

This girl is kind of small. Her black dress is skintight, short, and not nearly warm enough. I can tell because she's rubbing her arms and almost jogging on the spot. Long hair, possibly brown, hangs past her shoulders. Her body is a true hourglass shape. And her face makes my chest ache like I've been shot through the ribcage with a poison arrow. Despite eating enough crème brûlée to fill a beer keg half an hour ago, my gut feels hollow.

Two words ram my brain over and over, sending shock waves through me.

I want.

I want.

That's all I can think, like I'm a kid staring in a shop window at a toy I'll never be lucky enough to get for Christmas.

But why this awful longing? This powerful need to be close to her.

To touch.

When I look at this girl, I forget that for me, sex means fear and pain. I can't hear that voice—the one that lurks in the dark, taunting me from the past—from that long-ago bedroom full of nightmares. For me, sex equals *only* that voice. But at this moment, I can't hear it. And even if I could, I'd just tell it to shut the fuck up.

Because I want her.

I want her in *that* way. A way that should terrify me.

A laugh rumbles out of me because that's a stupid idea. I don't ever want anyone in *that* way. Never have. Never will. Well, except that right now, there's no denying that I badly want to fuck her.

I wouldn't know what to do even if I did get hold of her—really wouldn't have a clue how to proceed. I've never touched a girl before. Never wanted to. Well, maybe I've wanted to a *little bit*. I've definitely looked before and checked out some enticing curves and wondered.

But I keep my distance from the girls on the streets that stare at me. Even the ones that live rough like me. And then there are the college girls. The business ladies. I don't want to scare them. Women like that don't deserve my anger. My pain. No way. And

I've never wanted any of them enough to try... to see what would happen if I *did* touch them.

This girl in the black dress, for some reason, she's different.

I want to know everything about her. What she feels like, tastes like, sounds like.

I *need* to know.

Is her skin smooth? Soft? What color are her sad eyes? Would she care that my hair is dirty? My skin? My soul.

What would it be like to kiss her? Press my lips against hers and use my tongue in her mouth. I've only had guys try to kiss me like that. Then I fuck *their* mouths with my fist.

So, this girl would have to show me everything, guide me. I wonder if she would.

Pacing to keep warm, she peers across the street. If I don't move, she'll look right at me. I'm not ready for that just yet, so I duck into the shadows. I've never seen such a heartbreaking face before, so beautiful and sad.

My heart pounds. What will happen if I step from the darkness and walk over over and speak to her?

I could say, 'Hey, my name's Lightning. What's yours?' Then what? It's not like I can ask her on a date. Not in my situation. But maybe... maybe if things work out with Ariana...

I glance over again and take two steps toward her, then one back. I don't know what to do. I can't decide.

Would a girl like her give a guy like me her cell number? If she did, I could call her tomorrow on the phone Ariana is supposedly sending over. My brain buzzes and whirs uselessly. I could show myself and risk scaring the crap out of her or walk away and regret it forever. Guess I should go over... Wait—she's with someone?

She turns toward Joe Junior's, smiling as an older guy steps through the doorway and passes her a no-doubt greasy bag of food.

My brain screeches to a halt. No. Fucking. Way. Instantly, I lose control of my limbs and stomach, and the crème brûlée lurches up my throat and sprays over the concrete.

Fuck. That's Cooper. *Fucking Cooper.*

What the fuck is it with this goddamn night?

I'm dumbstruck. Feverish with shock. It's been a while since I've laid eyes on him, and all I can see is red blood and black murder.

And hate. Hate that goes on forever.

I'm gonna kill that fucker. I swear it.

He's not the first asshole to fuck me over. Things had gone to shit long before I met him, but a couple of years ago, Cooper was the first person on the scene when I most needed help. And the dirty cop that he was, he chose to wrap me in chains, torture the fuck out of me, and drive nails into my coffin.

My shock morphs into a rage that fires through every fiber of my being. I wipe my mouth and picture several ways to cause him pain. Somehow, I stop myself from rushing over to get started on the job.

Because with Coop's connections, if he sees me, I'm a dead man. For me to end him, it must be an ambush—a surprise attack. So I stay where I am.

But why is he with this girl? Why *her*?

My body shakes while I watch them eat fries and talk. She makes him laugh, but every time he looks away, her eyes turn haunted. She's beautiful, but in a tragic way. It distracts me from hating on Coop. Maybe it's her sadness that calls to me. But I can't believe she's associated with that dirtbag—the ex-cop who holds my soul to ransom.

What an insane night. I feel worse than I did at the beginning when I was starving hungry.

The rain has soaked through my top, and it clings to my chest in a suffocating way. I tip my head back and open my mouth, icy water splattering my tongue. It feels good. Cleansing. So, that's it then. I'm out of here.

Good fucking riddance sad-girl. And Coop. For now.

Walking fast, I head in the opposite direction. I need to get maximum space between my past and my future ASAP.

When I've stomped about two blocks, I hail a cab and give the driver Ariana's friend's address.

Enveloped in the car's warmth, I drop my head back against the seat and let my mind wander. Immediately, it snaps back to the girl. Even after seeing her with Coop, I still want to speak to her and find out her name. Ask if I can follow her to wherever she's going just so I can look at her. And dream about touching her.

Jesus, what the hell is wrong with my head? Pathetic.

And then I let myself think about *him.*

That asshole Coop.

The Coop-factor must have caused my bizarre reaction to the girl. I could probably sense him on her—all the stress and hate and anger and pain that goes along with that guy. It's got me all revved up. On edge. Ready to fight or *fuck.* It's such a weird thing—the fight or flight instinct.

Half an hour later, the cab slows in front of a multi-story apartment complex, one of those trendy, renovated warehouses. In fact, the street is full of them. This is the old industrial zone behind the beach—a cool area for those fortunate enough to live here. Now there's an art gallery next door and a cafe with huge rectangular slabs of wood for outdoor tables and seats made of wine barrels.

It's a promising sign. And the kind of place you could bring a girl with sad eyes home to.

Well, I shouldn't get too excited yet. Even hipsters can be psychopaths.

"Thanks, man," I say to the driver as I hand him a bunch of cash. "Keep the change." I might as well spread the good fortune around, and besides, if I get myself killed tonight, I won't need the money.

Loud rock music wafts down from a window. Party sounds. Laughter.

More good omens.

Just in case it's my last opportunity to star gaze, I give the sky a long look. It's too cloudy for any real satisfaction.

Man, even in my line of work, I know it's stupid to turn up to a stranger's house. Within the hour, I might be minced into sausage filling.

But, hey, fuck it. Here goes nothing. Before I can change my mind, I bolt up the steps and press the intercom.

Chapter 5

L

"Hey, Lightning? Is that your Ariana-blessed ass out there?"

I jump as a deep voice crackles through the intercom. "Yeah. It's me."

"Don't loiter on my doorstep, man. What are you waiting for?"

"I'm waiting for your maid to buzz me in, *you idiot.*" I mutter the last two words under my breath. No point pissing him off before we even meet properly. Plenty of time for that later.

He laughs, the rough sound rumbling like thunder. Then a long beep sounds. "At your own risk, ride the Starship Enterprise up to the top floor. Mine's the green door at the end of the corridor."

Being a smartass, I reply, "Yes, sir," and open the steel doors.

My jaw drops as I take in the massive foyer. A pressed tin ceiling hangs high as the stars, the space cavernous enough to house a nightclub. Blond wood, exposed brick, and metal everywhere—shiny, sharp, and cool as hell.

No doubt Angelo makes big bucks, which is reassuring, I *think*. I still might be plunging deeper into the shit with Ariana and her so-called *friend*, but there's only one way to find out. And that involves getting in the elevator.

Angelo wasn't kidding. The bling-filled contraption is full-on Star Trek. In five heartbeats, I'm ten floors up. And, of course, surrounded by mirrors again. I don't need a reminder of how trashed I look. Slumped shoulders, beat-up clothes, pissed as hell.

Glad to be away from my own reflection, I cruise down an eerily lit hallway, beams of light slicing over my skin. This whole place gives off serious Blade Runner vibes.

When I arrive at the green entrance, I knock twice. *Please. Please.*

I'm not sure what I'm silently begging for, but it sure as fuck *isn't* the sight that greets me when the door swings open. I find myself staring at a guy who looks like someone mashed a Nubian prince with a Rasta dude and then cranked the hotness dial to max.

Doe eyes wide, his pouty lips stay sealed.

"You Angelo?" I ask.

He flinches like he's amazed I can speak. "Shit, man, I'll be anything you want me to be." He grins and yanks me into his apartment by my T-shirt. Scratching his chin, he circles me like a shark while I give him my sharpest piranha smile. He'd better not touch me again or this will be the shortest friendship in history.

He whistles long and low. "*Damn*, you're really something else, you know? No wonder Ariana was tripping over her own words on the phone." He hoots like an owl on amphetamines. "Let me check you out, *Lightning Boy*. Yeah! You're as pretty as a pony and as hard as a muscled-up gangster. You're the real deal, my man."

I narrow my eyes and puff my chest. "I'm not a boy anymore. How old are *you*?"

"Twenty. Relax. I don't bite. Sit." He ushers me onto a king-sized couch and retreats to a high-tech kitchen. "Beer?"

"Yeah, sure." It might be my last—though this high-energy jerk doesn't exactly give off serial killer vibes.

I try to look unfazed while taking in his apartment but fail miserably. This place is insane. Tonight feels like hopping from one epic movie set to another.

Exposed brick columns, massive wooden beams, absurdly huge windows, a fireplace I could live in, and the largest flat-screen I've ever seen leave me speechless.

"It's cool, huh?" he says, handing me a bottle as he lounges across from me. He nods at the screen. "You game?"

"Never tried it, but I'm sure it's fun."

"You never gamed? Well, shit. You're a babe in the woods. We're gonna have us some fun in this bachelor pad, Mr. Lightning Boy."

I stare him down. "Don't call me that."

He laughs, not slowing his pace. "Ariana said Lightning was your name."

Yeah. But it's the addition of the word *boy* that makes my skin crawl and reminds me of *him.* The monster I slayed. The monster that never stays dead, no matter how many times I try to kill him.

So, you've been stuck on the streets, huh?"

I nod.

"And wild Ariana pulled your ass out of the gutter. Lucky dude. That woman can get you the easiest money you've ever made. Travel to crazy places, have your photo taken prancing down a runway. It's practically free cash. Worst part? Waiting around on shoots. But that's okay. You can always get your dick sucked while someone's painting your nails..." He trails off.

Probably because there's smoke billowing from my nostrils.

"What? You don't like that? Thought you hustled for cash."

I grunt. Hell yes, I hustled. For scraps of food. Cigarettes. Anything to survive another day.

"Yeah," he says. "Well, I guess that'd put anyone off giving blowjobs. Maybe you need to receive a no-strings-attached one. I'll pay it forward if you're interested in some stress relief. You're wound up tight."

I don't get it. Why does everyone want the same thing from me? "No thanks. I'm not into guys."

He glares, unconvinced.

"I swear."

"You're a *rent boy.* So how does the not-liking-guys thing work out for you?"

"Well, I need to eat. Plenty of idiots will pay to shove their dicks in my mouth. So..." I shrug, trying not to look pissed. "I just make sure it's over fast. That's why they call me Lightning. Can't say I like it."

"You fuck them?"

"I try not to. Sometimes... but only for a shitload of money."

His smile turns mocking. "Right. You don't like guys, but you somehow get hard enough to fuck their hairy, un-sexy bodies. Your story's not ringing true, my friend. I think you need to face facts and admit that you—"

"I can only do it if I hurt them," I blurt. I can't believe I finally said it out loud. The ugly truth.

His eyebrows leap. "For real?"

"Yeah, man. Tie them to a chair and make the fuckers cry. That'd do it for me." Not many chairs in public restrooms, but, hey, something to consider if Ariana's modeling gig doesn't work out.

"That shit turns you on?"

"Well, not traditionally. But the thought of making those jerks hurt has been known to get the blood flowing where it needs to."

"You're one fucked-up dude. Someday I want to know how you got that way."

Funny thing is... I have a feeling I might actually tell him.

He gulps his drink loud enough to make me grin and drops the bottle onto the coffee table. "One more question about your fascinating sex-life."

Or lack thereof.

"Do you do girls?"

I bite my lip. Should I tell him? My face scrunches up before I can stop it.

Angelo chuckles. "It's a simple question. Yes or no?"

"No."

His dreads swing as his head pulls back.

"I haven't... you know. Fucked a girl. I think about it sometimes, but then I—"

"No way." He cuts in, leaning forward. "You can't be a pussy virgin."

Man. Why did I bare my soul to this nosy guy? I zip my lips.

"Yes, you are! You ain't never done a girl. You want me to fix you up? I know plenty of lovely ladies ready to help you ditch your V card." He reaches for his phone.

Before I can think, I lunge and rip his cell out of his hand.

"Hey," he yells as I fling it across the room. "Not a great start to our friendship if you've broken that thing."

I lean forward and yank my hair. The pain helps. "Sorry. I just... I don't really do sex. It's complicated. Don't hassle me about it, and we'll get along fine." I hope. Because I want to stay here. This place is cool, and Angelo's a funny guy.

Lifting his hands, he says, "Peace, bro. No problem. Whatever cranks your plank. I'll leave you to it."

Instantly, my mind goes to sad-girl. My dick, too. I picture her body, her face. Fire burns through me.

I need Angelo gone fast, so I can get deal with this heat.

I yawn loudly, and he laughs. "Tired, huh? I'll show you the spare room. And tomorrow, I'm gonna give you the lowdown on this crazy modeling caper. After that, I'm gonna teach you how to cook a Jamaican curry, and then—because honestly, gaming is even more important than food—we're gonna play for twelve hours straight. Sound good?"

"Wait." I stand up fast, shaking my head as panic sets in. "I don't think I can do this."

"Do what? Sit down," he says. "So, you're not gonna stay?"

"No, man, I wanna stay. But would it be okay if I sleep on the couch?"

He looks at me like the zombie apocalypse is upon us, and I've just come out of the closet as patient zero.

"Why the couch? The spare room is awesome. It's no trouble, I assure you."

"I mean, I'm sure it's a great room. But I just can't handle too many doors between me and the outside, you know?"

"Are you worried I'm gonna lock you in and fatten you up to make you taste better, Goldilocks? That's okay. I get where you're at."

I flop back on the soft, comfortable couch. "I think that was Hansel and Gretel... you know, with the cage and the food."

"Well, since you're so savvy with your fairy tales, Lightning Boy, you should know that the handsome pauper-boy always turns out to be a prince. In this story, that's you. Things are looking up for you, kid. You're safe. You can relax."

Safe? I mouth the word, catching it before any sound forms.

"Well, that'd be cool," I say, stretching my arms overhead. My back cracks loudly. "No one's ever helped me before so..."

His eyebrows twist. Shock? Sympathy? Hard to tell.

I throw back the rest of my beer and stand again. "Where's the bathroom?"

"Wait until you see the six-head shower. You're gonna love it. It's intense."

Chapter 6

L

Angelo is right. The shower is fifty shades of fucking insane, the bathroom itself otherworldly. I'm talking about a massive plunge pool set deep into a stepped stone platform, the scale and design fit for the king of the underworld.

The walls are metallic mosaic tiles of blue, green, and orange. Spooky lights shimmer through a huge round window as if the damn thing is a portal to another universe. It likely just looks out over the bay. It's cool, though.

My head turns and turns as I take it all in. Okay, so I guess that crazy-looking alcove is the shower. Or a solarium. Or possibly a teleportation device.

I strip off and fumble with knobs until I find the right lever. Water jets from fucking everywhere as I yank it hard left. Then I step into the flow. Fucking hell. That's damn good. Light sparks off my wet skin while I stare at the lavish surroundings, still unable to believe my change of luck.

This whole scene is surreal, just like that girl on the street tonight.

Water pummels me, the heat almost too much to take. It's shooting from no less than six different outlets projecting from the walls. I've never felt anything so satisfying in my life.

Speaking of satisfaction...

I pump herbal-scented gel out of a ceramic bottle and soap up my chest. My dick pulses. I need to jerk off, get some relief. I wash every inch of skin until I smell like a flower farm. Well not quite everywhere. I've saved the best bit for last.

With my head pressing back against the tiles and water gushing over my face, I slide my hand down my stomach. My heart pounds as I picture her, my dream girl, the curve of her hips, her dark eyes sifting through the shadows where I lurked across the road from the hamburger joint. I give my cock an agonizingly slow pump.

Then another and another until it's hard to breathe.

Holding my base tightly, a groan vibrates through my chest, my dick pulsing. Right now, I'm so ready to sink into her warm, wet heat. Feel her body melt against mine.

My legs shake as I start to get into it, using my other hand to bring my balls into the game. My breath comes in harsh pants, and I keep pumping, wondering what the girl smells like. Feels like. Then my leg muscles lock, my head spins, and I freeze, hoping I don't pass out.

I picture her smile, the one she gave Cooper, and my hands drop to my thighs. Fucking Cooper. He's an instant buzz kill, every damn time.

The lever that shuts down the deluge of water squeaks when I flick it. Then I dry off with a velvety towel, my cock still twitching. I need to be lying flat on my back before I can deal with it. In bed where there's nowhere left to fall.

When my hair has stopped dripping, I go back to the living room where Angelo has laid out a huge white comforter and an actual pillow.

I scratch my head, calculating when I last used one of those, seems like forever, and stare around the empty room, the luxury trappings taunting me with their exoticness.

This is a fantasy world. One I don't belong in.

When I open my eyes later, will I be hogtied and drugged and possibly have a knife sticking out of my gut? Who gives a fuck. That probably isn't gonna happen. But if it does, at least I'll be warm and, hopefully, blissfully unconscious while I wait for my end to come.

The crisp cotton crinkles as I fold back the comforter and slip underneath.

Fuck, yeah. It feels amazing.

I pull the covers up to my neck. They smell like lemons. I glance across the room. Goddamn it. The standing lamp next to the fireplace is still blazing. It's fine. It can stay blazing. Then it might shine some light on Angelo when he comes for me with a kitchen knife, granting me some warning. *Fuck.* I can't let go of the idea that my good fortune just can't be real, and that I'll be dead by morning.

Even with the amber lamp glowing, the dark still slithers toward me from the corners of the room. And I wait, feeling shut up, locked in, defenseless.

Ah, just go to sleep idiot. I should be used to this feeling. After all, ever since Mom died, it's how I grew up.

Always waiting in the dark. Shivering and shaking, fighting back nausea. Always wondering. Will it happen tonight? Is he coming for me again? Night after night consumed by the same fears.

That voice from the past starts to whisper and snarl. I smack my fist into my temple hard, and I push the hated sound down deep. Nope. Nope. No way. I won't let the monster's voice wreck my first comfortable sleep in forever. Not fucking here. And not now.

Normally, being turned on brings the worst kind of feelings. Shame and hate. Disgust. Can't say I like it much. So, whenever I get myself off, I don't see any girl in particular. There's no whole person I'm getting into. It's just a swirl of imagined curves, soft skin, and secret places, crafted from how I can only guess a girl's body might look and feel.

And like the havoc I unleash on the fuckwits in the park, I make sure it's quick, get it over with fast. Because I'm Lightning. Just like they say I am.

But now, with my palm drifting down my hot skin, I think of the sad-eyed girl and let flames lick through my blood. It's shocking because I feel far from annoyed by the situation. Everything else fades, my past, all my fears, everything but the image of her haunted eyes.

Her face, then the dress, crushing her curves like a black bandage. I do the same to myself, squeeze hard, breathing loudly through four slow strokes.

My hands shake, and the feeling intensifies. Fuck, I might blow any second.

This is too fast. I can't let it happen yet.

My hands drop, fists twisting into the covers. The friction of the bedclothes will be enough to push me over. But I can't resist the slow torturous grind of my hips against the sheets, savoring every moment as I transport myself back to Jackson Street and picture walking through the rain and strolling right up to the girl.

In my mind, water hits my boots as I splash through puddles. I duck out of the way of a car, the screech of its horn loud at my back.

It feels and sounds and smells so real.

I've always had an overactive fantasy life—I've needed one to survive. At this moment, I'm thankful for it because it feels like I'm standing right in front of her.

I clear my throat, and she looks up, those dark, molten eyes widening. She takes a step away.

"It's okay," I say softly. I stretch my hand out, bridging the space between our bodies—only two feet, but it feels like an ocean. "Hey, don't be afraid. My name is—"

Cutting me off, her hand zips out and twists into my T-shirt. I lose balance as she tugs me around a corner and shoves me backward, a brick wall grating my skin. "—Lightning," I finish. "My name is Lightning."

She smiles, and fuck it's gorgeous, like a candle flame lighting a dark space, banishing every ghost. We puff and pant, staring and staring, and I'm starving for her. Hungry to get my hands on every inch of her.

It's *not real*, I tell myself.

It's not real.

But I don't back away. And it's a good thing that this is only happening in my head because I've never done this before, so it won't matter if I fuck it up. A raw sound escapes me as I lift both hands, slowly, slowly, and then, holy fuck, I'm exploring her tits. Well, her fictional tits, but even so, it's a stronger hit than any drug I can buy out on the streets.

Horns beep in the distance. People yell. But it all blends into meaningless noise.

Her eyelids flicker closed as I slip my clumsy paws into her dress, her skin silky beneath my fingertips. I drag the material below her breasts. Yep, my imagination is first-rate because, hell, what a sight—dark peaks and round, soft flesh to caress and worship. I pull her in tight, wrap her in my arms, and crush her way too hard. Lucky she's not real.

She grinds against me, her head falling back. When her eyes open, they're not sad anymore, they're hot. Blazing. Bright and fiery.

Then, she's got her hands in my jeans, and she's stroking me. Light then fast. Soft then hard.

"Lightning," she whispers. With a firm grasp on my wrist, she drags my hand down to her core, my palm scraping skin along the way. The black dress is hiked up around her waist and she's dripping wet.

I pant and groan like I'm dying. Any second I'm gonna come so damn hard... but no.

Not like this.

I shove her against the wall, grip myself, and push into her heat. She makes this guttural sound, and the feel of her body—glove-tight—is mind blowing.

I plunge in and out.

Long strokes.

Hard strokes.

And, hell, I don't know if a real-life girl would feel like this... but whatever... because this is *amazing*. Jerking off has never felt so good.

I heave her farther up the wall and piston my hips in time with her moans.

"Fuck yes," I say, my hand already buried under the covers and pumping frantically. Then I'm groaning and moaning like it's the end of the world. Everything winds tighter, coiling and spiraling. Up. Up. So damn good I'm gonna...

No.

Stop.

In the alley, my hand grips her hair tight as I balance on the knife's edge, the rest of my body frozen. Don't move. Don't move.

"What's your name?" I ask, my voice coming out in panted bursts. I need to know. Then as she begins to speak, I tumble over into oblivion, and I can't hear a thing.

I *need* to know her name, but I can't stop sinking—down, down, down—exploding like the mother of all fireworks until I hit the ground.

Fuck.

My eyes flare open. I'm crashed over the couch, my limbs shaking like jelly. There's no flame-eyed girl. No black dress. No smoking-hot body to hold on to. It's just me and my buzz-saw breathing.

I creep to the bathroom and clean up. I grab a wad of toilet paper and do the same to the bedclothes. Then I collapse back into the warmth of my temporary bed, my brain whirling with crazy thoughts.

This is what I want.

A home. A place where I can dream about the girl I saw tonight in peace and safety. Not looking over my shoulder, hustling for food, and feeling like shit all the time. I don't want to do that anymore.

I want to feel human. To be a guy who just wants a girl.

No forced blowjobs, no living with the pain of a hollow gut. No stench and cold and loneliness. No Coop. No memories.

Just a guy. A guy who wants a girl.

I think of Cooper and the last time I saw him, back when I ran.

It wasn't so long ago. I was seventeen. Now I'm almost nineteen.

So young.

But eighteen… eighteen is just a number, right? The word keeps looping around my head, driving me insane. My brain is fracturing and needs a full reboot.

But it's fine because I won't be this young and stupid for much longer. Soon, I'll be older. Stronger.

When that day arrives, Cooper better look the fuck out because I'll be coming for him.

An uncomfortable feeling smothers me like a too-hot blanket—the past and the future colliding together.

And I know. I know in my bones that time moves fast, like a river gushing by. Days will pass, nights too, and before too long, I'll be a man good and proper—a loaded gun, cocked and ready.

Closing my eyes, I summon the girl's image again, wishing I could know, maybe just once, what she feels like in reality. Not in a dream conjured up by lust. I drag her sad face to mine in the dark of my imagination. Picture taking her hips in my hands, trapping them again, and pulling her in. Not letting go this time.

Warmth spreads through my veins as I wish for this, even pray for it.

And, of course, this makes me an idiot because I've forgotten the warning, the one my mom gave me over and over when I was a kid.

Be careful what you wish for, she used to say.

Be careful, my little lion.

My angel.

Be careful because, one day, you just might get it.

Chapter 7

EDEN - ONE HOUR LATER

"Did you enjoy your birthday, Eden?" Cooper asks as he pulls up outside my apartment block. He flicks on the car's interior light, his beady eyes burning into mine as I contemplate his question.

Did I enjoy my birthday?

The restaurant was fancy, but I barely ate a thing.

Coop noticed, and since he's a control freak, he forced me to eat a bag of greasy fries on our walk back through the seedy part of town. He loves to take me there to remind me where I'd be if it weren't for his so-called benevolence. Believe me, kind and caring are two things that this guy isn't.

Now where was I? Right, my eighteenth birthday...

All night, Coop had been edgy, sick plans and schemes clearly brewing beneath his furrowed brow.

After dinner, it had rained heavily on our walk down Jackson Street, and my mood was gloomy.

So the truth is... no, I didn't really enjoy my birthday.

But the smile currently stretched over my face tells a different story—the version I hope he'll swallow without question. My fake smile is all gratitude and *oh-my-god-you're-the-best-guy-ever.* What a load of crap.

"Thank you," is the most I can force myself to say without choking.

He looks pleased, the self-absorbed fool. "Good. You're only eighteen once, Eden. You've gotta live it up." The navy suit jacket strains as he pulls an expensive wallet out of his breast pocket. Recently, he's put on weight. "I nearly forgot to give you your present."

Heaven forbid.

The wallet flips open, and his pudgy fingers dip and delve inside it. A creased photo lies across the middle. His thumb keeps it in place.

Who goes to the trouble of printing photos these days, anyway? I've unfortunately known Coop for two horrible years now—far too long—and I've never seen this picture before.

"Who's that?" I ask, leaning a little closer. I hate the smell of his aftershave. It's expensive and overpowering.

His grin flickers as he flaps the photo between us. "An old friend," he says, chuckling like a slob. "Or maybe I should say, he's a *young* old friend." He leers at the photo.

Coop is gross. "Can I see it?"

Eyes narrowed, he studies me. My long brown hair is in a wet tangle from the rain, my silly black dress tight like a bandage, and dark red lips pretending to smile. I don't know why he looks so suspicious; he made me like this.

After giving the picture a cherishing fondle, he hands it over.

I grip it hard, because Coop is likely to change his mind any moment and whip it away. He loves to play games.

I look down at the photo. "Oh," I say as I press a shaking palm against my chest.

"Oh, indeed," he agrees.

A boy who could be my age sits on a couch. It's Coop's couch. Broad back to the camera, the guy wears jeans, intricate ink swirled over his skin—and that's about it. Torso twisted, he looks through chunks of dark blond hair over his shoulder, directly at the photographer. Or, in this case, the person viewing the image. Lucky freaking me.

He's laughing, but he doesn't look happy. Arrogance shapes scorn into every feature. Even his eyes—those electric blue eyes are bitter and mocking as they hook me hard, drag me close, and ruin me.

"God. He's... I mean, this guy is something..." I let my words trail off before I accidentally say what I really think.

"Oh, yes." Coop snickers. "He most certainly is."

My heart pounds. "What's his name? How come you've never spoken about him before?"

"Thirteen months ago, I was negligent, and he slipped through my fingers. But I'm doing my best to remedy that mistake, Eden."

My blood chills at the violence in his eyes. Something else lurks in his expression, too. I'm not sure what it is, but ice shivers over my skin at its intensity.

"Well, who is he?"

"Somebody that I used to know. And plan to again. Very soon, I hope."

That poor guy. I really hope he's well hidden. "Coop! You're not answering my question."

"You don't need to know, Eden. He's my little secret."

A dirty one, I bet.

As my fingers stroke the photo, Coop breathes a sleazy laugh through his nostrils. "Nice, huh?"

Nice is absolutely not the correct word for this face I'm staring at. The smile. Those eyes.

Something claws deep inside me, a sick longing, as I pass the picture back. "He's okay, I guess." *Liar.*

Coop's bushy eyebrows hike upward, his brow tightening as he digests my unexpected answer.

It's never wise to let Cooper know anything has snagged your attention because the guy lives to take things away from people.

In the light of the streetlamp, rain streams down the car window in pretty orange rivulets. Preparing to head into the cold, I tug my annoying dress down my thighs. It's freezing enough out there I'm about to become an icicle with opinions.

"Here." His thick paw curls around my shoulder, the other holding out a wad of cash. "Your present. Buy yourself some textbooks for school. I know they're probably the only luxury you'll allow yourself."

True. He's right about that at least.

I need to get qualified. I need work. And I need to pay Coop back and then never ever set eyes on him again.

I don't know much about life, who I am or where I'm going, but one thing is certain—Cooper Martinez is a prick. I have to break free from him.

"Thanks," I say, tucking the money into my bag, already shuffling away from him.

I open the door, wobble onto the sidewalk, and then slam it shut. I imagine his smug laugh as he pulls off the curb. And because he likes to take his time letting go, he drives away slowly down my street.

I want to see the stars twinkle before I head upstairs, but the sky is overcast. Black and leaden, like my heart.

I'm lonely. Lost. Like the boy in Coop's picture.

That guy makes my insides melt. My body quiver. My heart trip over itself.

And as much as I'd like to lay eyes on him in the flesh, see that smile, and touch that face, I hope with every part of my being that the boy stays hidden.

A slice of sky appears between a break in the clouds, a bright star shining down through it.

I make a wish. I say a prayer and whisper a plea.

May that boy in the photo stay lost.

May he never be found.

Keep him safe.

And as far away from Coop as possible.

Chapter 8

EDEN - 4 Years Later

Before Sam died, he passed on two pieces of advice. One good and the other just plain questionable.

The good: if your heart aches every single time you look at someone, run and run fast, because it probably won't end well. Although bleak, that sounded fair enough at the time, considering what he'd gone through with my mother. She left when I was three.

And the other: lightning never strikes the same place twice. Sorry? Was that even true? I suspected a little googling would shoot that idea down fast, but I didn't pull out my phone to check. That would have been a waste of precious time. And Dad didn't have much of that left.

Out of all the corny lines he could've chosen to pass on to his teenage daughter, those two were kind of lame. I longed for special words I could hold close to my heart, meaningful words I could cling to after he was gone. So to be honest, I was disappointed.

"Remember those two things, Edie," he'd said, his bony fingers pinching my arm.

I nodded obediently and kissed his gaunt cheek. Then in the old cottage on our run-down lavender farm, I slumped over the bed, watching the cancer chomp away at his body, and decided that the disease must have finally reached his brain.

Why else would he waste his labored breath spouting mad theories about lightning?

After he'd fallen asleep, I called his oncologist. And within the fortnight, Dad was dead.

Then a whole six years later, it only took one meeting with a guy called L for me to realize that my father had been right about the heartache bit. One look at that man and he got under my skin, tore my heart out.

And not long after making L's acquaintance, I knew for sure that Dad had been wrong about the second thing—about lightning.

It *could* strike the same place twice. And the same person, too. Repeatedly.

I was the hard evidence, because that boy was Lightning with a capital L. And he blew me into pieces several times over.

And one horrible day, when I knew L a little better, I stared into his furious neon eyes that were way too close to mine, and all I could think was—why? Why the hell *hadn't* I run away fast?

Just like Sam had warned me to.

Chapter 9

EDEN

I despise Coop. He's nothing but a sweaty, dead-eyed, sleazy bastard. And this might seem a little over the top for a girl like me, who's generally kind to everyone I meet, but I dream about killing him one day.

I don't know when. Or how. He's an ex-cop and a dirty one, too, so it wouldn't be easy to pull off. But as I watch his name, appropriately saved as *The Devil*, flash across my cell screen, I fantasize the hell out of it. I picture wrapping my fingers around his throat, wishing my hands would miraculously morph into stronger ones.

But who am I kidding? When I watch bank commercials on TV, I cry.

So it probably won't be me who kills Coop, but one day he'll get what's coming to him. He makes life difficult for enough people. Therefore, it's only a matter of time.

I've just finished swimming laps at the local pool, and I'm tired. The last thing I want is his dreaded summons call. It's been almost five months since he's asked me to do something vile, but even before I answer my cell, I know. I know it will be bad. I pick up anyway because I'm too scared not to.

His gruff voice barks out instructions. I hang up before he's finished speaking because small victories are better than none.

The gray walls close in on me as I stand limp in the middle of the change room with my heart thumping, the smell of chlorine burning my nose and the thought of what Coop wants me to do stinging my eyes.

Wake up, Edie, I think. *It's one more step closer to getting Sam's farm back.*

The farm that belongs to me.

My home—it's all I want.

So, I haul ass across town to be there within the hour. Because that's what my Lord and Master wants.

Be there by four-thirty, Edie, or else, he'd said on the phone.

Since I have no intention of finding out what '*or else*' means, at exactly 4:30 p.m. on a sunny Friday afternoon, I find myself in the marble bathroom of a soulless city apartment, stripping down to my underwear with Coop's beady eyes crawling over me.

"Get a move on, Edie. The guy out there is a fucking wild thing, likely to bolt any minute, so I don't know how long he'll stick around. And I really need to pull this one off today." He gives me a foul wink and adds, "So to speak, you know."

Once upon a time, Coop was handsome. You can see it there in his bone structure. But his broad, princely features have long been ruined, puffed out by excess booze and depraved living. I'm sure the black heart pounding in his chest doesn't do much for his complexion, either.

Eyes rolling, I shimmy out of my stockings and slip off a black stiletto heel, leaning a sweaty palm against the green-tiled wall. "Why are you so worried? The word going around is that you've got this guy on a tight leash," I mutter, reaching for my second shoe.

I love biker boots and any item of clothing that adds a protective layer, but today, I've worn the come-fuck-me shoes because Coop believes they help get the job done. That they make it easier, like a tool belt on a carpenter. But I can't stand them a second longer, so I try to sneak them off.

"Not entirely. He's a loose cannon this one." Coop's laugh echoes around the room. "Hey, leave those shoes on. He just might like them. Who knows what will get this bastard jacked up. Don't think he's ever gotten hard for a girl before."

"Shit, Cooper! What if he can't? You promised this would be one of the last times you'd make me do this. No matter what happens today, please tell me that you'll count this toward my tally."

I wrench paper towel from the dispenser and pretend to work on my smoky eyeliner in the mirror. No way I'm crying in front of this asshole. "Hey, it won't be my fault if he can't perform. I showed up here just like you asked me to, wearing these stupid clothes."

In a flash, Coop presses me against the wall, his beer gut crushing into my stomach, stale breath hot in my face.

Beefy fingers squeeze my windpipe. "Mind your manners or you'll find out what the alternative to doing this is. I don't think you'll like it at all."

Suppressing a grin, he drops his hand and steps back. "If you fuck this up, we're all in trouble here, so shut up and listen to the deal."

He folds thick arms over his navy sports coat, leaning on the door. Behind that door, his kinky buddies wait. "Out there in the living room are three suits and my boy L. Now when you get in that room, ignore the suits, don't even look at them. Just do whatever the fuck L says. He's been briefed, and he'll be ready for you. Mentally at least. And you'd better damn well hope you can inspire him physically. When you're done, come back in here. I'll be waiting."

"You're not watching?"

"Not today."

I breathe a sigh of relief. I hate it when I'm forced to perform in front of Cooper's repulsive, leering eyes.

"Stop looking at me like I've kicked your freaking dog and get a move on, Edie."

Right. Wonderful. So, I simply have to turn on a guy who, according to Coop, bats exclusively for the other team. Great. With my obvious feminine attributes, I'm going to be at a distinct disadvantage.

Coop strokes a lock of my long hair, making sure to press his thumb over my nipple through the red bra as he pushes dark strands over my shoulder. "You're looking good, Edie."

I repress the urge to smack him. "Only my friends call me that. I'd prefer all you other assholes to call me Eden."

"Feisty today, aren't you?"

Coop smirks as I shrug him off. I don't want to speak to him any more than I must, but curiosity gets the better of me. "So what's he like, anyway?"

"Who? L?" Coop snickers. "He's broken. Angry. And a completely ruthless prick."

I snatch my brush from the vanity and drag it through my hair briskly so Coop can't see the terror in my eyes. Hopefully, he's just trying to scare me with that description of the guy I'm about to meet.

"L is a stupid name," I say to cover my nerves. "No mother calls a baby that."

"True. When he was a kid, he was called something else. But living out on the streets, he earned a different name." Raising a bushy, gray eyebrow, Coop pauses for dramatic effect. "You wanna know what he's called?"

I puff a loud breath through copious layers of lipstick. "I asked, didn't I?"

"Well, that boy out there answers to the name of Lightning."

I freeze, skin prickling as an image of Dad's face strobes through my brain. Panicking, I push it away. I don't want Sam's memory polluted by Coop and his filth. The hairbrush feels like a brick in my palm as I set it down on the counter. "Lightning? Really?"

"Yep. But mostly, he just goes by L."

"Why is he called Lightning? I mean it's a weird name."

"He got the name because the little bastard was flash-fast at everything. Stealing your wallet. Running away. And most impressively when it came to getting people off. He could make a guy come in his pants within seconds. And he doesn't mind making them suffer either, which they love. Made him famous in our little circle of twisted money makers. Speaking of which, those suits out there have paid a great deal of money to watch L try to fuck you, so quit stalling and go make it happen."

What does he mean by "*try to*"?

God, these little sex-party setups of Coop's are disgusting, but this must be the sickest one yet. *And* the most dangerous.

What kind of lunatic pays money to watch a guy attempt the impossible anyway?

Well, I won't have to wonder about the brains behind this sick voyeurs' scheme for much longer. I'm about to walk through the door and meet him.

And I'll also meet this L person, my partner in crime today. The guy sounds like he'd rather make out with a pillow than a girl trussed up in red lace. But according to Coop, he might enjoy making me cry. So that's awesome for him. But for me? Not so much.

Hopefully, L has a first-class imagination. It might help him get the job done.

Luckily for me, my body responds even when my brain doesn't want it to, and that's both a curse and a saving grace. It certainly reduces the pain factor whenever I have to take part in these terrible scenes that Coop cooks up.

"Want a hit of coke?" Coop asks. "Something stronger? Might help if this goes badly. I know exactly what L's capable of. How far he's prepared to go. And believe me, Eden, it could hurt."

"No, thanks." Not even the fear of what's waiting for me out there is enough to make me go down that dark path. In a couple of hours, this will be over. And I'll be that much closer to freedom.

That is if *Lightning* can play his part and the suits out there get the kicks they've paid for.

Picturing the psychotic ex-street hustler that I'm about to grind up against like a sad cat on heat, I take a big breath and push through the door, then nearly fall flat on my barely covered butt.

Completely naked, a scowling god stands next to a padded bench, hands on his lean hips, inked biceps flexing, and his impressive package looking far from fired up.

He's the opposite of the guy I pictured and undoubtedly the most beautiful creature I've ever laid eyes on. And he looks strong. *Extremely* strong.

Well, if I die today, at least I'll have a spectacular view as he squeezes the life out of me.

That's something, I suppose.

Chapter 10

L

The girl wobbles toward me in her stupid sky-high shoes. A snail could go faster. "Do you think you can get a move on? I turn into a pumpkin at midnight," I say.

She stumbles slightly, then keeps limping forward.

For the first time in our long and completely fucked-up association, Coop has surprised me. To make this a sure thing, today of all days, I thought he'd serve up a chick who looks the part. Beautiful but hard-edged.

Or at the very least—one who can walk properly.

It's not that she's ugly, quite the opposite. But she looks fucking scared and not at all what I was expecting.

Tilting her head at the sun streaming through the floor-to-ceiling windows behind me, she says, "Don't worry. I should make it over to you by eleven o'clock. There'll be plenty of time for you to spank me or whatever you like to do. So relax."

A puff of air parts my lips, almost a laugh. A sense of humor was the last thing I expected from one of Coop's girls.

She comes closer. Dust motes swirl in the light between us, the air buzzing with tension. The pricks in suits have stopped talking about stocks and market forces, zeroing in on each unsteady step she takes.

I stare too, my eyes tracking from the creamy skin of her forehead all the way down to those dumbass shoes and back again. Something fizzes in my brain—a feeling like déjà vu.

Red lace. Long brown hair. Wide-set dark eyes. Big tits. The whole package is hourglass shaped and kind of clean looking. Clean isn't right. Innocent or sweet maybe

Funny that, considering the fucked-up event she's about to participate in.

Again, what the hell is Coop playing at by setting me up with this girl?

Given what he thinks I like to fuck, it's hard to believe he hasn't found the scrawniest girl in town, hoping she'll confuse my dick into putting on a worthy show.

That thought makes me smile because Coop doesn't know. He has no fucking clue that when I look at a well-stacked female, my brain yells *hell yeah* while my body, dumb fuck that it is, grumbles *hell no*.

When that happens, I tell my brain to listen to my dick. Because the sad fact is, after all these years of shooting load after load with nothing to inspire me but a guy's sharp angles and the thrill of causing pain, soft-fleshy curves won't get me off.

Not that I've ever dared test the theory. But against my will, for years now, I've been programmed to get hard for the exact opposite of girls like her.

There is no way I want soft and breakable. I need something I can hurt. Someone who can take a whole universe of pain—swallow down my blackness in one greedy gulp. And, honestly, this girl doesn't look very hungry. Not for what I can provide, anyway.

She stops a foot away. Covered in red lace, her nipples rise and fall with each shallow breath. Oh, yeah. She's beautiful but terrified.

With great effort, I haul my eyes up to her face and recognition hits like a wrecking ball.

Fuck.

I've seen this girl before with Coop. A long time ago. Four years to be exact.

The night I met Ariana, the lady who ended my homelessness for good, this girl stood on a rainy street smiling at Coop, looking haunted every time he glanced away. And later that night, when I bedded down on Angelo's couch—safe for the first time in thirteen months—I thought about her. Her sad eyes. That sweet smile. And back then, I did something I rarely do. I imagined my hands on every miraculous curve and brought myself off like the mother of all Fourth of Julys.

Again, *fuck.*

I can't believe she's standing in front of me. My sad-eyed girl.

Coop has no idea what he's unleashed; how much I want this. And how in an instant, I've gone from not giving a crap to fucking scared that I might fail and not experience what I'd pictured all those years ago, back when I was eighteen and one girl's suffering had whipped through the night air, slashing up my insides and setting me on fire.

I want this so badly. I want to silence the voices that fuck with my head, get turned on and touch a girl. It's everything I've fantasized about since that rainy night when I fixed my twisted longings on a pair of sad eyes.

The weasel hovering on my left speaks. It's the nasal-voiced little fucker who gets his kicks out of these stupid scenes. Pays for it all with his immorally gained fortune.

It seems that having me hurt him isn't enough to get him hot these days. He needs to see me fail at something. Well, someday I'll knock the head off his fucked-up shoulders, and in that venture, my success will be guaranteed.

I wonder if he'll get off on that.

But, sadly, that's not gonna happen today. After seeing my sad-eyed girl materialize like something from a wet dream, today I aim to please. I will do exactly what he wants and try to fuck a girl for the first time in my sob-story of a life.

And like I said, the brain is very willing, but I don't know if my body will get on board. It hasn't been trained for this. Not on the streets and not since Cooper got his rotten hands on me again.

"It's not too late to take something, L," says the sick fuck, holding out a handful of pills. "You don't seem inspired by this pretty little filly. And we've paid a bundle to see you service her. I'll speak frankly. There's no room for pride today. If you require a little assistance, we won't think any less of your prowess. Will we, gentlemen?" He points to his two anemic cronies, and they nod like sickly servants. "So come over here. I have a wonderful treat that will help you."

Slowly, I turn my head and stare at his pasty face. Let the hatred shine through. He swallows and opens his mouth to wheedle out more shit, but before he can get a sound out, the girl speaks.

"L," she calls in a sweet voice, like she's summoning me to the table for a piping-hot Thanksgiving supper.

With a smile wobbling on her face, she picks up a green tube from what I like to call Coop's *fuck-bench*. Then she grins as wide as the Grand Canyon. I'm dazzled by straight teeth and two cute-as-pie dimples.

"Hi! I'm Edie. How are you doing over there, Lightning?"

I shake my head. It's all I *can* do. Edie. Her name is Edie.

"Or do you prefer L? No comment? Okay, I guess I'll just call you L, then."

Flipping the lid on the lube, she sniffs then rubs some over her fingers. "That's awful. We can't use that. Hold on. I'll be back in a flash."

She kicks off her shoes and runs for the bathroom. Ten seconds later, she's rushing at me, holding out a jar. "Here, smell this."

This girl is nuts.

I dip my head and sniff. Warmth floods my brain. I see sunsets on tropical beaches, and my arms feel heavy, like I've been swimming all day.

"I made it myself. It's coconut oil with ylang-ylang and sandalwood," she says, looking more than a little proud. "Much better, huh?"

"Um. Yeah. I guess..."

The three suits snicker at the bizarre scene as they shuffle into their front-row armchairs, shrugging out of jackets and mumbling to themselves. I can't make out their words because this chick has just fried my brain.

Raising the jar between us like an offering, she says, "Is it all right with you if I put some of this on?"

Instead of throwing her on the padded bench and inducing terror—usually the fastest way to make my dick work—I just stand there and frown. "Ah. Sure."

This must be Coop's weirdest setup yet. And given the crazy-ass scenarios that he's created over the years, that's saying something.

The jar lid falls to the floor. Her eyes bore into mine as she scoops out a glob of oily cream and spreads it over her arms, making long, sweeping strokes.

Up and down. Then up and down again.

Transfixed, I swallow hard, the exotic smell of oils making me lightheaded.

She rubs circles over her chest, not dipping into the red bra to touch herself up like other girls in this situation might do. Considering what we're here for, it's weirdly chaste.

And fucking sexy.

When she takes a step closer, a sick kind of thrill hums through my stomach.

"L? I'm gonna put some of this on you. Is that okay?" she asks, placing the jar on the bench.

I clear my throat. Fuck, what's wrong with my voice? "Fine. Okay... yes," I finally say, sounding like I've just leaped off the planet Stupid spaceship.

She scoops out more thick oil and wraps her fingers around my throat, stroking lightly and gently squeezing my neck muscles. Jesus, it feels good.

Goosebumps prickle over my skin as she dips her hand back into the oil. This time, she works my shoulders and biceps, and waves of bliss roll over me.

My mind loosening, my stomach and balls tighten.

I fucking hate feeling weak like this. Desperate to break the spell, I try to summon anger, the violence of lust. But it doesn't work.

I'm frozen where I stand, chest heaving and my fingers itching to reach out. To touch her.

Coop is going to be livid because for this to have any chance of working, I need to be in control—scaring the living crap out of her. It's the only way I might be able to do it... to fuck her.

So this has to change. There's no alternative. To get my blood pumping in the right direction, I need to hear her cry.

Moving fast, I get up in her face, but she steps sideways before I can grab her.

She turns away, and I watch her ass as she bends to pick up a leather ottoman. What the hell is she doing now?

"I'm going to kiss you," she says as she drops the thing at my feet. "Wow. Pretty tall, aren't you?"

Speechless, I stare. Four years ago, I would have sold my soul to know what kissing her felt like, but my soul is long fucked and these days, I don't want anyone near my mouth. I don't allow it.

The sharp tang of the oil makes me suck in a breath as her soft palms frame my face. Her hands tremble. She gives me a sympathetic smile—like we're in this together—and my mouth opens in panic as her face comes close.

And then closer.

Shit. I'd better tell her not to. "I don't—" I say as her lips meet mine. I hiss the word "*kiss*" into her lungs.

And then I'm drowning, spiraling down into blackness. Her mouth... her lips.

Fuck. No. I can't do this...

I wait for the voice to start. The one that tells me I'm good, then bad. Worthless. That everything's my fault.

I wait and wait. But the words in my head don't come. There's only lust zinging through my cells.

I must make a noise because she breaks away and makes a soothing sound like she's settling a freaked-out stallion, which is kind of what I feel like. And for some reason, her voice, her hand pressing against my cheek, works.

I settle.

Mutterings come from the sicko-voyeurs, but staring down at her lips, I don't give a fuck about them anymore. All I need is to feel it again. Her kiss.

When her arms wrap around my neck and her lush curves press against me, I step closer, my gut churning at the strange sensations.

She is so soft. I could break this one easily. Snap her in half. Crack bones without even raising a bead of sweat.

She kisses me again, slow and coaxing, like she knows I need guidance. My arms lock around her, and I try to follow the push and pull of her lips, to learn the tempo. The glide of her tongue.

Our teeth click together hard. Fuck! I don't know how to do this properly. But, oh, man, no wonder people do this kissing thing. It feels amazing.

Panting, I practically eat her up, probably squeezing her too tightly as I try to get closer. Take more. And more.

The room around us disappears. The amazing city view. All those roof gardens and windows opposite that probably look straight in on us. Today, I don't care about them.

"Hey," she whispers. "Do you think you could slow down a little? I wasn't sure if you'd be able to do it... but you're as hard as steel. So... great job."

Going by the mix of fear and relief in her dark eyes, she seems to think I'm worried about the situation with the suits and their expectations. And maybe I am a little. Because if I can't stay hard and fuck a girl for these freaks, Coop might make some phone calls. The calls that he's been threatening to make since I was a teenager.

But I'm too astounded by how turned on I am to be worried. I put my hand on the back of her head, pull her close, and kiss her deeply, sucking on her bottom lip. I'm getting the hang of this kissing business, and like I always do when I get a bit of confidence up—I go into full attack.

"L, wait." She pulls back. I press forward. The weirdos snicker and start unbuttoning shirts. They think it's funny, me fumbling and groping at her, but that doesn't stop them from getting off on it.

Maybe that's the whole point of this exercise. To watch me make an ass of myself.

The back of my neck tingles where her fingers lie. She slides them down, rubbing and squeezing my biceps. The flames under my skin burn hotter. No one dares to touch me like this. No one ever touches me at *all* if I can help it.

The air coils tighter, the only sounds sawing through it are our loud breathing and the low hum of the city below.

"It's good, isn't it?" she asks. "This feeling is so good."

I can't deny it, so I just frown at her.

"Well, we can take it even higher than this."

Ah, here's the part where she pulls out her favorite chemical trick—whatever party drug she thinks will help me keep it up.

"You don't have to hurt anyone, L. All you need to do is let it build bit by bit. Tease. And everything gets even hotter."

What is she talking about? I'm already burning up and thinking of that final moment. Those seconds when the killer rush hits and all notion of who I am and everything I've done disappears.

"So, that's all we need to do. Draw it out for as long as we can. Until the waiting itself hurts."

Now she's talking my language. Pain and unfathomable darkness.

"Shall we try? Let's ignore those guys over there and do it our way."

Liking the sound of that, I grab her ass, round and juicy as a summer peach, and press her against my hardness. I take her mouth like a pro, like I've been doing this kissing thing forever, and try to summon the focused anger that always gets me through these close encounters. Because outside of this, when I'm not fucking, I don't get close to anyone. Not ever.

It's only the dark fury that can get me off. That black feeling kindles in my balls, in my gut, but as I grind against her, she makes these sounds. Soft moans that tighten my muscles.

Oh, man.

It feels so fucking good.

I lift her knee, nestling it against my waist, my mouth taking more, my hips grinding harder. She fights back by brushing her lips against mine, persuading me to go slow.

In about the stupidest move of my life, I relax and let her lead. And the second I surrender—everything stops.

The world blows apart, and I'm remade.

Even the perverts, moving their hands over their feeble little dicks don't exist.

As we kiss, she wriggles, making space between us. Just enough to move her palm over my skin. Over my chest. My stomach. Inching down.

And it's exactly like she said it would be. Better. Hotter. And if she doesn't stop soon, I'm gonna come in her hand. I can't let that happen because these fuckers have paid for bareback fucking. We've both been tested and cleared, and these suits have paid, so... that's what we'll be doing.

With my hands cradling her face, between kisses, I say, "Hell... I'm sorry. I don't think I can wait."

Fuck, I think, as I lift her off the ottoman. They're probably the nicest words I've ever said to anyone I was about to stick my dick in.

I lay her on the bench, crank it to the perfect height, and then I let my eyes feast.

Her hair is spread out over the dark-green leather, her panties wet, tits rising and falling fast. Jesus. It's the most beautiful sight I've ever seen.

Her hand goes to the strap on the red-corset thing she's wearing, readying to pull it down.

"No. Leave it on."

I want to feel the lace over her nipples and her soft, round stomach. I jolt forward, and she flinches like she's expecting pain.

"Slowly," she whispers.

My head lashes to the left. The sharks are circling. I'd forgotten all about them.

The biggest asshole hovers beside me, his crisp white shirt hanging open, custom tailored pants around his ankles, and cock shoved in the mouth of his equally disgusting associate who's on his knees. The third sicko lies back in the chair, jerking leisurely at his dick.

"Fucking move back," I say to the creep. "*Now.*"

He stops moaning. "L, that's not very sporting of you."

I'm about to reach out and choke him when the girl speaks. "*Hey,* hey, L. I'm waiting for you to touch me."

I press my shaft against her slickness, then place my palms on her breasts and squeeze. Man, they feel so good.

She moans, then winces. Oh, right. I'm hurting her. I stop squeezing and run the pads of my fingers along the bumpy lace.

My fingers play in the damp material covering her stomach. I can't stop touching her, enjoying how I've messed her up. Marked her as mine.

But I need to see more skin. "Okay, now you can ditch the outfit," I say.

Sitting up, she peels the top off and shimmies her panties down her legs.

"Go on and fuck her, L," the weasel says.

"*Shut up*," I snarl.

The idiot loves it when I yell at him. He snatches the lube from the guy next to him and squirts it over his reedy dick. He starts pumping his cock, and the guy on his knees in front of him waits, his mouth open and ready, obedient and empty-eyed.

Soft fingers grasp my hand, and she tugs me down. Bracing myself on my elbows, my mouth hovers over her nipple. "Come on," she says. "Take it. I know you want to."

I close my teeth around it until she writhes and moans. Then I attack her mouth, then move back to the nipple, to her mouth again, and then the other nipple, taking and taking.

I want to come so badly, but I don't want to stop devouring her. Not ever.

She grips my wrist, dragging my hand down to her pussy, and I flinch. I had no idea a girl could feel like this. So wet.

The sound of the suits slapping skin against skin, moaning as they watch, doesn't even distract me.

She slides me in her juices, and it feels like a miracle. No lube needed. When she slips my fingers inside her, my heart stops beating.

"F—*uck*," I say, so strung out I can barely curse properly.

She strokes my dick, making me pant harder.

And then... and then she stops guiding my fingers over her clit and brings the tip of my cock into her body. I make a sound—a helpless groan, and then push in to the hilt.

Oh, hell, yeah.

Everything but her and our connection falls off a cliff. I'm so present in this moment. Only here. Now. As if nothing existed before I touched her. I have no future—only this. And I don't care. I'm flooded with gratitude, burning with longing, and there is nowhere else in the world I'd rather be than right here touching her.

Fuck, it feels so good.

"You can go for it now, L," she says. "Get it done as quickly as you need to."

Quickly? Yes. I want that. I want to pound. I want to make her yell. I think for a hot second about doing that. Imagine what it will feel like hard and fast.

But when I move, I do the opposite.

Lodged deep, I grip her hips, then drag her to the end of the bench. Slowly, slowly, I pull back. Heart pounding, I stare at my cock pressed against her slick folds. It's an image I thought I'd only see in fever dreams, never in reality.

I stare at her—spread-eagled, impaled on my dick—until I can't take it anymore. I plunge back inside her. Then glide out, millimeter by hot millimeter, savoring the feel. I manage six blisteringly slow strokes before I'm driving into her. Fucking her good and hard.

"Fuck. Fuck," I grunt through clenched teeth, announcing each time I push deep.

With my dick gripped in her heat, I need to suck on her lips, but I'm too tall to make that work while I'm inside her. So I pull out, replacing my cock with my hand, my fingers working her pussy while my tongue works her mouth.

Then she squirms, whimpering like I'm hurting her.

What? *Am* I hurting her?

My eyes flick down. A liver-spotted hand lies on her stomach, making its way down south. I snap my fist out before the hand can move any further.

Bone crunches. Someone screams.

"That prick broke my nose!" Blood pours out of the suit's face, the one who looks like a pig.

"Keep your filthy hands off her or it'll be your arm I break next," I say, growling like a rabid dog.

"L," says the boss-weasel beside me. "Ignore him. We need you to finish this. And you," he turns to the guy who's still bleeding and squealing, "sit down and be quiet."

I sneer at him, a hot surge of anger running through me. Yeah, *now* this feels like my kind of normal. Sex and anger. Anger and sex. This is how I usually roll.

Staring at my face, the weasel lets out a sickening moan. He's digging the aggression. Bet I could break *his* nose as easily as I did his friend's. Wouldn't mind trying.

The girl—Edie, her name is Edie—puts one hand on my shoulder, the other on my dick, drawing me inside her again. Then she rests back on her elbows, digs her heels into my butt, and makes me forget about the weasel. The blood. Even the anger.

I fuck her like that, watching her tits move with each hard thrust. I've always hated this bench, the pathetic shits that usually lie on it, begging and moaning, but right now, *right now*, I love it. The way it puts her at the perfect height. Makes it so easy.

"That's it, L. Listen to that bitch loving every second."

As I turn and glare at the weasel, she pulls my head down and kisses me, and keeps kissing me while I dig my fingers into the lush flesh of her hips and fuck her. Her sounds go rough, like she's losing it. She's so close to the end. Pulling at me. Meeting every hard thrust with her hips.

I picture the night I first saw her. The glistening, wet street. The black dress. My hand on my dick that night as I lost my mind to the memory of her sad eyes. I want to fuck her, keep fucking her until we're blown into tiny pieces. Until we're nothing. Annihilated. Gone.

I won't stop for anything. I push her back on the bench, cover as much of her as I can, and pump faster.

She says, "God. God. God," then goes tense and shakes like a hurricane. And my cock, skin to skin, bears the brunt of every sweet clench and rolling wave as she comes. *Oh, fuck.* It's too much.

Don't go over.

Don't go over.

But I want to give in so badly.

She keeps spasming around me, but I don't move. I tremble and groan. Then everything stops. Just stops, like I've been absorbed into a black hole. And I'm nothing.

Then whatever is left within me contracts hard and explodes. I shudder over her chest while hot waves of come spurt again and again inside her.

Fucking, hell.

I am lost.

We lie there, our skin slick as we puff breaths over each other. After a minute of this shocking inability to think or move, I sense a foul energy move close.

It's the weasel, of course.

"Oh, dear boy. How absolutely sublime. I had no idea you were capable of *that.* What glorious noise. Such unsophisticated fumbling. Anyone witnessing that would think you were an untried, callow boy."

I'm not sure what that means, but I have enough of an idea for heat to wash over me. I swear I hear the girl make a long shush sound. A noise meant to soothe.

But the fuckwit keeps talking. "Anyone who saw that would have no idea of the expert fucking machine that you are, silent and ruthless. Well, let me reiterate—that was beyond beautiful and worth every single dollar I paid. Possibly more."

I stare into Edie's wide eyes and consider what I'll do to the weasel if I turn around.

My gaze drops to her lips. What would kissing her feel like now that the rush is over? It shouldn't feel as good.

But I already know it will, and I'm keen to find out for sure. With my dick softening inside her, I drop my face and get my answer.

Yep, it's the same as before. Kissing her makes everything but the two of us disappear.

For five seconds, my head spins slowly as my blood heats. Her lips and tongue move gently, then she presses my face away.

"Thank you," she whispers as she shimmies away and sits up, gathering scraps of lace.

What the fuck does she mean by thank you?

I look around at the late-afternoon light softening the scene. The weasel is wiping himself down with tissues. When he finishes, he holds a bunch out toward Edie. I snatch them from him and shove them at her. "Here," I say, sounding rougher than I should.

Giving me a quick smile, she takes them and dabs the wad between her legs, then fumbles to her feet. I feel nauseous.

That's weird. Ever since I've been a so-called adult, I haven't allowed anything as pathetic as guilt to seep in after fucking someone. Pretty much no matter what I've done; the more badass I am, the more Coop's scumbags like it.

Speaking of scumbags, the suits shuffle around the room, putting their respectable selves back together, while I silently throw my jeans and T-shirt on.

"So nice to meet you, Eden. I do hope we see you again soon," says the weasel.

My eyes shoot up just in time to watch her mouthwatering butt disappear through the door. That ass was mine only minutes ago.

"You had better shut that gorgeous mouth of yours, L, or we might start thinking lovely Eden rocked your world." Scratching his chin, the weasel laughs. "We might need to book her again to please you, Lighting. Or perhaps to torture you, we won't invite her back at all. Tell me, my beauty, which option would you prefer?"

Even if I knew the answer to that dumb question—which I sure as fuck don't—nothing and no one in the world could make me tell that weasel in a suit.

Not even Cooper.

Chapter 11

EDEN

Coop is an asshole.

I flush the toilet, then rearrange my street clothes in the mirror, wiping tears with the back of my hand. I snatch my discarded lingerie off the tiles and throw it into the trash bin.

When I push through into the adjoining suite, my tears flow freely again. "How could you do this to me?"

Coop closes his laptop, gets up from the couch, and strides around the coffee table with his arms stretched out like his greatest desire is to offer me comfort.

Yeah. That'll be the day.

"Eden... are you okay? Do you need a doctor? Come here. I'll drive you," he says, wearing an expression of concern that doesn't reach his eyes.

I push his hand away and point at the door opposite. "Don't touch me. Is that the way out of this hellhole?"

"Wait... So L couldn't do the job?" he asks, frowning at me as if he gives a crap.

"He did the job, Coop, and it was horrible." I dig around in my backpack, pretending to look for something. "It felt like I was deflowering a virgin. Like I was the sexual deviant instead of those suited-up lowlifes out there..." I trail off, my heart in my mouth as Cooper bends in half, his manic laughter bouncing off the stark, silvery walls.

He pulls me toward the black sofa and pushes me on to it. "Sit down. Fucking hell. Tell me everything."

There's no way I'm telling this asshole a thing.

"I'll make it worth your while, Eden." He sits opposite, narrowing his eyes.

Through massive windows that run along the west wall, city buildings reflect the sky's stormy patterns. As I stare at them, I keep my expression perfectly blank, hiding my inner turmoil.

Elbows on his knees, he leans forward, pulls out his phone, and taps at it. "I'm taking five grand off your debt. That's how keen I am to hear your version of events." Rubbing his chest, he chuckles like the pervert I know he is. "So we achieved the impossible, then. Got L to shove his end in a female at long last. No offense, Edie."

My eyes widen, but my mouth stays shut. Is it really possible L has never had sex with a girl before? Never even wanted to? It doesn't seem likely given the way things played out back there. He seemed so into it. But then again, he was skittish in the beginning.

"No deal, huh? Tell you what, because I'm feeling generous, I'll take ten grand off."

My stomach rolls as I stare ahead.

"Fuck it. How about twenty, then?" His thumbs jab the phone screen then he flips it around and holds it close to my face to taunt me with the balance sheet. Wait. He's serious.

I slowly suck in air. The things he's made me do over the last couple of years are so anti who I actually am, it's laughable. I'm no brave exhibitionist. No confident seductress.

And what happened in that room—the way my skin, my heart, and my soul were all grated raw by the pain in that boy's eyes. His intensity. His fear. Something long buried inside me cracked open. The physical act with L felt sacred and strangely familiar. And the last thing I want is to trade that precious feeling like a worthless commodity to the scumbag sitting across from me.

"I'm emailing the updated spreadsheet to you now," Coop says. Frowning, he fiddles with his phone. "So start talking, Edie, and remember I'll get the suits' take on it anyway. So, if your tale doesn't match theirs, you'll be in deep shit."

With my temples aching, I whisper, "Fine. What do you want to know?"

"For starters, show me where he hurt you. Was it... was it grisly?"

I shake my head.

His eyebrows knit. "But... it was bad, right?"

Focusing on the lush white carpet, I shake my head again.

"But he *did* hurt you?"

"No. He didn't."

"*Bullshit.* But you did say he fucked you."

I breathe out. Then nod.

"That's impossible. He can't even get it up without making someone suffer... *Christ.*" Unbuttoning his sports jacket, Coop flops backward, the couch cushions sighing in protest. "This calls for a drink, Eden. Want one?"

"No."

He throws off his jacket and goes to the Balinese sideboard, grabs two glasses, and pours double measures from a crystal decanter.

"Here." He shoves a glass in my face.

I grimace at it and sniff. It's scotch. Maybe a sip or two will stop my hands shaking.

I think of the farm. Of my dad back before Mom left us, before everything fell apart.

Rubbing my mouth to remove the taste of L's skin, I force myself to speak slowly. "When I walked in there, I got the shock of my life. That boy was the last thing I'd expected. Because he'd been a street hustler, I thought... I don't know." I glance at the ceiling, collecting my thoughts.

"He'd be a bit effeminate maybe?" Cooper laughs. "How narrow minded of you."

"Oh, shut up. I didn't say that. You did. I just didn't think he'd be so strong, okay? I hadn't expected someone who could snap me in half without meaning to."

"Why do you think he's so valuable? Lightning is a legend to those guys in there is because he's the real deal. Hard as nails and a beautiful fucking nightmare. Quite literally."

Right now, my still-humming body agrees with Cooper's description.

"So, does he do this stuff for you for the money?"

"L doesn't need the cash, believe me."

That seems unlikely.

"Anyway, keep going. So you get in there and you're terrified by the sight of him."

"Well you made damn sure that I thought he might hurt me, Coop." The scotch burns as I gulp it down. "So I had nothing to lose by trying to... at least calm him down a little. Be gentle."

"Gentle? What do you mean?"

I sigh. "You know, touch him. God, it sounds so dumb, but I tried to slow things down. Used a bit of massage oil. You know how it works, Coop, tame the savage beast by kissing him and..." I trail off as thunder rolls over Coop's features.

With his eyes glued to mine, he thuds his glass on a pile of magazines. It topples over, amber liquid pooling on the paper and underneath his laptop. He doesn't spare it a glance. "Hold it right there. You're trying to tell me, Eden, that you greased him up like a fair day hog and then kissed him, and he just stood there and let you?"

"Yes. He let me. He even kissed me back. Quite sweetly." I would love a photo of Coop's stunned face right now. I want it printed, turned into a poster, so I can stab it with a kitchen knife several times a day.

"It was like he'd never been touched that way before. With kindness. Like he'd never had sex that started slow. Sex that kindled from a gentle spark and blazed into a wildfire. And, Coop, he was into it, too. *Really* into it."

Coop's mouth thins to a furious line. "Tell me what happened next." His voice rasps low. "What did he do? Tell me, Eden."

This story isn't pleasing to Cooper Martinez. Not one bit. But he's paid for the truth, and I'm going to give it to him.

I lock eyes with him and go for it. "I thought L wouldn't be turned on by me and that your whole stupid plan would fail. And he'd have to beat the living crap out of me to entertain those evil shits out there. But I couldn't believe my eyes, Coop, he was hard almost straight away. He *wanted* to do it. So badly that he fumbled like a boy who'd never even kissed a girl before. Or at least like a guy who hadn't had much practice. But it didn't take him long to work it out... to learn how to go with the feel of it... just like any boy who was into girls would do."

Except for the hard rap of Coop's nails on the coffee table, the room is quiet.

"So, I guess you're wrong about him only being into guys. He must be bi."

"Nah." Coop reaches for his glass. "I've never seen him even look at a girl..." He frowns down at the mess on the coffee table, pushes his laptop clear of it, and then fixes me with a dark stare brimming with something ugly. "But there's no way in hell that he came while fucking you—"

"He did."

Coop shuffles to the edge of the couch, white-knuckled hands gripping his knees. "But was he... was he quiet?"

"Pardon?"

"Did he make any sound when he came?"

Wrapping my down coat tightly around my middle, I get to my feet. This is ridiculous. Why is Coop obsessed with the details? It's almost as if... unless he... Wait. I step a little closer, gaze into his steel-gray irises, and see it glittering there—raw obsession.

Un-*freaking*-believable.

Coop must have it bad for Lightning.

Then again, maybe it shouldn't shock me. I'm sure that *I'll* be dreaming about him. Probably forever. Those crystal-blue eyes. Cold. And at the same time flaming hot. The delicious curve of his mouth. The whole package, really. It wouldn't look out of place on a billboard. One that would cause nasty traffic pileups.

Well. Praise be and hallelujah. I finally have a weapon I can use against Coop.

The truth.

With my face only inches from his, I say, "No, Cooper. He wasn't quiet. He moaned, and he groaned. He said no. He said yes. Cursed over and over. And at the end, he even begged and said please, Jesus, and fuck repeatedly."

His mouth slack, Coop edges backward, his hands shaking on his thighs as I press forward and show him no mercy.

Smirking and trying to hide the frightened wobble in my voice, I say, "And I'm pretty sure he chanted an apology to someone as he came hard, shaking inside me."

Coop winces.

"Although, I'm not sure who it was he thought he had let down in some way—himself or me. I couldn't tell because by that point, I was too close to passing out from the volts of electricity he was pulsing through me."

Slumped against creases of soft leather, Coop looks withered well beyond his fifty years.

"You're lying."

I pluck my backpack off the carpet. "No, I'm not lying. Ask your filthy friends in there. They heard every moan. Watched every clumsy stroke of his hands, his mouth, and other impressive parts."

Violent intent flares in Coop's eyes, sending an icy shiver up my spine. He opens his mouth but doesn't speak. Shocked, I watch him tug his long-sleeved shirt over his head, messing up his wiry, salt-and-pepper hair.

In all the years I've known him, I've never once seen him in just a T-shirt. Never noticed the numbers etched in black ink running down his arm. The ones he's scratching and rubbing. Funny, they're the exact length of a cell phone number. The red letters underneath, crafted to drip like blood say: *This changes... you die.*

Coop sweats, squeezing the tattoo. And as his eyes skate between mine and the Persian rug, the truth suddenly hits me, and I know. As sure as I know that I prefer dark chocolate over milk, have a thing for storm clouds and guys with eyes so blue they hurt to look at, I'm certain whose number it is tattooed on Coop's arm. It's a sick reverse-brand. A statement of ownership. And a warning.

It's also an easy number to remember.

I straighten to my full height, all five feet three of it, rolling my shoulders back. "I'm going home. Don't make me do this anymore, Coop. I'm not the person you force me to be. And it's killing me."

I wait for a response but get none.

Feeling his glare on the back of my skull like a blowtorch, I sprint to the door, fumble it open, and slam it behind me. I fall back against the wall, pull out my cell, and plug the numbers from Coop's tattoo into my contacts. There is no way I want to risk forgetting them.

Now, how shall I save it? Under his name? No... maybe I should hide it. That would be the most sensible choice. I chew my lip, which makes me think of L's mouth—sensuous and lush.

Nope. There'll be no hiding. My thumbs speed over the screen as I save the number.

My work boots clumping against floorboards, I head down a brightly lit hallway toward the elevator, praying that Coop doesn't follow me because if he does, it will only be to strangle me. And I'm not ready to die yet.

First, I need to learn everything I can about L. If Coop is obsessed with him, maybe I can exploit that somehow to get the farm back sooner. And since Lightning is lick-the-plate-clean delicious, it'll be a pleasure to make him a research project.

The elevator door zips shut behind me. I grin down at the contact details on my phone screen before clicking it off, a hot thrill panging through me at the sight of his name.

Lightning Boy.

I shove the cell into my backpack. Hell, if I use that number and call L, I will definitely go down for it. Because when Coop finds out, he really *will* kill me.

Chapter 12

EDEN

A gusty wind crashes the waves together over the shore. The sound is so loud and constant that I can't make out the pimply teenager's words.

I lean over the counter of the beach-side coffee truck and say, "What?"

He sneers down at me. "I *said* you probably haven't got enough money in your account. The transaction was rejected."

Damn. I forgot payday is tomorrow, not today.

My best friend, Jess, pushes my arm out of the way and shoves her phone at him. "I'll get this. You paid last week, Edie."

"Cool, thanks," Grabbing my coffee, I ask, "Shall we sit on the wall and drink these?"

"No," she says deadpan. "I think the public restroom might be a nice choice today."

Jess's dry sense of humor can be harsh, but it's one of the reasons I love her so much.

She rubs her butt. "A few more of these jogging sessions, and I'll have a firmer ass than Chris Hemsworth's. I wouldn't mind if you relaxed the pace a little, Edie. As far as I know, we're not in training for the Olympics."

I give her a friendly hip bump as we walk. "I'm no expert, but I think you'll need to exercise more than once a week if you want buns of steel."

Jess sips from her biodegradable cup. Everything in this trendy beach-side neighborhood is beautiful, eco-friendly, and certified organic-fairtrade. Hence the apartment rents are unattainable for most humans of ordinary means. "Ouch!" she splutters. "That's hot. Hey, stop laughing."

"Okay," I say while snickering at her coffee-froth mustache. It makes her look like an unhinged Emma Stone.

"Ahh," she sighs, licking it away. "This is definitely the best part of exercising, when it's done and you can sit back and criticize other people's jogging styles as they go past."

I kick a stone off the path. "Well, they won't have to try very hard to look less ridiculous than we did."

"You're not wrong, Edie. A school of stingrays out jogging would be more elegant than us."

I laugh as we sit on the stone wall. It's our favorite place to recover from jogging because it has a gorgeous view across the bay.

Bright sunshine filters down through clouds, making the sea glow like it's made of shattered moonstones. Every few minutes someone jogs or power walks along the path in front of us, puffing and sweating. Jess gives them a sly thumbs up or thumbs down and manages to say a plenty about their styles just by wriggling her eyebrows. I'm glad I'm not a jogger parading past her. She's a brutally hard judge.

The sky is an intense blue streaked with inky swirls. "I hope that blows over," I say, pointing at the storm gathering on the horizon. "I was going to do a stint at the community garden after this, but I think I'll give it a miss if it's going to pour."

"You should just go home and relax for a change." Jess pulls a strand of bright red hair from her scarlet lips. Even exercising, her look is pure glam.

She once admitted her dream of being discovered by a talent agent while she's out rollerblading or working at the grocery store. Despite never having taken an acting class in her life, she's certain she'll one day be an A-grade Hollywood star. Her self-confidence is an admirable if not completely deluded trait.

"You've been at college all day," she continues, "and you've just run up and down the bay three hundred times. Chill out. Or even better, *go* out. Find a random sexy guy to have some fun with for a change. Do you even remember what a penis feels like?"

Oh, boy, do I remember.

Immediately, I'm transported back to that room. I can see L's beautiful face, his features drawn tight as he drives in and out of my body with a delicious intensity. I should probably keep that memory to myself.

Yeah, no need to involve Jess, I think, just as my mouth opens. "I *did* have a recent close encounter with a very sexy guy. Two days ago, in fact." I slap a hand over my traitorous mouth. I can't believe I told her.

Her head whips around. "*What*? Don't say things like that when I'm sitting on a wall. I nearly fell off! How? Who? Tell me everything."

I don't have many friends, and other than Jess, the only person I let close is Nico, the emo kid I work with at the nursery.

Friendship with Jess has many perks. She works at an organic store down on Main Street and regularly supplies me with boxes of free vegetables. She never has low-vibe days. And she also talks a lot. That last one is my favorite Jess perk because it means she rarely asks questions. Today, unfortunately, is an exception.

We met nearly two years ago at one of Coop's parties, which I'm aware is a bizarre way to make a friend. Jess is lucky. She's only done a Coop party once for the money, and I thought I'd never see her again. Then one day, I was surprised to find the girl I'd last seen cozying up to a Norwegian businessman smirking at me behind the counter of my regular grocery store. I smirked back, and then we went out, got drunk, and debriefed on the weirdness that is Coop and his repellent buddies.

So Jess understands what I'm involved in and mostly doesn't make a fuss when Coop calls a few times a year requesting my presence. But she does enjoy a little scold now and then. Like I said, she's a harsh judge.

"Well, Edie? I'm waiting here. Spill the beans."

"It was at one of Coop's things." I cringe, waiting for her to start bitching and moaning at me.

Her gray eyes narrow. "Where you met this guy? It was at Coop's thing?"

"That's what I said, didn't I? He was a... he was a participant. I had to... *you know...* do it with him."

"I think after what you've allowed Coop to make you do over the last couple of years, you should at least be able to say the word *sex* by now." Shaking her head, she collects her thoughts, then takes a big breath to keep sniping at me. "Why?"

"Why did I have sex with him? Because I had to."

"But that demon Coop! Stop saying yes to him, Edie. When will you wake up to the fact that he is never going to give you your dad's farm back? He'll just toy with you until you're old and broken. Or worse, dead."

Hot shame rushes through me. "He only makes me go to those things twice a year at the most. And you've attended one yourself out of pure greed, so you really can't talk." I lean forward, readying to push off the wall and stomp away.

"Sit down." Jess knocks me backward. "Tell me about this guy."

I blow out a breath and start gushing like I'm fourteen with a crush on the high school quarterback. "I've heard Coop talk about him before, but he's never actually named him, just raved about this ex-street kid with a reputation as a real hardass that he sometimes ropes into his parties. Coop said he only does it with guys and can only have sex if he hurts them. For kicks, Coop's sleazebags wanted to see this guy try to fuck a girl. Thought it would be exciting to see him fail and probably kill me trying."

She shakes her head. "Do you see what I mean? Coop is not gonna stop until he turns you that special shade of blue that's reserved for the no longer living. And this guy you screwed, did he hurt you?"

"No. He was gentle, even kind of reverent." I laugh at Jess's stunned expression. "Just looking at him was enough to break my heart. He's tall, tatted, built like a god, and has this wild mix of danger and fragility. You know when you meet someone and they seem so familiar, but you can't work out why? It was like that. And I can't stop thinking about him."

"So you had sex with this gorgeous god while those perverts watched."

Heat prickles behind my eyes. "Yes, and he was so into it, Jess. Awestruck and shaking like he really hadn't done it with a girl before, just like Coop said. And somehow, he made me forget that those gross idiots were in the room with us. Isn't that incredible?"

For once she's speechless, but in typical Jess-fashion her silence doesn't last long. "That's horrible. And kind of amazing."

"I can't believe a guy like him would do anything for Coop. I'm going insane thinking about it—about him. I need to know what his deal is. And guess what? I've got his number!"

Her fingers snap around my arm like a bear trap. "You should call him, and I'll use my psychic powers to read his intentions through the phone. I'll be able to tell if he's trouble."

She's joking. Mostly. Jess does have an uncannily accurate black-heart detector.

I pull up Lighting Boy in my contacts and press the call button.

The breeze whips my hair around my face while I wait, heart in my mouth.

After three seconds, L answers. "Who's this?" he barks.

"And hello to you, too. This is Eden. We met the other day at Coop's thing and—"

"I know who you are. How did you get my number?"

"From Coop."

There's a drawn-out silence.

"From Coop?" he asks.

"Uh, yeah."

"Nope. Not possible. Try again."

"I saw Coop's tattoo," I say. "The one on his arm. And I guessed what it was."

"What?" He groans. It's deep and gravelly and sexy as hell. Then he goes quiet.

Jess stares at me, and L's silence drones on, making me scramble to fill it.

"I don't know how I knew it was your number. I guess... I just did. I'm calling because I want to talk to you about this crazy stuff with Coop and—"

"Yeah? Well, I don't wanna talk to *you* about it. So back off and leave me alone."

"L, wait!" Even though this guy is shockingly rude, I don't want to let him slip away yet. "Think about it. You've got my number. Make sure you save it. And call me anytime you want to talk. It's such a weird situation... with Coop... and I'd love to hear your story. And maybe I can tell you mine."

"Listen, I figure that you're someone who whores yourself out to lowlifes because you need money or maybe you do it for fun. Either way, I don't give a shit. I don't need to know anything else about you. Is that clear enough for you?" Without another word, he hangs up.

"Shit." I stuff my phone back in my jacket. "What a jerk."

Jess laughs. "I think he's really into you."

"Shut up," I say.

"Listen, Edie. It's rare for you to be interested in a guy, so it kills me to say this, but no matter how attractive this one is, don't call him again. He's bad news."

I give her a sulky look.

"Listen, he's somehow got himself messed up with Coop's sick weirdos. And going by that phone call, I don't think he likes you. So, if you happen to see him out and about, I suggest you run like hell."

That's probably a good idea. And it's also the exact advice Dad gave me all those years ago.

I'm beginning to think maybe Sam had psychic powers. He'd mentioned the running and the lightning practically in the same breath. How else could he have known about L—dangerous as a bolt from the sky and currently messing with my head?

As I mull Dad's words over in my mind, I recall that he'd mostly warned against an aching heart, and for now at least, that organ is safe. I plan to keep it that way.

All I have to do is stop thinking about L.

That should be easy.

Or maybe not.

Chapter 13

EDEN

"**H**ey, Edie. Quick, catch this!"

A huge bag of organic compost sails through the air. I fold my arms and watch it hit the ground at my feet.

Nico laughs, pushing dyed black hair out of his bright green eyes. "You'll have to work on your muscles if you want to be a farmer. You can't just cross your arms at stuff that's too big to deal with."

"And you'll need to quit being such an annoying pest if you seriously hope to land a girlfriend sometime before you turn twenty-one," I tell him.

His dirt-stained fingers twist the silver ring pierced through his bottom lip. "Hey, I'm only eighteen. There's still lots of time for me to enjoy being irritating." He struts across the nursery storeroom and bends to pick up the bag. "And in case you haven't noticed,

I'm getting better looking every day. So if I ever want a girlfriend, which is doubtful, it shouldn't be too hard for me to get one."

That's true. For a skinny emo boy, Nico is very cute.

As an only child with no living relatives, he's the little brother I've always wished for, annoying as hell but generally lovable. Nearly all our nursery shifts are together, and luckily for him, I mostly manage to stop myself from reaching out to pinch his lily-white cheek whenever he does something particularly adorable. Which is often.

"What is your actual hair color underneath all that dark dye?" I tease, pulling a face like I disapprove. I adore his indie style, and honestly, Nico could be bald and still pull it off.

"The color is like my mom's. Kinda blond, I guess."

I nod. "Honey blond like Zsofia's? I doubt it. I was picturing that you had a nice shade of dirty dishwater underneath all that inky-black angst."

He whips off a glove and throws it at my stomach. Covering his gaping mouth, he says, "Sorry! I don't know how that happened. Damn gardening implements around here have minds of their own."

They certainly do when Nico is around.

Frowning, I check the time. "Shit, it's one-thirty already. I've gotta go. I'm late for class, and I need to swing by the mall and get some money before I head to school. I bought these textbooks from this girl who insists on cash payment. Who does that these days?"

"My mom. Aren't you finished that course yet?" he taunts.

I lift the tray of seedlings onto the potting shelf behind me, dirt sprinkling over my boots. "Only six more months and then I'm done." I give him a stern look. "As you well know. And then my life will be all about slaving away until I'm fifty-five so I can pay off that asshole and get my dad's farm back."

"That guy sounds like a complete dick bag. Oh. Not your dad, Edie."

I laugh. "Oh, you have no idea how big of an asshole Cooper is, and that's exactly how it needs to stay. That man is a no-go topic, remember?"

"Well, if you can't give me any details about him, whatever you've got going on with him must really be fucked up. Why don't you just give up on the idea of that farm? You could travel and work overseas. There are other lavender farms to do good with. Ones that you could even manage. You don't need to *own* one, Edie."

"That farm is mine. It's all I have left of my dad. I want it more than anything."

He turns back to the pile of compost bags, shaking his head. "Let it go. Move on. Cut your ties with that guy."

Grinning, I stroll closer, and his eyes narrow. Probably bracing for impact. "Okay. Thanks for the life advice," I say, giving his back a hard whack before heading for the staffroom.

"Hey," he calls. "Mom asked me to invite you for a movie night Thursday. She's making goulash again."

When Nico was a baby, his dad left. He has no siblings. It's probably why we clicked instantly. We're both abandoned children.

"Awesome. Tell her thanks. Nothing could keep me away." I grab my bag. "Can you finish transplanting those seedlings for me before you leave? There are only two trays left."

"Yeah. Cool. I'm desperate for tasks because there aren't many cute girls coming through today."

Over my shoulder, I say, "That's because I posted on our Facebook page that *you* were working. Public service announcement."

I head out, climb into my wreck of a car, and drive toward the nearest strip mall as fast as I dare.

I hate stumbling into tutorials late, feeling fellow students stare and judge me as I try to find a seat. It's humiliating, but I can't avoid it today.

After driving around the mall parking lot for ten minutes, narrowly missing several poles. I give up and park my car, Olive, so far from the stores it's almost in the next neighborhood. Then I give myself a stomach cramp racing toward the corner convenience store—the one with the flickering sign and ATM jammed just inside the door.

As I enter, I'm hit by the smell of burnt coffee and cleaning spray, fluorescent lights buzzing overhead.

Dammit, the place is busy, and I haven't got time for this. I stand puffing near the drink fridges, staring at the broad back of the guy queued at the ATM. His shoulder blades keep me captivated for longer than they should. I ogle them shamelessly. He even rocks a baseball cap attractively, his longish, sun-kissed hair falling in an artful mess. I have to stop myself from reaching out, his hair is that adorable.

After three minutes, my blood is simmering with impatience. I give silent thanks for his carved muscles and first-class butt encased in pale denim. Without them, I might have erupted in a full-blown rage by now. Or probably just cried in frustration.

Finally, the customer ahead of him shuffles away clutching a receipt and a coffee, and I prepare to move forward in spirit, if not in body.

Other than his thumb flicking over his phone screen, the guy stays frustratingly motionless, and my insides threaten to boil over. It's your turn, dickhead.

I peer around his shoulder. What could he possibly still be doing? Arranging a hookup with his drug dealer? Nope. He's scrolling TikTok, and judging by the follower count, he's surprisingly popular. Going by his build and the tattoos winding down his muscular arms... Wait... they look familiar...

I shake my head. No. It couldn't be him. What would be the odds?

Anyway—right. If that's his own account, with that many followers, he's probably full of himself. Popularity aside, I'm late and need him to grab his cash and move on. Immediately. Which means... shit. I'm going to have to speak to him.

I despise talking to these hot-alpha types. They take every glance as an invitation, like you're desperate and begging for it. It's exhausting. And humiliating.

Sighing, I step to the side, trying to get a proper look at him. He pulls off his cap, flicks his eyes up, and pins me with an intensely frowning, tropical-blue stare.

Oh, no. No, *no, no*. It's him. L. In the flesh.

Like cartoon characters, our eyes widen at the exact same time.

Oh my God. It's the guy whose face, and maybe a few other very specific body parts, have been running a nonstop highlight reel in my head over the past few nights.

He steps back, growling, "Eden," like he's choking on the word instead of greeting me. His manners haven't improved since yesterday's phone call. And still, my heart kicks into overdrive.

The normal reaction would be revulsion. I should be freaked out by the party, by what those assholes forced on us.
Instead, there's clearly something wrong with me, because I haven't been able to stop thinking about him. A bad boy with a brutal reputation, shaking like a virgin. So fragile. So unfairly hot.

And the whole V-card thing? Coop must've been lying. Or L played him. Because there is no way a guy who looks like this made it to his early twenties untouched by female hands. It's just not possible.

He stares at me.

I don't look away.

Crap. I guess it's up to me to speak, then. "Oh, it's you!" I brilliantly commence my ramble with. "Sorry, I've been standing behind you for ages, but I didn't recognize you in that outfit. You know, the jeans. And instead of just... um—"

"Skin," he states flatly.

Red-faced and with my jaw dangling unattractively, I nod.

The corner of his mouth lifts slightly. Not quite a smile, more like amusement at my expense.

Golden hair all disheveled, as if he's just rolled out of someone else's bed, he looks at me as though I've either shot his dog or offered him a shit sandwich.

Okay, this is going nowhere fast, and I really need to get him out of my way. Out of my head would help too.

I point at the cash machine. "Do you think you could—"

"What are you doing here?" he interrupts instead, not taking the hint to finish up and move along.

Feeling strangely guilty, I say, "Well, I live around the corner, but I've just come from work, which is also around the corner. So. I end up here a lot."

"Where?"

"What?" I ask, unsure what he means.

He rolls his electric-colored eyes. "Where do you live?"

I shift my feet. No idea why that's any of his business. "Um..." is my scintillating answer.

Thrusting his disturbingly handsome face well beyond polite boundaries and into my personal air space, he says, "Which. Street.

Edie?" Each word lands separately, deliberate, like he's talking to a slow child and resenting every second of it.

"Blackchapel," I reply, sounding like I'm not quite sure where I live, which probably confirms his theory that I'm an idiot.

He takes a step backward, which is a relief. I can breathe again. "Oh, yeah. I know it. You live in one of those Art Deco apartments with the curved windows, right?"

I nod. "How would you know that?"

"Our mutual friend owns the building. Makes sense. Also makes you an idiot."

Ah, ha. There it is—his low opinion of me clearly stated.

"You should move out of that place," he says. "Cut your ties with Cooper."

Well this guy certainly has strong views about other people's business, and he's not afraid to share them. Also, he's not the first person to give me that advice today.

At this point, it would be quite appropriate for me to tell him to back off. Like he did to me yesterday on the phone. Honestly, it's surprising he's even acknowledging me today—out in public, no less—let alone handing out life advice.

"I know I probably should cut ties with Cooper," I admit. "But it's not that simple."

"No. It never is with Coop. But you need to get as far away from that prick as you can. And by that, I mean like yesterday. Does he hurt you?"

"Not physically," I reply.

"Good. Tell him if he does, I'm gonna rip his head off and shove it so far up his ass he'll be able to speak through his gut hole. Understand?"

"Sure," I lie. "By gut hole, do you by any chance mean bellybutton?"

Ignoring me, he points at the Heaven and Earth Garden badge stuck to my nerdy, green-collared T-shirt, his finger only an inch away from my breast. He might as well have tasered my nipple for all the crackling awareness it sends through me.

"Work there, do you?"

I glance down, just to make sure my boob is still attached to my chest. "Yep. Sometimes. I mean—yes. Part-time. I'm studying farm management full-time."

His eyebrows shoot up above dreamy, azure eyes, and he lifts his chin, looking down his nose at me in a get-the-fuck-outta-here way. Not sure why it takes that expression to do it, but intense lust pools in my belly and a few other places I really shouldn't think about right now.

Maybe because it's so like the defiant expression he'd given those perverted suits the other day. That dangerous look that had warred with his other stare—the hungry one he'd fixed on me as he bent me over that bench.

"So what about you? Where do you live, L?" I ask, sounding prim and nervous, like a wallflower at a Regency-era party talking to an out-of-my-league duke rather than a guy who'd, not that long ago, been sweating and groaning over me like an animal.

Eyes on the pavement, he steps back, shoving his phone roughly into his back pocket. The flexing of his arm muscles makes his Yakuza-style tattoo dance. The black-and-gray ink swirls down his right arm, a knife blade ending near his elbow. I picture the snarling dragon hidden beneath his sleeve, the ink coiling over his collarbone—dusky pink and bright blue flowers popping against the black wave patterns cascading over his chest like a warrior's breastplate.

Biting his perfect lip, he glares at me while I stare at his arms. "Like them, do you?" he asks gruffly.

"What?"

"My tattoos."

"Oh! No."

He raises an eyebrow.

"I mean... they're fine. If you like dragons. But you haven't answered my question. Do you live around here as well?"

"I've gotta go," he says, dismissing me and scowling down at his heavy black boots. Tough-guy boots. They suit him.

He backs away like he thinks I'm armed and dangerous and that keeping me in his line of sight is the safest option.

Interesting. He's decided not to get his money out after all.

Fine.

That works well for me and my running-late-for-class situation.

Face flushing, I turn swiftly toward the ATM, stomach panging at the thought that I'm missing the perfect opportunity to find out more about my current obsession. My mystery boy. The guy whose hetero-sex cherry I had apparently popped.

"Oh, okay then," I say over my shoulder. "It was good to see you again, L."

"With clothes on this time, too," comes his deep voice from behind me.

It sounds suspiciously like he's smiling. No. That couldn't be. He looks like he's never been amused in his life. His mouth is permanently grim. Unfortunately for me, still lush and sexy.

I fling my head around for one last ogle and freeze. He's grinning. A real one. Lopsided and wide across his gorgeous face. The light gold stubble on his chin makes him look scruffy, and I ache to reach out and touch it.

I wish I had the courage to invite him out for a drink. We could get drunk, make out in the hallway near the restrooms, and I could pretend he was just some guy from the neighborhood—someone who knew nothing about teenage prostitutes, the streets, or sex parties.

This man is the farthest thing from boyfriend material I can imagine. But that doesn't stop me from fantasizing. It should. Except maybe late at night, lying awake in bed. That might be allowed.

Pulling out my wallet, I turn back to the ATM.

"Hey," he calls, already walking backward into traffic. A car skids to a stop, nearly taking him out. He doesn't even look. "Don't call me again, Edie. Ever."

And just like that... there goes my asking-him-out fantasy. Struck by lightning. Reduced to ash.

Oh well. Reliving this encounter with Lightning should at least keep me awake in accounting class, which—damn it—I am now officially ten minutes late for.

I don't answer him. And even though it nearly kills me, I don't turn around for one last look.

I just let him walk away.

Chapter 14

L

It's midnight. I'm standing on Jackson Street across the road from Joe Junior's burger joint, and I don't know what the hell I'm doing here. That's bullshit. I know exactly why I'm here.

I'm staring hard at a particular spot on the pavement. It's the exact place Edie stood four years ago—with Coop—the night I first saw her.

Dropping my forehead into my palms, I smother a laugh and scrub my face until it hurts. A long whistle pierces my ears, so loud it cuts through the racket of the traffic. Then a fast-moving object slams into my shoulder.

"Get the fuck outta here," yells a gravely voice. "What are you doing here, L, my man?"

Oh, hell. Please, no. Don't let it be who I think it is.

I raise my head and find myself staring into the drug-fucked eyes of Reno the lunatic, an associate from my time on the streets.

Skinny as a drinking straw, *Christ*, he looks bad. Like the last time I saw him, his narrow head is still shaved, only now it's covered in festering crusty scabs. I'm amazed he's still alive.

He cackles like a psychopath, his breath almost making me gag. Shit, man. He doesn't have a single tooth left in his head.

"Been a long time," I say, tipping my chin at him as I cross my arms and widen my stance.

"You can say that again, motherfucker."

Right now, I can think of a lot of things to say to the dude, but I don't say anything. He stole from me more times than I care to remember.

Silver eyes raking over me, he flicks up the bottom of my T-shirt. "Look at you! Fuckin' fancy."

I look down at myself and see jeans, T-shirt, scuffed boots—nothing flash.

He leans close and sniffs. "You smell real pretty, homeboy."

I plant my palms on his chest and shove him back. "Yeah? You don't."

He cackles like a crackhead. "So the rumors are true. You got off the streets. Wasn't sure if you were dead, Lightning, but damn you done good, my dude. Hey, you got something for me? Just a little bump for an old friend."

I shake my head. "Don't touch the stuff anymore."

"Shame," he says, radiating bad vibes as he paces back and forth, shaking his hand at me like a revival preacher. "Hey. Hey, Lightning. Walk with me, man."

I haven't visited this part of town since the night Ariana rescued my sorry ass from the gutter, and it's just my luck to run into the biggest lowlife from my time living rough. And I definitely don't want to go anywhere with him.

He watches me bite my lip. "Nah, man. I'm cool. Really. Would old Reno here fuck with you?"

Yeah. He most absolutely would.

"Come with me, brother. I need to show you where your friend old Nelson is sleeping these days. The guy's in a whole world of trouble. You wanna see?"

For a second, I forget how to breathe. "Nelson's still alive?"

Giving me a toothless grin, Reno nods, and I shake my head at how crazy the fucker looks.

"Come on. He's in the park... just around the way."

Oh, perfect. The site of my last stand as a half-starved teenage hustler. This gets better and better. But old Nelson... he and I used to crash in the same spot every night—under the Shardpoint Bridge. If that poor fucker's still alive, I want to do something to help him.

We walk fast, dodging cars and weaving through people out boozing and pimping and scraping by exactly the way I used to. It's a shock to smell the desperation in the air, taste its sour flavor on my tongue again. This sense of danger buzzing over my skin feels as regular as breathing. So familiar. And far too normal.

While we walk, Reno dances around me—in front, behind, in front again—and all I have to do is say yeah, nope, yep, uh huh every so often and he doesn't even notice my unease. He's too busy rattling his own jaw.

The park is empty when we enter, and besides Reno's constant jabbering, the only other sound is our boots scuffing over the gravel path. His voice grows louder, no doubt waking up any critters who were hoping for some shut-eye. My eyes skim over the shadowy trees and shrubs, skin prickling even though the breeze is warm.

"So where's Nelson?" I ask.

Reno points to an ancient oak over by a drinking fountain. He's strangely silent as he turns and strides toward it. Moving out of the lamppost's glaring light, I follow, the darkness heavy at my back.

Smoke coils in the air as Reno lights a cigarette. He doesn't even bother to offer me one, so it's lucky I don't do that shit anymore or I might be offended.

"Hundred bucks," he says, the red tip glowing hot near his mouth.

"What are you on about?"

"Hundred. To fuck me."

First, I laugh. Then heat slams through me as sweat breaks out on the back of my neck. "I don't wanna fuck you, you idiot. Got much better things to spend my money on."

His smile turns nasty. "I'll do you, then."

"I don't think so. Just tell me where Nelson is."

I blink and he's in my face, his fist gripping my T-shirt. *Fuck.* I don't wanna hurt the dickhead, but the edges of the park start to dissolve around me, whispers from past nightmares slithering inside my skull. Taunting as they come for me. They're always coming for me.

Growling, I push Reno's chest hard, and he stumbles backward. "Fuck off," I say. "The drugs have really fucked your brain, man."

"Stay cool, Lightning. I've always been into you, man. Hell, I'll suck you for free."

I can't catch my breath. It's ragged. Uneven. But no matter how much I want to punch Reno and make him stop talking, I need to keep my shit together. "Just tell me where Nelson is."

"Dead, of course, you stupid fuck."

Taking my time, I crack my knuckles, and then lunge for him. He drops into a squat like he's about to pull up his socks... or... *fuck*—he's got a knife. I throw my fist at him, grunting as it crunches into his temple. He slumps to his knees on the grass. His shoulder clicks as my palm slams into it. Then he flops backward. I straddle his waist, my hands wrapping around his scrawny neck.

"I should fucking kill you," I snarl.

And just as the voice in my head gets louder—the one that tells me I'm *beautiful and bad, so fucking bad*—Reno starts having some kind of bizarre attack, his hands slapping his tank top. He grimaces and holds a palm up, fingers spread wide. "You're bleeding, L. You're fucking bleeding on me."

Really? I grope around the burning sensation on my stomach. My hand comes away wet. "You sliced me, you moron."

I give him a half-hearted smack to the chops and launch up onto my unsteady feet. I feel lightheaded, but I think it's just the shock. I'm never coming near this dump again.

"Sorry, man," he starts to grovel. "I didn't mean to—"

"Shut up," I spit over my shoulder. "You ever see me on the street again, Reno, do me a fucking favor and keep on walking."

I press hard against my wound, but I don't lift my shirt to check it out. It stings bad. I don't reckon I'm dying, but if my innards are hanging out, I really don't want to see them. I should probably call Angelo, get him to pick me up just in case I pass out. Nope, that won't work. He'll be out drinking. Or knowing him, at some kind of orgy.

I head back toward Jackson where the buses are, again wondering why the hell I came here tonight. I'm such a loser because I'm still kidding myself. Pretending I'm all at a loss when I know exactly why I'm here.

And the reason is: *that* girl. Nearly a week ago now, I had sex with a female for the first time. With *her*. And I'm pretty sure it's ruined my life. It's definitely done something to my brain because now, it's all I can think about. Edie. Fucking her. And that rainy night four years ago when I saw her standing on the opposite side of the street. The amazing bolt of lust she'd inspired—my first experience of pure violent longing. Now thoughts of her feel like oxygen. What I need to survive.

But why is she still messed up with Cooper?

He's the reason I need to stay away from her. And he's the reason she needs to hate me, not call me up for cozy little heart-to-hearts like our lives are somehow aligned and we're going through the same shit together. My life has completely transformed since that long-ago rainy night when the mere sight of her rebooted my heart. Seems hers hasn't.

I'm an asshole to her for her own good because I'm dangerous. Not the best guy to hang out with. She could ask anyone who's ever been close to me, and they'd confirm that fact. But wait—she can't because they're dead.

So I'm *helping* her by being a prick. That's what I keep telling myself as I walk along clutching my burning gut. I'm performing a noble deed by staying away, not acting on what I really want, which is to see her again. Touch her again.

All I have to do is avoid that girl.

Stay away.

Don't think about those sweet dimples. The way she tasted. The hypnotic movement of her body underneath mine. Fuck!

To distract myself, I chant a rap to the beat of my bootheels on the pavement. I riff about trees and knives. Streetlights and psychosis. Car horns. Dumbasses with no teeth. And then, unfortunately, wind up describing a pair of sad, dark eyes.

It takes me a while to get back to Jackson Street because halfway there, my pace slows right down. When I finally arrive, I turn in the opposite direction to home.

I stop and stare at Joe Junior's where tonight's unwise adventure began and realize that the way I'm facing leads to Edie's apartment. It's quite a hike though. And I'm still bleeding. I should turn around. But I keep walking, guided by my unreliable dick compass.

I must be crazier than Reno, because every instinct I have is dragging me toward her. Like if I don't see her face tonight, something in me is going to die.

Chapter 15

EDEN

The light in my stairwell is out again. Damn Coop. He rarely acts like a proper landlord or fixes anything, despite his endless promises to do so.

I bolt up the steps to my apartment, grating the pads of my fingers along the internal brick wall as I go, praying I don't trip in the dark and snap my neck. As I reach the second-floor landing, so close to the sanctuary of home, my cell rings.

Unwisely, I answer it.

"You deserted me," Jess slurs.

"Impressive," I say, digging around in my canvas satchel for my keys. "It only took forty-five minutes for you to figure out that I'd split. Much better than last weekend when it took you almost three hours to realize."

"What's your point? I was hammered last week, Edie."

I laugh. "And what about tonight?"

"I'm only a little drunk."

I snort down the line at her lie.

"You sound all echoey," she says. "Please tell me you're not calling me from the toilet."

"The stupid stair lights are on the blink again, and I'm standing out here trying to find my keys in the dark, wishing I actually *was* on the toilet."

"Okay, nope. Get inside. Right now. Find your keys, lock the door, and then call me to confirm you're not dead. Actually, just text me. Tommy-too-cute-for-his-own-good is here tonight and he's giving me bedroom eyes."

"Just make sure that's *all* you let Tommy give you tonight," I scold. "I'm pretty sure you caught herpes the last time you did something you shouldn't with him."

"Only the oral kind." She laughs. "But seriously, Edie, you need to get inside. That place gives me murder vibes."

"Relax. The neighborhood isn't quite that bad."

"What did you say?" she yells.

A loud guitar riff blares in the background.

"I *said* it's not that bad around here."

"Tommy's heading my way." Jess whoops. "Okay, I'm going. Please lock your door."

"Sure, if you promise to stop drinking tequila," I nag pointlessly. She's already gone.

As I finally find the keys in my bag, dread slides through my bloodstream, the tiny hairs on my arms standing to attention. I resist the urge to glance over my shoulder and instead focus on getting the door open and then locked tight behind me.

Ten minutes ago, when I'd turned off the main street into the courtyard my apartment overlooks, I'd had the unsettling sensation that someone—or, perhaps worse, some*thing*—was watching me from the shadows of the elm trees. So I'm a little spooked right now and wishing I hadn't watched that horror movie with Nico and his mom last night.

My front door opens onto a large living space and adjoining kitchen. It's sparsely furnished with sturdy but plain thrift-store pieces. Colorful cushions and jewel-toned rugs brighten the somber dark wood floor and make the place feel like home.

After my dad died when I was sixteen, I spent two years getting tossed from one bad foster home to the next. So even though my one-bedroom apartment is small, it's all mine, and I love it with an almost irrational passion. Every time I come home, I usually feel happy, like I've walked into a roomful of puppies waiting to greet me.

Except tonight, I just feel jittery.

I've lived here alone since I was eighteen—nearly four years now. And solitary time is mostly wonderful, just like the apartment itself. Mostly. Because it comes with one massive drawback attached to the lease. A mean, dirty ex-cop called Cooper Martinez.

After buying my father's farm when he died, Cooper kept tabs on me throughout my stint in the foster care system. And when

I was released into the big, wide world as a so-called adult, he barged back into my life wearing the mask of a benevolent uncle. I stress the word mask. He helped me apply for college, got me a job at the garden center, and even moved me into one of his investment properties—this very apartment—graciously charging minimal rent.

At the time, I thought, *wow*, what a great guy. Looking out for a girl alone in the world and all that baloney.

But there was a catch, of course—the parties. "Oh, hi, Eden," he'd say every six months or so. "I've got something outstanding in the works for next week, so I need my special girl. You free?" I'd clear my schedule if I wasn't, because after all, Coop is the world-class prick who holds my dad's farm hostage. My birthright. The only thing that truly matters to me.

Good memories are buried in the rich brown soil of that farm. The few happy ones I have of my mom, before she lost her mind and abandoned us. Beautiful rolling fields of purple lavender. Sam's hearty laugh. And whatever innocence I had left.

And bingo—there it is. The quality that makes me special. At Coop's shindigs, my sexual naivety practically glows under a spotlight, dampening the lace I wear and shining up my skin. The creeps can smell it. They can tell I'd sooner poke myself in the eyes with those dumb heels than attempt to sashay across a room in them. It's obvious I'm playing a role that doesn't fit me. And badly, too. But that doesn't matter to the suits. If anything, I'm sure it makes them like me more.

Anyway, I'm home now. Alone at one-thirty on a Friday night, *scratch that*, Saturday morning, admiring the patterns on the pressed-tin ceiling from the doorway.

I dump my bag on the narrow sideboard by the door. A warm, lazy glow spreads through the apartment as I flick on lamps, yawning as I reach the living room's best feature: the huge Art Deco bay window. By day, afternoon sun drenches everything in gold. Now it only reflects the room back at me like an eerie black mirror.

I should shut those blinds.

I stare into the dim courtyard as I tug the cords. There is definitely a person-shaped shadow lingering near the trees. It could be Ivan, the British marketing whiz, returning home late, as he often does on a Friday, to vomit noisily into the fountain while bellowing for help getting up to his third-floor apartment. He regularly forgets where he lives. Tonight, he'll be fending for himself. I'm not going anywhere near that courtyard. Not after that horror movie.

My skin prickles. I sprint for the bathroom, yanking my phone out as I go. I cue up a classic punk playlist and abandon it on the kitchen counter mid-song, already breathing easier. Music grounds me. Keeps my imagination from sprinting straight into serial-killer territory.

For the thousandth time tonight, I curse Nico and his bright idea of "just one mildly scary movie. It's not too bad."

Bladder relieved, I head for my bedroom, stripping off my stretchy black dress and flinging it onto the bed without looking. Relief loosens my shoulders. I'm home. I'm safe.

And then something horrible happens.

Three heavy thumps sound against my front door.

My heart tries to claw its way out of my chest as I rush down the hall and stare at the door's red paint.

Thump. Thump. Thump.

Oh no. No. Absolutely not.

It has to be the shadow-person from the courtyard. I do not want to know who that is. If I stay quiet, maybe they'll go away. People give up eventually, right?

Bang. Bang. Bang.

"Hey, Edie. Open up. It's me, L."

My stomach drops.

L?

What the hell is he doing here?

My heart goes feral, ricocheting against my ribs. I can't speak. I don't even breathe. Three seconds pass.

"Edie! I know you're in there. For fuck's sake, open up. I'm bleeding all over your welcome mat."

"What?" I yell, already grabbing the handle as adrenaline steamrolls common sense.

I wrench the door open.

He's right there, too close and frowning. One big palm pressed flat to his dark T-shirt. Blood slicks between his fingers, black in the low light.

My pulse spikes hard as his gaze drops slowly to my chest. And stays there.

Unbelievable. He's bleeding and still managing to ogle my tits. I glance down at my lacy tank top and matching panties. Okay. Fine. I walked into that one.

I clear my throat. "Inside. Now."

He steps over the threshold and stops. Just stares at me, his expression predatory. Dark, golden hair hangs in messy chunks over his forehead, framing a jaw that looks carved from granite.

My legs absolutely betray me, and for a moment, I wobble as I walk backwards into my apartment.

"L, what the hell—"

"Awesome," he cuts in, crooked grin flashing. "You're playing The Clash. This is a fucking great song. Didn't have you pegged as a punk fan."

I fold my arms over my chest. I don't know why. He's already seen everything. Touched it. Tasted it.

"Would you fancy a quick slam dance before I call an ambulance? Shit, L, forget the music. What happened to you? Should I ring 911—"

"No." The word falls like a slammed gate between us. The dining table creaks as he braces a palm on it, jaw tightening. "Please don't.

Cops are the last thing I need. It's nothing. Just a scratch. I fell into something. It was just—"

"The pointy end of a blade," I finish flatly. "You're leaking on my floor."

I step into his space and plant my hands on his chest. His heat envelops me, his heady male scent flooding my senses and erasing every sensible thought. I ignore the low curl of want in my belly and shove him toward the couch.

"Contrary to your opinion," I add, "I'm not completely stupid. I have an idea what you've been up to."

The paisley couch is mostly red. A mercy, really. He can bleed on it all he wants.

"I never said you were stupid." He drops onto the cushions with a groan, eyes never leaving my face.

"Do not move," I tell him. "If you pass out, I'm calling an ambulance whether you like it or not."

I grab a towel from the hall closet and toss it at him.

"And L?"

He looks up, pupils blown wide, mouth tight with pain.

"If you get blood on my favorite rug," I say sweetly, "I will kill you myself."

With my nervous system still buzzing on pure adrenaline, I stumble into my bedroom, yank a light summer robe from the bedpost, and speed toward the bathroom. From the cabinet, I grab disinfectant, cotton swabs, and a packet of bandages. On my way past the kitchen, I snatch a bowl from the stack of clean dishes.

When I return, L hasn't moved an inch. That surprises me. He doesn't strike me as the obey-instructions type of guy.

Unhelpfully, my brain drifts to Coop's party. To what I showed L that night. What we shared. How fast he learned. Then I shove the heated images away and kneel beside the couch.

His head rests back against the cushions, eyes tracking the ornate patterns stamped into the tin ceiling, like he's counting each tiny sunburst. Like he's disassociating. I sit beside him, but he keeps staring up.

"It's stopped," he murmurs.

"What has?"

"The music. Your playlist or whatever. It finished. Can you put it on again?"

"No." I pop the cap on the disinfectant. "I want to talk to you."

"That's what I was afraid of." His mouth twists into a scowl. Still stupidly kissable. Annoyingly so.

"Three days ago you told me to go to hell," I say. "So showing up on my doorstep bleeding is... odd. What exactly do you think you're doing here?"

He exhales a slow breath. "I didn't know where to go. Couldn't get your face out of my mind. All I know is I wanted to see you before I bled out. Remembered you live close by. But I hung around the fountain for a while, trying to decide if I should keep walking."

"I'm glad you didn't."

His eyes flick to my face, then quickly away.

"So," I say, reaching for his hands and prying his fingers away from his stomach, "what happened to you?"

Blood seeps from his wound again but not too much. The cut's a couple of inches long. Not deep. It'll probably stop bleeding soon, though stitches wouldn't hurt. Failing that, butterfly bandages, a whispered prayer, and he'll be fine in a few days.

He sighs, gaze still glued to the ceiling. Maybe he's secretly passionate about 1930s interior design.

"The least you can do is explain why you're bleeding on my couch," I say, glancing sideways. "I'm not calling the cops, if that's what you're worried about."

His lips quirk. "I ran into an idiot I knew from when I lived on the streets. Before I got my life vaguely together." He drags a hand through his hair, dark-gold waves going feral. "Hearing I lived on the streets, does that make you want to kick me out?"

"No. I already knew about that," I say quietly. "Coop told me."

"Right." He swallows. "I had a disagreement with this asshole in the park, and he pulled a knife. Scratched me before my fist could introduce itself to his face."

"Hold your shirt up," I say, dabbing at the wound. "I can't see what I'm doing."

He pushes my hands away, grabs the hem, and yanks the T-shirt over his head in one fast motion. A grunt escapes him as he sinks back against the couch.

Oh. Okay.

Guilt hits me square in the chest as my eyes betray me, skating over his muscled torso. This is not the time for ogling. He's injured. This is inappropriate, and I am a menace to my own sanity.

I force my focus back to the cut and clean it carefully. The scent of antiseptic burns my nose, a sharp counter to his heat and the way his scent makes my head spin.

"Why?" I ask, smoothing antiseptic over the wound.

Four beats of heavy silence thud through the room.

"Why what?"

"Why did you fight him?"

His hips shift, but his mouth stays shut.

I press the edges of the cut together and guide his fingers to hold them in place. Then I tear open three packets of plasters. My hands are steadier now, focused. As I smooth the last one onto his skin, I say, "So tell me, are you one of those guys who thinks a night out doesn't count unless someone ends up hurt?"

He finally looks at me. Really looks. Then he leans forward. "I fought him because he was insisting I fuck him." His voice is slow and deliberate. "I didn't want to do that, and he didn't take it very well."

"Why not?" The question slips out before I can stop it. "I thought that was your... thing."

Anger flares in his eyes, quickens his breathing.

For reasons I don't examine too closely, my hand presses more firmly against his warm stomach. I should stop touching him, but I don't pull away.

"Because," he says quietly, "I don't like fucking guys. And the truth is, I don't really like fucking anyone."

That gives me pause. It doesn't line up with what I saw the other night. With what I felt.

Silence hums through the room. Restless, he bounces his knee, staring at the floor like it might give him answers.

I wait.

Finally, he draws in a breath and lifts his gaze to mine. There's something raw shining there, something that frightens me. "But here's the strange part, Edie. I *have* been thinking about fucking *you.*" His eyes flick to my mouth. "A lot. Thinking about how it felt. How present I was. How much I didn't hate it. The complete opposite, actually."

His words surprise me, and I absorb them silently. What they imply. What it costs him to admit it. My chest tightens.

"Usually," he continues, "sex is just noise in my head. A bad noise, and I'm not really there for it, you know? This was different."

He watches my face closely, waiting for my judgment, for me to recoil.

I do neither. Instead, I stand and take the bowl to the sink. I need to move, to create distance between us. I rinse it under water that's far too hot, welcoming the sting in my fingers.

Suddenly, his hand settles on my hip with no warning. He's crept up behind me, making no sound. Heat blooms at my back. His body is so close but not quite touching mine. I close my eyes.

"I haven't been with anyone since you," he says low. "I can't stop thinking about it. About you. It's been a week, and I feel like I'm crawling out of my skin."

He edges slightly closer.

"I need to have you without an audience," he continues. "I want to know what it's like to choose this. To want someone and mean it."

Yes, my mind echoes. I want the same thing too. And badly.

His hand slides up my back, gentle now. He moves my hair aside and presses his mouth to my neck. "So," he murmurs, "can we—"

I nod before he finishes the sentence. Because I already know I want this too.

I turn, reach for his neck, and then his mouth is on mine, his lips soft, his intent the opposite.

Breathing hard, he backs me into the wall beside the fridge, every movement urgent and raw. It's too much, too fast. I turn my head away, needing a second, needing my pulse to settle and my brain to engage. Only moments ago, I was playing Nurse Betty. Now I'm falling apart.

This is escalating out of control. His intensity is frightening.

His hand tangles in my hair and yanks my head back. His mouth crashes into mine, hot and forceful. He palms my breast hard, then drags his hand down my ribs, over my stomach, lower. His breath comes fast, his erection pressing insistently into me. He nudges my panties aside and pushes two fingers inside me.

Even wet, even wanting him, the way he drives into me hurts.

"L. Hey—stop."

"What?" His eyes are unfocused, too far gone.

I slide my hands over his shoulders, grounding us both. "You're hurting me. You need to slow down. Be gentle."

Confusion tightens his features. He removes his fingers from my body and stares at the floor, jaw clenched. For a beat, he looks lost. Then something hard shutters his gaze, and he leans in again, kissing me rough, one hand fisted in my hair, the other shoving my robe to the floor.

"Wait. Stop."

He groans and breaks the kiss, breath ragged.

Oh. I get it now. He has absolutely no idea what he's doing.

My chest tightens. "Hey," I say softly. I run my fingers through his hair as he keeps staring at the floor. "It's okay."

I hesitate, then say it anyway. "You're used to being rough, aren't you?"

He nods once.

"And you're usually in control."

Another short nod.

"Well," I say, my voice steady now, "if we do this, it has to be different. It has to be my way. Or we don't do it at all."

"I don't know if I can," he admits. "I'm not sure I—"

"You can," I say gently. "This time, you're not in charge." I meet his eyes. "You listen and follow my lead. You stop when I say stop. I'm in control. Okay?"

He shakes his head, then speaks fast, "I can be gentle. Look, I'll show you." His hands cup my face and he kisses me again.

It's hot and sexy, but it still isn't gentle.

I press my palm to his chest and create space between us. "If you can't rein it in, you should leave."

"I can," he says, brow furrowing. "I'm trying. I just—" He exhales sharply. "I don't have much practice with this kind of thing."

"With what exactly?"

"With not... overpowering people."

Something in my expression must change, because he flinches, and then freezes.

"No," I say quickly. "It's okay. That wasn't a criticism of how you're kissing me." I soften my voice. "That part's perfect. You just need to slow down."

His mouth curves into a slow, hopeful smile. The kind that makes me want to hold him close forever. And that terrifies me.

"Do you think you can let me be the boss?" I ask.

He stalks back and forth, the floorboards creaking beneath his boots. "No. Probably not."

The kitchen faucet beside us goes drip—drip—drip. The toilet next door flushes.

I fold my arms, keeping my expression flat. "Okay. Then we stop, and you can leave."

Grimacing, he drags his hands down his face. "Fine." He drops curled fists to his sides and looks at me. Stripped of bravado. "Whatever you want. You tell me what to do, and I'll do it."

"All right," I say. "Good. Come here."

He steps closer.

When he's directly in front of me, I cradle his face and meet his eyes. They're open, completely exposed. Nothing like the man who shoved me into a wall five minutes ago. "You have to say it," I tell him. "Say that I'm in charge."

"But, Edie," he says quietly, "you don't know what you're asking."

"I do." I let my thumb brush his jaw. "I have a pretty good idea why control feels non-negotiable to you. And I get it." I keep my voice steady. "But trusting someone enough to let go? That can feel incredible. You deserve to experience that."

He breathes out, long and shaky. "Okay. You're in charge." A pause. "I'll stay still unless you tell me otherwise. And if I can't do what you ask, I'll leave."

I kiss him.

He doesn't move a muscle, letting me set the pace.

I pull back just enough to smile. "Kiss me," I say softly. "As slowly as you can. Don't touch. Keep your hands right where they are."

Heat coils low in my belly as his mouth brushes mine lightly, his tongue moving with careful restraint. His breath ghosts over my skin, and three times his hand twitches upward. Three times he stops himself, fist clenching midair.

He wants to touch me badly but chooses to follow my instructions instead.

I take his hand and smile. "Come on. Let's move to my bedroom before this gets out of control."

A shy, almost disbelieving smile tugs at his lips as he stills.

"Don't tell me you've never done this in a bed," I say gently.

"Not like this," he admits. "Not since I was a teenager when things got... uh, complicated."

I don't ask for details. Now is not the time. All I know is I need to tread so carefully with this broken boy. Protect him from the horrors of his past.

My gaze drifts down his bare chest to the hard line of him beneath his jeans. He doesn't seem traumatized now by what we've been doing. What we're about to do. He's all in. Shivering with desire. Choosing this. Choosing *me*.

Without another word, I squeeze his hand and lead him toward my bedroom.

Chapter 16

EDEN

When I pull him through the doorway, he pauses, taking it all in—the old vinyl stacked beside my turntable, band posters sharing wall space with gardening charts, books and clothes in cheerful disarray. Curiosity softens his posture. Maybe even awe.

The bed creaks as I perch on the edge and let myself look him over slowly. "Okay," I say calmly. "Take off your jeans."

Moving fast, his fingers fumble at the buttons. Frustration flashes across his face.

I smile and scoot back on the bed, bracing on my elbows. "Slow down," I tell him. "We've got all night."

He drops his hands, breathing hard, staring at me like he's overthinking every move.

"Go on," I say gently. "You're doing fine. Don't stop."

He takes a steadying breath and does as he's told. When he's naked, his gaze falls to the floor, teeth catching briefly on his lower lip, his vulnerability disarming.

I soften my voice. "Look at me."

He lifts his head.

I crook my finger, beckoning him close. He crawls over me as I press my palms into his chest and run them down his abs. Eyes on my mouth, he brings his lips within an inch of mine.

"Did I tell you to do that?" I whisper against them.

He stares. "What?"

"Did I tell you to come that close?"

"No."

"That's right, I didn't. You should say sorry."

His Adam's apple bobs. "I'm sorry."

"Lie on your back."

Without a word, he shuffles over.

Wow.

What a sight. From his endearing frown, tousled hair, hewn-marble torso, and the perfectly proportioned cock straining in my direction, every part of him is scrumptious. Okay, so maybe one part is a trifle over-proportioned... but still perfect.

Clad only in my tank top and panties, I straddle him. He leans up on his elbows, but I push him back. "I told you not to move unless I asked you to. Is that unclear?"

"No. But..."

I study his face. "Are you having second thoughts about this?"

"No," he says quickly. "I just… can't you lie down here and let me go on top? That way I'll feel more—"

"In control? I'm sorry, L, but no."

His hand reaches for my face, and I push it away.

"I'm wondering if this position reminds you of something. Back when you were forced to do things. A long time ago?"

His eyes squeeze shut. "How do you know I—"

"Well, you've hinted at it. And I don't need a psychology degree to work out that you've been hurt and…" I take a big breath so I can say the word. Speak the truth. "…been abused."

Turning his head, he fixes his attention on the cherry blossom patterns on my window blind.

"I don't want to hurt you, L. I want you to feel good. I like you a lot. You're beautiful. I think maybe both inside and out."

His detailed inspection of the window furnishings continues.

"Let me show you what it feels like when you allow yourself to trust someone. Someone who cares about you."

Silence hangs between us as he stares deep into my eyes, my very soul.

I rise and grab an amber bottle of massage oil from the dresser.

Unscrewing the lid, I straddle him again, hovering over his erection. I rub oil on his upper body, leaning forward and back, pressing gently against his hard length, teasing with light friction repeatedly.

My panties are quickly soaked, my thighs trembling. L's eyes roll back, his eyelids fluttering, palm rising toward my waist.

"No touching," I remind him.

"Fuck. You're killing me."

"Pretty sure you'll live." I rub oil over the rippling muscles of his stomach, then peel my tank top off and toss it aside.

His hand rises again. "Come on, Edie, please let me touch you."

"Not yet." With my thumb, I trace the moisture on the head of his cock, his readiness confirming he isn't freaked out by this light, submissive play.

I press his shoulders into the bed and kiss him. Tension radiates from every muscle, coiled tight and trembling slightly. "Okay, you can kiss me back," I instruct. "Use only your mouth. Take as much as you want."

He gasps and surges forward, attacking me with his mouth, the perfect rhythm of his tongue making my head spin. As I pull my face away, he tries to follow. I shove him back slightly and kiss his throat, chest, moving downward.

His stomach muscles flinch. "What are you doing?"

I smile. "Exactly what you think. And all you have to do is stay perfectly still."

His mouth opens and closes.

"It's fine, L. Just lie back and enjoy it."

"But I haven't had anyone do that... I mean, not since..." His words trail off, and my chest softens.

"It's okay. I'm not that person who wanted to hurt you... the one who probably made you feel good and bad at the same time. And I'm guessing they shamed you for it, left you confused."

"Edie, I really don't think I can—"

"You can. Just try. Or don't. That's fine too. If you'd rather leave, I get it. You can come back anytime you want and we can give this another shot."

Gently, I palm his balls, and he groans. My confidence surges, and I feel powerful, like I do this kind of thing all the time.

I don't. Far from it.

Other than a self-absorbed boyfriend who took my virginity at seventeen, a single random hookup after a gig, and handful of Coop's parties, my experience is limited. But L's lost-bad-boy vibe draws me in. His fragility makes me want to protect him. His anger makes me want to soothe him. His beauty makes me want to consume him. I ache to taste him everywhere.

My hand circles his shaft, stroking lightly. "I want you to feel good. Feel what sex is like when there's no fear, no anger. Only trust."

Not that I've fully felt that myself yet. But I can imagine it. Something we can explore together.

"So," I ask, hand still stroking, "what do you think? Shall we just have fun?"

He nods warily as I shift down the bed.

Gripping the thick base, I lick his tip, apply light suction, and take in as much as I can, just once, slicking him up. I blow lightly over his skin, then bob up and down slowly three times.

"Oh, fuck," he moans.

I go carefully, making sure this feels different from anything he's experienced before. I want him to know it's okay. There's nothing wrong with desire. Even when it's a little kinky, if it's consensual, there's nothing to be ashamed of.

I press my lips over the velvety head, tasting pre-come, and suck lightly. While I work him, I cup his balls. "You taste so good." At my words, his thighs tremble, his breathing turning ragged and loud.

I lick and suck, again and again, my moans soft, his loud.

When he thrusts gently into my mouth, I pull back, fingers still wrapped around his base. "That's good, huh?"

Looking shattered, he nods.

"Just like you. You're good, too. Every part of you, L. You don't need to hurt me to do this." I keep my voice steady. "You just want to feel it. Enjoy it. Right?"

He nods again, eyes bright with something close to awe.

"Do you want to fuck me, L?"

"Yeah." No hesitation. No doubt.

I stroke him and smile. "You said you haven't been with anyone since me. Is that true?"

"Yes." The word strains past his tight throat.

"Same," I say. "And we both had tests before the party, so that means we can go skin to skin. No condom." I crawl up the bed and settle my hips over him.

He frowns, rigid with restraint, like a dog told to stay with a steak inches from its nose. His mouth twists as something inside him wrestles for control. He takes a sharp breath, fingers hovering near my panties.

I nod. "That's okay. You can touch me there." I wait a beat. "Over my underwear. And gently."

He cups me, thumb gliding feather-light. "Fuck. You're so wet. Is that normal? I mean… is that how you normally feel?"

"No," I reply, my voice low and husky. "It's because of you. You do this to me, L. So easily." I roll my hips into his fingers, and he shudders.

"I need you inside me. Do you want these on or off?" I ask, flicking my panties.

"Off. *Please.*"

I shed my underwear, and he watches every movement hungrily.

The distant hum of the neighborhood—hip hop drifting from somewhere, cars rolling by—fades as I climb back over him, lining him up. I sink down slowly. In this position, I can't quite reach to kiss him and keep him fully inside at the same time.

Between panted breaths, I murmur, "You can touch me anywhere you want. Just… don't try to flip me. I need to stay on top tonight."

And then his hands are everywhere—on my breasts, my stomach, my hips. Eyes dark and intense, his fingers stroke where we're joined. He circles my clit, amazed by my reactions, the way my hips roll and my head falls back. I drag slowly up his length, then plunge down. Over and over.

"Does that hurt your stomach wound... should I go easier?" I ask.

"What wound?" He laughs, then mutters, "Fuck," again and again.

I'm on fire. Every nerve a live wire, every part of me tightening, spiraling. I try to go slow, but everything ramps up. My moans, my movements, growing louder and faster. I have to check. Make sure he's still with me. That he's okay.

"Is this good, L?" I breathe.

"Yeah... yes. Oh, fuck, yes." He bites his lip, thrusting up into me. I don't know why I even asked. His hot groans, the taut muscles, the expression on his face—they say it all. But hearing him confirm it? It's thrilling.

I want to watch him go over.

"Let go, L. Come."

"I can't..."

"You can," I say, face close to his. "Just fuck me harder... without anger. No rage. Just feel... feel how good it is, and let yourself go."

He grits his teeth, grips my hips, and slams into me over and over until we're both groaning loudly.

The intense buzz grows stronger, electricity crackling around us, inside me, as I claw at the edge of bliss. "Please, L."

He grips my waist, holding me still. His hips slam mercilessly, thunder rolling over me, through me.

"Shit... Edie..."

Then he drives deep, his cock pulsing, body shuddering. I can tell he's trying to stifle a long groan, holding back, afraid to let it out. The low rumble in his chest makes me cry out, and I come hard, muscles clenching around him as he gasps, trembling, huffing through ragged breaths.

I collapse over him. His hand rests on my back, then lifts, hesitates, and drops again. He laughs. "Do I have permission to touch you yet, or is that still off-limits, boss?"

I laugh too. "Go for it. You can touch me anywhere."

We lie there, hearts thudding, waiting for our bodies to settle, his palm tracing lazy circles over my skin.

It takes a long while to come down.

Finally, I lift off him, leaving a mess on his thigh and the sheet. "I should probably head to the bathroom and deal with that."

"No. Don't go yet," he says, smiling. Then he shocks the life out of me by pulling me into his arms, wrapping me up like he's afraid I might disappear.

Shouldn't he be bolting for the door?

I inch back so I can see his eyes. "Was it... okay?" I ask quietly.

He scrunches his face. "Well... yeah. I guess it was okay."

I do my best not to look offended and obviously fail.

He laughs. "I'm teasing you. That was the best thing I've ever done. I'm going to start getting into fights every day just so I can turn up bleeding and get nursed by you, if this is what happens afterward."

My heart melts. I stroke his cheek.

With his expression so open, he looks sweet, tired, and dazed. "Does it always feel like that?"

I pause, collecting my thoughts. No it doesn't. Not for me.

I can't quite meet his gaze when I answer with a lie. "Yeah. Pretty much. There are plenty of people out there to sleep with if you want to test the theory yourself."

His eyes harden slightly as he removes his arm from around me. "So... would you let me fuck your ass if I wanted to?"

Interesting question. "Um. I don't know. Would I like it? Doesn't it hurt?"

"Usually the way I do it, yeah, it hurts."

I grimace. "Oh. You're not exactly selling it."

"I've never tried to," he says flatly. "That's why those guys like it."

"I don't get it," I admit.

He rolls onto his back, blowing out a hard breath. "The thing is, I'm not bi, Edie. I'm just... messed up."

I prop myself on my elbow, quirking an eyebrow at him.

Studying my face, he says, "I like girls. I always have."

"Only girls?" I ask. "But I thought you—"

"Yeah. That's what everyone thinks." His jaw tightens. "Look, if I were gay, I'd own it. I've got friends who are only into guys. That's fine. But me? I've only ever been with men because I was forced to."

My chest tightens.

"When I was homeless, I did the blowjob thing just so I could, you know... eat. When I finally got out of that mess, somehow Coop found me again. He uses me as a toy for his sick friends sometimes because he's got something on me." L trails off, raking his fingers through his hair. "It sounds like bullshit, I know. But I swear it's not."

I wonder what on earth Coop has over him. It must be something big for a guy like L to do that horrible man's bidding.

"But Coop said you'd never slept with a girl before me."

"That's true too. Until six days ago, I hadn't."

My eyes bulge, my mouth falling open. "But if you were into girls, why hadn't you slept with one?"

"Because I hated sex," he says quietly. "It was just this thing I'd been made to do—or had to do to survive. Sure, sometimes it felt good. But you were right earlier. When I liked any part of it, it only made me feel worse. For letting it happen. For sometimes getting off on it when it was so obviously wrong."

His eyes drift back to the cherry-blossom blind. "I didn't think I'd ever be capable of doing it with someone I actually liked."

I grip his chin and turn his face toward me, forcing a soft smile onto my own.

He flashes a quick grin. "But tonight... this... you've blown my mind. It felt incredible." He exhales, almost laughing at himself. "I can't believe I don't feel like hurting myself—or you—afterward. Not even a little bit."

"Well, I'm really glad to hear that," I say, aiming for easygoing, even as my body buzzes with shock and thrums with curiosity. I have so many questions. Too many. But they'll have to wait. There's no way I'm risking scaring him off now.

Trailing a finger from my throat down between my breasts, he asks, "So when can we do it again? Is now too soon?"

I laugh, fumbling over the covers for clothes. "After we eat some noodles and maybe drink a beer, then sure."

He gives me a strange smile, and I pause, studying him. It's odd. Then it clicks. He looks happy—that's it. Genuinely happy. My chest tightens.

"Stay there and relax. I've got leftovers I can heat up."

"Hell, don't feed me as well. I'll be back tomorrow if you do that."

"Oh, I'm not worried," I say lightly. "There are plenty of girls who'll be keen to help you create positive sex memories if you show the slightest interest. I can promise you that. You'll branch out soon enough."

His lips quirk sideways as he watches me pull on yoga pants and an old band T-shirt. "What if you're the only one I want helping me?"

"Believe me, you won't want that for long. So just kick back. Enjoy the afterglow, and I'll bring you something delicious." I give him what I hope is a sassy smile and head for the kitchen.

God, I lied. Of course I'm worried. But not about him. About me. About my brain. My thoughts. And whether I can survive such a devastating encounter with a damaged boy made of lightning and pain—a guy custom-built for breaking hearts.

Mine in particular.

Chapter 17

EDen

I'm in an environmental chemistry class when my cell rings, my ringtone blaring from my lap. Judging by the hundreds of scowls aimed my way, my fellow students are not fans of ear-blistering indie music.

"Turn that off," the girl in front of me snaps, rotating her glare around like an angry barn owl.

"I'm sorry," I whisper, fumbling to silence the call. I *hate* it when I forget to put my phone on silent before class starts.

Bright white against the black screen, the words *Lightning Boy* flash up, shocking my eyeballs and sending my heart ricocheting against my ribs.

L is calling me.

I lurch to my feet, frowning at the lazily splayed undergrad limbs blocking my exit. I take a big breath and then start climbing.

"Excuse me. Sorry," I say politely on repeat, while internally I'm screaming.

Honestly, you'd think people could recognize an emergency when a girl in the middle of an emotional meltdown crawls straight over their laps.

At last, I tumble out of the lecture hall and into the blinding midday sunshine. By the time I find a quiet corner and lean against the brick wall of the Science building, reality catches up with me.

No voicemail. Of course he didn't leave a message. That figures.

Three nights ago, after a bowl of spicy noodles, a snuggly snooze, and another round of sex—slow and tender this time—he kissed me stupid and then vanished into the gray dawn, leaving me to my own devices. Those devices turned out to be moping around the apartment, staring blankly at wardrobe doors and light fittings, while seeing only L's eyes, his smile, his golden skin. Remembering the way he smelled. Musky. Warm. Unfairly delicious.

Now, I picture the shape his lips made as he slurped noodles. I think of his arms, biceps bulging as he lay back against my pillow, hands linked behind his head, the pose turning his smirk lethal.

Why is he calling? Maybe to issue an invitation to watch the sun set and eat burgers down at the grungy marina bar tonight. The thought is wildly optimistic, but my skin buzzes anyway.

Well. I refuse to waste any more time wondering and hoping. It's time to find out what he wants.

My thumbs move fast. His phone rings. And rings.

Answer the damn call.

Just as I'm about to give up, he does.

"Edie," he says. Only two deep syllables, yet they brim with warning. Or maybe he's nervous. But probably not.

"Hi, L. I just missed a call from you."

"Yeah."

Silence.

I wait as long as I can, which turns out to be about three seconds, then ask, "So... how are you?"

"Crazy busy. You?"

Seriously? He's busy doing what, exactly? Friday, after he'd bled on my couch and caused permanent damage to my heart, I'd asked how he spent his time and earned his keep. He'd responded with head-spinning kisses, successfully derailing the interrogation, then promptly scurried back to his lair, which I imagine is somewhere close by in the city.

Drowning in the dense silence, I mash my phone harder against my ear and remember L's hordes of TikTok followers. Maybe he's a high-profile male escort.

Yeah. That makes a horrifying amount of sense.

"Edie?" he finally asks. "You still there?"

I fist-pump the air, absurdly pleased that he's the one who cracked first and ended our childish silent standoff. My technology and agriscience teacher strolls past, beaming. She probably thinks I've just aced a mid-term exam.

Right, enough stalling. It's time to break the impasse with some aggressively uncomfortable small talk. "Yeah, I'm busy too. My study schedule's brutal, and I'm dreaming about sitting exams every night."

I count five full heartbeats of resounding silence.

"So... what did you call for?" I ask.

"I, uh... I just wanted to make sure that I didn't give you the wrong idea the other night... You know, at your place?"

"Okay," I say carefully. "What kind of idea?"

"I might have accidentally sounded like I wanted something from you."

A girl on a green bike cycles past. I love her old-fashioned cane basket, the multicolored ribbons threaded through it. For no reason at all, that detail makes my chest ache.

I shake the stupid, treacherous image of pedaling along country paths with a certain messy-haired boy from my head and glare at my boots. A picnic date with L is clearly not on the agenda.

"Sorry," I say. "I don't understand what you're trying to tell me. What exactly do you think you sounded like you wanted?"

He sighs. "That's just it—nothing. And what I said after we slept together... well, it could be misinterpreted. Might have sounded like I wanted something regular with you. And it was wrong of me to say those things. Because, Edie, I don't want anything at all from you. I really don't."

Wow. This guy totally lives up to his brutal reputation. There is nothing gentle about his tone, no letting me down easy by just ghosting me, like most guys would have done in the same situation.

"Oh, right. Sure. I understand," I say.

My own mother ran away from me. Why would a man I barely know want anything more than sex from me?

"Listen, it's not you. It's just... I don't do relationships. I don't want that kinda deal with anyone. So, I just thought you should know."

And there it is—the classic it's-not-you-it's-me cop-out.

"I've got a class to get to. In future, do me a favor and try not to visit any ATMs near my place or show up bleeding on my doorstep. Enjoy your life." I end the call and thud the back of my head twice against the brick wall.

What an asshole L is. Or maybe it's a good thing that he shoots straight. Not many guys have the courage to be so honest. Or so ruthless. But coming to terms with that fact doesn't lessen the pain in my chest. It honestly hurts that he wants nothing to do with me.

But only an idiot would allow someone like him to cause them pain. Only a fool would fall in love with a guy because he's gorgeous and because the sex is transcendent. Because of the hunger in his eyes.

It's madness to pine over him. The guy is rude, secretive, damaged goods, somehow involved with Coop's little band of freaks, and the clincher—he's one hundred percent uninterested in me.

Guess that makes me stupid, then.

With a black hole expanding in my chest, I suffer through a lab tutorial, play a late afternoon game of basketball with Nico and his school buddies, which I suck at, all the while reciting a vow. Never again. Never again.

That's right. Never ever again will I call L. Or chase after him. Or speak to him. Even if the guy falls from the sky and lands at my feet bleeding from every orifice, my head held high, I'll simply step over him and let someone else deal with the mess.

Yeah, that plan will keep me on the path that leads to peace, happiness, and a joyful life as a lavender farmer.

So, fuck you, L.

I have six months of school to get through. Grants to apply for. A farm to claim back and get on its feet. I don't need some cold-hearted guy distracting me.

Henceforth—L is dead to me.

<h1 style="text-align:center">Chapter 18</h1>

L

Angelo hasn't heard a single word I've just said. He's too busy mowing down *Call of Duty* zombies and hooting into his headset. The guy might look like a young Beyoncé with muscles, but he acts like a frat boy who never learned basic social skills.

And me? Tonight, I don't give a shit about *Black Ops* whatever. I'm skimming the comments on my latest post and trying not to think about a certain girl or that amazing bed in her Art Deco apartment.

"That's what I'm talking about," Angelo yells, short dreads bouncing as he aces a mission. He looks like he's been fused to the couch for a week and has no working relationship with personal grooming.

He's been gaming for hours. And even though the place is a pigsty right now, it still somehow manages to feel warm and inviting. Very Angelo. One of my favorite places to be.

Four years ago, I spent my first night off the streets passed out on this very couch. Back when I was barely functional, and Angelo was funny, patient, and kind—fast becoming my first real friend.

Not long after that, I started landing lucrative jobs through Ariana's agency and moved into the apartment across the hall.

I went from crashing under bridges to my very own luxury pad. Thank fuck Angelo helped me furnish it, because I had no idea what I was doing. Still don't. So, yeah, he's my neighbor, colleague, and friend. Despite the gaming addiction, he's a good guy. The kind you want in your corner. And like me, he's raking it in.

"Hey," I say. "Turn that shit off for a minute."

His dark eyes flick my way, then snap back to the screen.

"Come on," I coax. "You know you want to head downtown with me and get dinner. It's nine-thirty already, and I'll gouge my eyes out if I have to watch you open another bag of Doritos."

Without looking away, he says, "I'm planning on demolishing a tray of donuts next. Call a pizza if that doesn't appeal. I'm kicking ass here and not moving."

"There'll be a rooftop swarm of barely dressed girls drinking cheap cocktails at Liberty tonight," I say. "So many hot girls. It'll be fun. I can watch you pick up, like I usually do."

"Yeah," he says. "Right after *you* turn them away. Ah, shit. Look out! He's behind the wall, you fuckwit."

"Angelo," I say. "Stop yelling at the screen. I'm starving."

"So go eat. Why don't you call on your new girlfriend? If you're nice to her, she might even feed you."

I choke on a mouthful of beer. "Who?"

"Your girlfriend. The one you've mentioned about twenty-seven times tonight."

"I didn't think you were listening, let alone counting. And if you had been paying attention, you wouldn't be calling her my girlfriend. You know I don't do that shit."

Smirking, he laughs through his nostrils. "Man, for you to even bother bitching about a girl basically means you're in love."

I throw a beer coaster at him. "Fuck you!"

"Admit it, bro. You're obsessed. And I'll bet a wad of cash that as soon as you leave here, you'll be heading straight to wherever that girl is. No matter what bullshit you're telling yourself."

My mouth opens and closes.

"Honestly, L, I wouldn't believe it unless I'd seen it for myself, but you..." He takes a hand off the controller long enough to point at me. "Are fucked up and pussy whipped. You should hear yourself. Edie this and Edie that. And also... poor me. And then... Edie blah blah blah. That's basically all you've said all night."

I hadn't. No way.

Angelo's smirk swings my way. "She popped your hetero-cherry, didn't she?"

Staring at the fireplace, I say, "She might have," then shove my hands through my hair.

I still can't believe Edie is the same girl who shot a lightning bolt of want through my chest on that life-changing night four years ago.

My thoughts tumble back to that crazy night: how Ariana, the woman I'd met only an hour before, ended my life on the streets and changed my life forever, the way the rain fell and the streets glittered like some sci-fi movie set as I glanced across the restaurant strip and saw a girl in a skimpy black dress out front of Joe Junior's burger joint.

It was Edie.

At the time, I didn't know her name. All I knew was that she looked cold. And fucking gorgeous. Then Cooper, a monster from my nightmare past, strutted out of the café and joined her on the pavement. Thirteen months had passed since I'd escaped him, and every second of that time, I'd been dreaming of finding him and making him pay. And there he was, showing up out of nowhere with a girl who'd just blown my mind.

She didn't look pleased about hanging out with him. Far from it.

Even knowing she was with that guy, her unbelievable body and sad eyes had me jerking off later that night like a regular lust-filled guy. Like I was normal.

I never thought I'd see her again, let alone actually fuck her—not once, but three incredible times. It was even worth getting my gut sliced by knobhead Reno last Friday, because it led me straight to her apartment and probably the best experience of my life.

And now she's haunting my every thought. On top of everything, she's still tangled up with that fucker Coop.

She's a complication I don't need. I'm a dangerous person to get close to, and that's a fact. Best for both of us if I stay away.

Annoyed with my own thoughts—and my growing obsession—I groan.

Angelo laughs. "Please! Just go bone her."

I skull the last dregs of my beer and flop back into the cushions, fingers tangled in my hair. "Fuck."

"Exactly, man. Go make sweet love to your lady."

"To my what?" Hell. "I've been telling her to stay away from me."

"That's fine, Lightning Boy. You're irresistible. Go woo her and do the dirty all night long."

"How many times have I asked you not to call me that?"

Grinning, he slaps his controller on the coffee table and whips out his phone, ignoring the chaos on the screen.

"Hey, look out," I warn. In the game, he's about to get blown to pieces. "You're dying there."

He laughs. "That's fine. Worth it."

"Worth what?" I ask as my phone bleats. Shit. It's Ariana.

Angelo snickers as I answer the call from my agent.

"Hey," I say, trying to sound cheerful. She's the closest thing I have to a mother, the woman who saved my life, so I make an effort.

"L darling," she purrs. "My advice? Go see your girlfriend. *Immediately.*"

"What?" I choke out.

Angelo snorts and slaps his thigh. I give him a death glare.

"Did he put you up to this?" I ask.

"Are you talking about Angelo? Well... maybe," she admits, trying not to laugh. Angelo, of course, is rolling on the couch like a sugar-high toddler.

"This isn't funny," I mutter.

"Falling in love tends to make a man lose his sense of humor," Ariana says.

"What the fuck? I'm not in love—"

"Sh, darling. We get it. This must be hard for you. You've never liked being at anyone's mercy, L."

I can't argue with that.

"She's just some girl, Ariana."

"That you slept with," she points out.

"You're fucked," I mouth at Angelo. The little snitch just shrugs and keeps gaming, explosions and gunfire filling the room.

"I know what a big step this is for you," Ariana continues as I move into the kitchen to hear her better. "Giving yourself to someone freely... she must be special."

Giving myself to someone? What am I, some kind of mail-order toy?

And yeah, Edie is something special. But that's not the point. I can't tell Ariana the truth about Coop, about being forced to fuck Edie. She doesn't know that part of my life, and she doesn't need to.

"I've gotta go."

"I do hope you're going to see her, L," she says.

I grunt noncommittally.

"Be a darling and remind Angelo about the Brazilian shoot. He's forgotten to confirm his schedule again."

"Sure. Talk soon.

"Kisses, darling."

She hangs up, and I stuff empty pizza boxes into Angelo's recycling bin. Fuck, he's a slob.

Hanging out with Edie is a terrible idea. That much is obvious.

Four years ago, Coop saw my face on a billboard, tracked me down, and tried to blackmail me into doing his stupid parties. I told no one about him. Not even Angelo.

When Coop wormed his way back into my life, I decided the smart move was patience. Let him think he had me under control. Do what he asked while I figured out how to end him without finishing up in a cell.

The plan's coming together. My bank balance looks better every week. I'm closer to revenge than I've ever been, and the last thing I need is to get tangled up with a girl. No matter how good she makes me feel.

I drift back toward the couch but can't bring myself to sit.

Angelo jerks his chin at me. "Jesus. Move, L. Your boner's blocking my view."

I don't have a boner. Not yet, anyway.

I shake my head and shove my phone into my pocket. "You still going to Brazil Friday?"

"Nah. Flying out tomorrow. Extra shoot."

"Figures. Confirm your schedule before Ariana has a meltdown. And get some sleep."

His eyes never leave the screen. "Go. Get outta here."

"Okay, okay. I'm leaving."

I stride out and instead of striding across the hallway to my apartment, I head for the elevator. And Edie's place.

Chapter 19

L

I'm riding a mild beer buzz and need air, so I decide to take the subway and walk from the station.

Less than thirty minutes later, I'm at her door.

I knock three times and shove my hands into my pockets. The landing's dark. There's a fancy wall sconce, but when I flick the switch beside the door, nothing happens. My boot starts tapping against the tiles. I hate that I can't make it stop.

Come on. Open the fucking door.

Footsteps thud inside. Then I hear her voice, warm with laughter as the door finally swings open. "Nico, you're way too early. I just got out of the shower and..." Her eyes lift from my boots to my face. "Oh! L."

She looks pissed. And totally, devastatingly gorgeous.

"Hi," I say, leaning my arm against the doorframe, aiming for casual.

She arches a brow. "Really? That's what you're going with? Fine. Two can play at that game. How are you? Had a nice night so far? And, also, what the hell are you doing here?"

"I was passing by. Saw the light on."

"And?" she prompts, crossing her arms over her chest.

God. She's furious. And so lovely the sight of her makes my chest ache.

"So... can I come in?"

My pulse spikes. My palms dampen. I suddenly realize I hadn't planned for her saying no.

I want her so badly I might drop to my knees and beg if she sends me away.

A flood of words pours from her lips, too fast to catch a single one.

I lean closer. "What was that?"

"Nothing. And, *no*, you can't come in. I'm busy."

"Busy with what?"

"Washing clothes... studying. Lots of studying."

"Right. Sounds very clean and scholarly. Can I just grab a glass of water before I go?"

She frowns, but I slip past her to the sink.

"The glasses are above your head," she says.

"I know," I reply, opening the green cupboard. Leaning against the sink, I sip water and fix a hot gaze on her. Damn. That lacy-black tank top, matching panties, and see-through robe—it's all killing me. But if things go my way, that robe sure won't last long.

Hands on her hips, she says, "After that phone call today, I don't see one good reason for you to be here."

I think about that call. Best to act like it never happened.

Wiping my mouth, I set the glass on the bench. "Really? You can't think of a reason?"

"No. I can't." Her gaze drops, cheeks pink, catching the obvious outline straining against my jeans. "Now that you've quenched your supposedly urgent thirst, time to go."

"But I'm dry as a desert," I say, arms folded, taking in every inch of her. "I feel like I'm dying here."

Her brow furrows in confusion.

I close the gap, and she shuffles back until she hits the wall behind her. Around the corner is the hallway to her bedroom. I love that room. Can't wait to see it again. "I'm also starving." I lift a damp curl from her shoulder, letting it slip through my fingers.

"Well, you've come to the wrong place. I'm not feeding you. My fridge is empty, cupboards almost bare. And I'm not cooking. Not for you."

"I'm not talking about food," I say, even though I could do with some of that, too. Up close, I can smell how turned on she is, and that wipes out every other bodily need, except the one only she can slake. "Because you're busy studying?"

"Yes, that. And... other reasons."

"I can't see your textbooks out here. Laptop's off."

"Listen, I don't owe you an explanation. Go drink and eat somewhere else. Okay?"

I press my palm to the base of her throat and step closer. "I can't. It's *you* I'm hungry for. You're the only thing I need. More than anything."

Her breathing turns shallow, and her nipples push visibly against the thin fabric. My mouth goes even drier.

I lower my voice. "You're the only one who does this to me, Edie. No one else. No one even comes close."

I'm a walking contradiction. Mixed signals, bad timing, even worse judgment, showing up here like I have any right to touch her again.

I lean in anyway, my cheek brushing hers. She exhales a shaky breath.

"I tried to stay away," I say quietly. "But I can't. I'm bad news, Edie. I'm fucked up. All wrong. You know that, right?"

Slowly, her hand comes up to rest against my jaw. The other fists in my shirt.

"But around you, for some reason, everything feels right." My voice cracks despite my effort to keep my cool. "I feel like a normal guy who just wants to be with a girl. Without the violence. Without the shame. Without—"

Her eyes sharpen. "What did you come here for, L? Just say it."

I drop my gaze to her purple-painted toenails. I can't tell her the truth—that I want to test the silence again. See if the voices stay gone, like they mostly did the last time I was here.

Was it just because I was fucking a woman? Or because I was fucking *her*?

Her fingers grip my chin, and she jerks my face up until we're eye to eye.

"What did you come here for?" she asks again. "I want the truth. Was it for sex? Is that all you want?"

Up close, her eyes flash green. They're hazel, not brown like I'd thought.

I nod. A rough sound scrapes out of my throat.

"What's that? I didn't hear you."

"Yes," I say. "I came here to fuck you."

She smiles and pats my cheek. "You're honest, at least. I'll give you that much."

I lean in without thinking, and she turns her head away. I blow out a frustrated breath over her shoulder, already bracing for the walk back to Angelo's place. Another night of guns blazing on his TV, another of his conquest stories queued up.

Then Edie inhales slowly and visibly steels herself. "Okay," she says. "Let's do it."

My head snaps up. "What?"

"I changed my mind," she says, resolve sharpening her gaze. "I think we should have sex. But only if you do it the way you usually do."

My pulse stutters. She can't be serious.

"You take control this time," she continues. "Be rough. You don't have to hurt me, but take me right to the edge. As close as you can." She holds my stare. "Show me."

"What the fuck, Edie," I say hoarsely. "Why would you want that?"

"I need to know what it feels like when you take control," she says. "I don't know why. I just do."

"No," I snap. "That's not what I want with you. Not ever."

"Then leave."

"But you don't get it," I say, shaking my head. "That dark shit makes me feel bad—"

"It shouldn't," she cuts in. "And it doesn't have to. There's no shame in hard sex if both people want it." Her voice softens, but her eyes don't waver. "The problem is, it was never your choice before."

I drag a hand through my hair. I don't want to poison this. Don't want to take something good and turn it into another reason to hate myself. Or hurt her.

She steps closer, fingers sliding into my hair, gentle and grounding. I close my eyes despite myself. Then her mouth is on mine, and I lose whatever fragile control I had left, gripping her hips, kissing her back like I'm drowning and she's the only thing that can save me.

Jesus. The kissing. It's the best drug, the best feeling. I could live on this high alone. How did I survive twenty-two years without it?

When I moan into her mouth, she pulls away just enough to speak.

"So you agree?" she asks quietly. "You'll take charge? And I want you mean, L. Or not at all." Her gaze pins me. "Do you understand?"

Fuck. This is so unfair.

"Okay," I say grimly, dragging my palm down the valley between her perfect breasts to rest on her stomach. "I don't get why you want this. But if it's the only way, then fine." I pause. "I just want to know one thing first."

"Okay. Sure."

"Who's Nico?"

She laughs. "That's what you're stuck on? He's a friend. Someone I work with."

"Must be a close one if you're opening the door to him half naked."

Her eyes flash. "Yeah. He is. And our relationship is none of your business." She lifts her chin. "Now where do you want to do this? Here, or the bedroom?"

I don't answer. Instead, I bend, haul her over my shoulder, and head down the hallway. When I toss her onto the bed, she squeaks out a surprised sound.

Yeah. This might be fun after all.

She scrambles back and reaches for the bedside lamp. Warm orange light spills over her skin. We stare at each other, breathing hard, the air thick and charged.

I twirl my finger.

She frowns.

"Turn over. Wait... pass me the bolster and those pillows first."

She swallows and obeys. As I catch them, I can't help but smile. I stack the pillows, set the bolster on top. "Come on," I say quietly. "On your stomach."

She rolls halfway, then looks back at me over her shoulder. "Do you want me to take these off?" She hooks a finger into her underwear.

Ignoring her question, I say, "Do what you're told. On your stomach. Now."

She flips over.

I grab her hips and pull her into position, adjusting her over the cushions until she's exactly where I want her. I peel the robe off her shoulders, tugging her arms behind her back. Her breathing turns rough. My cock responds immediately.

I slide the black panties down, baring her, her ass lifted at a devastating angle. I take my time looking. Letting the image sink in.

"Don't move," I warn, stripping fast. My boots hit the wall beneath the window. She stays still, except for the fine tremor rippling through her body. I can't tell if it's nerves or need. Maybe both.

The floorboards creak as I grab the oil from her dresser. "This'll make things easier," I say, unscrewing the cap.

I shove her top up just enough, leave it clinging to her skin. Lace, heat, softness... fuck. She gasps when the oil spills over her back, cold against her warm skin. I straddle her thighs and work it in, palms sliding over her spine, her hips, her ass. She groans.

Then I let my fingers drift lower. She's soaked. I keep touching her there, slow and relentless, until she's squirming and I'm leaking pre-come on her body. The sight makes my dick pulse hard.

This is every filthy fantasy I've ever had crashing into real life. It's almost too much, a brutal effort not to lose control and fuck her senseless in ten seconds flat.

In the end, it's her soft little moans that undo me, make me lose it. I sit back, slide my knees to the perfect angle, spread her ass cheeks and rub my thumb around her rim, massaging and dipping in.

Her moaning gets louder, her legs and hips restless. I can't wait any longer and press my cock between her cheeks, sliding up and down in the slickness. Now we're both making noise.

But the best thing, the most incredible part, is that there's no voice in my head telling me I'm an evil, dirty, piece of shit. I just feel horny and hot, my skin buzzing so hard with the need to come. But I can't let that happen. It's too soon. I don't ever want this to end.

I slip my hand underneath her, pinch and roll her nipple hard, and keep doing it. I stroke my dick back slowly, then press forward again. Backward once more, and then I push into her hard.

As I ram inside her pussy, she makes this amazing sound and goes still. Even with my balls drawn tight, my cock ready to explode, I laugh. Guess she thought I was planning on a different entry point.

I fuck her hard and fast, wrenching her hips back against mine, my fingers digging into her flesh.

"Does that... hurt?" I manage to grunt out.

She tries to look over her shoulder, but with me pounding into her body roughly, it isn't easy. She gives up and muffles words into the mattress. "Yes, it hurts in the best possible way. But this... you're cheating. Do it the way you always have... how you did it before you met me."

With my hips still hammering, I slide my hand around her throat and squeeze. But only lightly. Gently. I could never treat her the way I do Coop's idiots. No way.

My fingers increase the pressure just a fraction, then I give her five more hard strokes and she starts shaking all over. I take my hand from her throat, find her clit, and give it perfect pressure while I change the game completely and fuck her slowly.

She moves like an earthquake underneath me. "No, L. Please. Oh, wait... *yes*," she whimpers, gripping the covers. Her back arches, long breathy sounds spilling out, and my body tightens with hers. I focus, letting the moment stretch, savoring every shudder, every gasp.

I feel her come, clenching around me, and I fight so hard to not explode along with her.

"Good girl. Fuck. That feels like heaven." My voice trembles as I slide in and out, my body shivering and shaking, my brain on fire. She keeps whimpering and moaning, and I fuck her sweetly all through it.

Her fist pounds the pillow. "Please, L."

That's all it takes for me to detonate. "Oh, fuck." An explosion big-bangs its way from my balls to my heart, and I pull out in time to shoot over her spine, coming like a broken fire hydrant.

Making a strangled sound low in my throat, I flip her onto her back and kiss her. Sorry about the bedcovers, I think—then immediately forget them and kiss her again.

Chapter 20

L

When our breathing finally slows, she smacks my arm. "You little shit."

"What?" I roll onto my back, forearm over my eyes, hiding the smile I can't quite kill.

"That's how you do it with Coop's dirtbags, is it?"

"Not exactly."

She snorts. "Not *exactly*. Lucky dirtbags. Must be nice for them."

A bitter laugh scrapes out of me. She has no idea what she just asked of me tonight. "I'd never hurt you like that, Edie. You have to hate someone—really hate them—to do what I've done to those guys. Wish them pain. Wish them dead. I couldn't summon anything like that with you if I tried for a thousand years."

She studies my face. "You couldn't, huh? I thought you might at least do the anal thing."

I bark out another laugh. "Don't sound so crushed. That can hurt like hell if you're not prepared. And when I was younger—"

Her eyes go wide.

"Fuck. Forget I said that." I shake my head. "It takes effort to make it good. Believe me. We can talk about it someday if you want. But not like this. Not because you're trying to prove something. Not because you want me to treat you the way I treat those scumbags." I scan her face, her sweet expression. "Why would you even want that?"

She doesn't answer.

Just stares at me, her gaze soft.

"When you've got time to play around and aren't buried in term papers, we can give it a whirl." I grip her wrist just before she smacks the smirk off my face.

"Okay, smartass. So, I lied about studying before, but I... Oh, shit—that's the door. Nico. I completely forgot!" She scrambles for clothes, pulling stuff over her head, wiggling panties up her hips, wiping herself off with a towel from a laundry basket. "Stay there," she commands, then shoots out of the room.

The front door opens, and a deep male voice echoes, followed by laughter—hers and his. Curious, I pull on my jeans and swagger out.

In the hallway, I spot a wiry, pretty boy leaning close to Edie. "You smell good," he says, his emo look offset by a lip piercing and bright green eyes. He sniffs her neck. "Lavender and ylang-ylang?"

"Yeah, and also probably sex," I reply, arms crossed over my bare chest.

Edie and the boy jump apart, staring at me.

He rattles the chain hanging from his black jeans, checking me out, his eyes widening. Good. My four-times-a-week MMA sessions aren't for nothing, then.

"Oh, hi, L," Edie says like I just showed up at a garden party. As if she doesn't remember what I was doing to her five minutes ago.

I rub my thumb over my lips and take her in slowly.

Her eyes flick to the guy, and with a practiced hostess smile, she steps to the center of the room. "Nico, this is L... Say hi."

Nico sticks out his hand. I give it two hard shakes, then drop it like it's a steaming turd.

"Okay, Tarzan. No need to break my hand. I'm a little too young for Jane here—or so she keeps telling me. Now that I've seen you, though, I think I finally get why I'm not her type."

"The name is L," I say.

"Sure, sure. Like the letter, right?"

I nod, mouth a grim line.

"Nice," Nico says. "Very different."

"Your name's cool too," I say. "I once knew a Pomeranian named Nico. Lived in a burned-out warehouse. One hell of a mangy mutt."

He throws his head back and laughs. "Ah, that's a good one. You're funny."

This kid's got guts, I'll give him that.

"Sometimes Edie thinks so," I say.

He glances at her, snickering. She gives a tiny shake of her head, but I catch it anyway. Old habits die hard. On the streets you learn to see every detail, every micro-expression.

"Nice tatts," he says. "You look familiar."

"Yeah?" I say. "Could be."

Edie stiffens.

Nico's eyebrow lifts. "I wonder from where?"

I shrug. "No doubt places most people don't go. You could've been a client of mine."

That earns me a longer look, like he's trying to decide if he should interrogate me further.

Edie appears horrified. She has nothing to worry about. I haven't hustled since I was eighteen. I stopped when I got off the streets after I found easier ways to get money. And other than Coop's infrequent soirees, I'm practically asexual. Until several days ago at least. Now sex is all I think about. And Edie.

"What line of work are you in?" Nico asks, taking a step toward me.

Edie cuts in fast. "Okay. No. We're not doing this right now. Nico, you've got a gig to get to."

"Oh, right." He glances between us. "So it's not *we* tonight anymore?"

"I'm not sure," she says carefully. "I might make it later."

I hold his gaze. Don't smile. Don't move.

He stares a beat too long, then laughs it off.

Edie exhales, and I roll my shoulders, cracking my neck. The kid's gaze slides over my tattoos while he waits for me to say I'm heading out the door. But I'm not going anywhere. Not a chance.

"Sorry about this, Nico," Edie says. "Next time you play, I promise I'll be there." She turns to me. "Nico sings in a band."

"Does he?" I say, stepping in beside her. "What are you called?"

Nico wanders to the fridge like he lives here, peers inside, then shuts it a little too hard. "Fist Fuck."

I snort before I can stop myself.

"He's lying," Edie says. "They're called Burntbad. Which is somehow worse. Wait there, Niccy, let me grab the fifty I owe you."

As she passes, I catch her shoulder, my hand sliding briefly over her side, making my claim. Nothing subtle about it. She disappears into the bedroom.

The kid steps closer. Too close. His eyes are bright and reckless. "You look like you're scared she'll bolt."

I arch a brow. "That so."

His mouth twitches. "What does L stand for anyway? Loser? Lazarus—"

I laugh. Properly this time, and he jerks back like he wasn't expecting it.

"Careful," I say mildly. "You seem to be thinking about me a little too much. Not sure I like it."

That gives him pause.

Edie comes back, cash in hand. He takes it, already edging toward the door. Smart guy.

"See you at work," he says to her before giving me a nod. "Take care of her."

"Better than you ever could. You can count on that."

Edie laughs and loops an arm around my neck. "Don't worry about him, Nico. I promise he's harmless."

"Harmless?" I say, tickling her side until she squeaks. "Keep on thinking that if it makes you feel better."

She grins over her shoulder at the kid. "Honestly, I've got this one under control."

The door slams shut behind us.

We dash back to her room, and I show Edie exactly how well she's taught me to fuck a girl. Gently. And as sweet as sunshine.

Chapter 21

EDEN

The next morning, miraculously, L is still lying unconscious beside me—his body a warm, heavy weight, shoulders and chest rising and falling slowly, like bellows.

Trying not to wake him, I fumble quietly out of bed and tiptoe to the bathroom. According to the clock in the living room, it's already past eleven. Damn. I've got an exam to study for.

When I return and open the blind, sunshine pours over L's face, and he rolls onto his back. Grinning, I prance around to my side of the bed and hop in, deliberately bouncing the mattress. Time to wake him.

A shot of turquoise flares as his eyes open, then widen. Breathing hard, like he's surfacing from a nightmare, he springs up against the headboard, hands sweeping frantically over the covers, searching, perhaps for something he can use as a weapon.

I grip his arm firmly. "Hey, everything's okay. Relax. You were exhausted last night. You fell asleep by accident, I think. And then you acted like a boulder for about seven hours straight."

His lips pull sideways. "You're lying. I don't sleep. Well, not much anyway." Hair a beautiful mess, muscles flexing under smooth skin, he stares blankly down at me.

"Well, you did last night." I trace the swirling clouds of ink over his chest. "Come back down here. You're not in a combat zone."

I really want to ask what's rattled him so badly, but I don't want to scare him away just yet.

His thumb brushes my lip, and his gaze drops, giving my breasts a hungry perusal. A crooked smile tugs at his mouth as he shuffles down under the covers, reaching for me.

I ignore the heat simmering in my belly. "Can I ask you something personal? Or is it a pointless exercise because you won't tell me the truth?"

"Probably pointless," he says gruffly. "I don't like answering questions."

That tracks. It's certainly a tricky conversation style and must make it difficult for him to make friends.

"But I guess I can give it a go," he finally says. "At least then you'll owe me the same, Edie."

That's the problem with wanting to know other people's secrets... sometimes they get curious about yours, too.

I try not to be distracted by his warm fingers sliding through my hair. "Fine," I say, choosing my words carefully. "So, what you do for Coop... is it for money? Is that how you make a living? How you survive?"

His eyes freeze over, his body going still. "Are you asking if I whore for him? Fuck, no. I wouldn't take his money to save my dying horse. If I had one, that is."

My tentative smile tugs upward despite myself.

Cheeks darkening, he says, "Stupid analogy. The horse thing..."

Seconds drag by while we stare at each other—L embarrassed, me quietly spiraling. Because if Coop doesn't pay him, then why the hell was he at that sick voyeur party? "Okay. So now I've got two questions for you."

A muscle in his jaw twitches. "Shoot, if you must."

"You're not sleeping rough anymore, so that means you've got rent to cover. And if Coop doesn't pay you, then who does?"

He looks at me like I'm an idiot. "Well, there are these things called jobs. Ever heard of them?"

"So what, you're a mechanic? An Uber driver? Or maybe a... pastry chef?"

He laughs, rolling onto his back, one arm slung over his eyes. "Sure. Something like that."

I tug his wrist down. He fixes me with an icy-blue stare but says nothing.

"L. Come on. Tell me."

He gives me that wide, infuriating smile, and still doesn't answer.

"Oh, forget it. I can figure this out for myself. My best guess is you're all three rolled into one, and you hire yourself out to the rich and famous. Drive them around, fix their cars, whip up a mean carbonara, and if the client's interested, throw in some incredible head."

Color flushes over his sharp cheekbones. He sits up fast, shoving the covers away like he's about to bolt.

"Wait." I grab his arm. "I'm sorry. That was a really bad joke." My hand slides over his back. "L. Come on. I didn't mean it like that."

He shrugs me off and perches on the edge of the mattress, shoulders tight.

"Just tell me," I say more softly. "Not the cleaned-up version you think I want. Is it really so terrible? You're clearly doing okay. I've seen your phone. Your clothes." I pause. "Whatever the truth is, I can handle it."

With his torso twisted toward me, he stares at his fingers clawed into the bedcovers, jaw clenched so hard it might crack. After a long, suffocating silence, he pushes to his feet and yanks on his jeans. They're faded, broken-in, but they definitely aren't cheap.

"I model," he snaps over his bare shoulder, and then he's gone, leaving me staring at the doorway with my mouth hanging open.

He *models*.

With the social grace of a feral cat and the emotional volatility of a live wire, it's hard to picture him surviving the kiss-kiss machinations of the high fashion world. But he does look like a walking billboard, so… fine. It kind of makes sense.

Scrambling out of bed, I drag on a T-shirt, then chase him down the hall.

I find him shirtless, hunched over on the couch, losing a fight with a pair of red Converse sneakers. Apparently anger makes putting shoes on impossible.

Willing my pulse to slow, I stroll past him into the kitchen. "I set the coffee last night," I say lightly. "I'll make you one. Smells good, right?"

His eyes narrow. "Fuck," he mutters, flinging the sneakers aside and collapsing back against the cushions, knees spread wide, defeat written into every line of his body. The view is absolutely criminal. I take it all in shamelessly.

He stares at the floor, drags a hand through his tawny hair, messing it up further. I have to lick my lips and look away. The guy is dangerously hot, and I need to focus on the dangerous part before I lose my head. And that other wretched organ. My heart.

"Sugar?" I ask, dropping a cube into his mug before he can object. Too bad if he likes it bitter.

I hand the coffee over and set mine on the table. He stares straight ahead, fingers curled loosely around the mug resting against his thigh like he's forgotten it exists.

"Say thank you, L."

He glances at my black flat screen and gives it a crooked smile. "Thank you, L."

I smack his arm.

"Smartass. Do you want to watch a movie? I've got to study, but you're welcome to hang out and entertain yourself."

I clap a hand over my mouth the second the words are out. Idiot. I should ask him to leave. But the tight pull in my belly, and worse, the one in my chest, says I'm not quite ready for that yet. Sadly, this feels like the start of a very bad habit.

He blows across the mug, then takes a careful sip. "No. I want to get outta here."

Fine, I tell myself. Absolutely fine. It isn't. But I can fake it.

I grab yesterday's paper and flap it open, eyes fixed on the entertainment section. "So. How often do you model? And what kind do you do? Is it your only job?"

I tuck my knees under my chin, stretching the blue T-shirt tight over my legs. His gaze locks onto me like I'm his favorite meal. I follow his eyes and glance down.

Oh. Right. I've stolen his vintage Atari shirt from the end of my bed.

I give him a sheepish smile. He grins back, slow and sexy.

"So you're just not going to answer?" I press. "How about telling me how you got into it... modeling, I mean."

He sets the cup down with a careless clunk and rubs a hand over his brow, face angled toward me now. "You're not going to let this go until you get the whole story, are you?"

"Probably not," I say.

He picks at a tear in his jeans and lets out a long sigh. "I was hustling one night when a guy gave me five hundred bucks instead of fifty. I lost my mind and spent most of it on an incredible meal. Walked into this French grill place with gold practically dripping from the ceiling, dressed more or less like this."

He glances down as if shocked by the sight of his flexing abs. "Had a T-shirt on, though. I'm still amazed they let me through the door."

I'm not. Looking like L does, he could walk into a royal palace wearing flip-flops and still improve the view. Men like him sell desire just by existing. And desire is excellent for business.

He takes another swallow of coffee. "I'm sitting there, basically a hobo, eating ribs like a caveman while every suit in the place stares at me. Like they're waiting for me to lose it and flip a table."

It wouldn't have been his ripped clothing that fascinated them. I can pretty much guarantee that.

"Anyway, this elegant older woman sits down and shoves her card at me. Says she represents a top agency and claims she can get me work." He snorts. "I assumed she meant sex. Turns out she was legit. I was almost nineteen, and she got me off the streets. Now I do it all—shoots, European catwalks, travel a lot, and make stupid amounts of money." His jaw tightens just a fraction. "And not a day goes by I don't thank fuck for Ariana. She saved my life."

"A very fortunate meeting, then," I say.

"Yeah, unbelievable, huh?"

So much for my American Apparel fantasies. This man is talking Milan, Paris, paparazzi, the whole deal, and I'm spiraling so hard, recalibrating who he is, that it's a miracle my eyes don't fall out of my head and land in his lap.

I smile like I'm not rattled. "So I should start keeping an eye out for you between the pages of GQ and Vogue?"

"Yeah. The covers, too." Reaching out to touch my cheek, he lets out a short laugh. "Don't look so shocked."

"So was that your own socials you were checking on your cell at the cash machine last week when I was rudely looking over your shoulder?"

He laughs, then nods.

"Now I understand why you've got so many followers. You're kind of a supermodel. It makes complete sense now."

"Yeah. It goes with the job. Our agents make us do it. But the cool thing is, some brand sends me a shirt, and I take a grumpy selfie with it on, when I'm still lying in bed half asleep, and get paid for it. It's easy money."

"It sounds like you could afford to move anywhere. Go far away. I don't understand the Coop thing. Why would you do it if you don't have to?" To avoid his glare, I take the mugs over to the sink and rinse them out. "You must enjoy it."

The energy in the room changes, a pressure drop, the unnerving sensation of an incoming storm prickling over my skin.

Wearing a savage expression, he stuffs his feet into his shoes, nearly breaking the laces as he ties them with unnecessary vigor.

"I fucking loathe those parties. And I fucking loathe your prick of a landlord."

I totally agree with L. I'm not proud of it, but I've lost count of the times I've wished Coop rotting six feet under.

L snatches his wallet off the coffee table.

"But then why do it?" I ask.

"Use your brain, Edie. He's got something on me." Hair falls into his eyes as he rifles quickly through his wallet, pulls out some notes, then pushes them back in. "And it's something bad."

For a terrible moment, I think he's going to offer me payment for services rendered, but he's probably only checking I haven't stolen his cash. A marginally better option.

He shoves the whole thing back in his pocket and stomps to the door, standing motionless for four beats. Then he turns, thunder in his eyes, electricity crackling in the air. "That asshole could put me away until the end of time."

"I don't suppose you'll tell me what you did?"

"No chance, Edie."

"But with your money, you could start afresh anywhere. Change your name. Your whole identity."

"Yeah. That's my plan. To get out of here when I've saved enough to lay low and never need to work again."

"Okay. So, how close are you?"

He smirks. "I'd say pretty fucking close. Last week I exceeded my goal. I can go any time I want."

My chest tightens. "Oh. Right." I fake a wide smile. "That's wonderful, L."

He opens the front door.

"Wait. Hey... don't forget your T-shirt."

"Keep it."

"You can't leave here half-dressed! You're on public transport, aren't you? You'll start a riot looking like that."

"Relax. It's hot out. No one will blink an eye."

Oh, yes, they will. There'll be plenty of eyes on him, drinking him in. I drag the T-shirt off and throw it at his ink-covered chest. "Everyone will look at you."

He laughs at me as I cover my breasts with crossed arms, the T-shirt now hanging defiantly out of his back pocket and his chin raised. "Who cares? I'm used to it. And you know what, Edie? Fuck you and your petty judgment. Stop telling me what to do."

"Charming," I yell as the door slams, rattling my brain and the apartment walls.

Something on the floor catches my eye. His shiny driver's license. Squinting, I pick it up and stare at his photo, a smile spreading on my face. I grab my phone and take a few pictures. Okay, sure, it's a bit stalkerish, but his face is important to me. I need to remember every detail. And his address, too. Who knows when I might need it. Too bad there's a suspicious splotch of black paint covering most of his name. I can barely make it out.

But his legal first name definitely starts with the letter L.

Chapter 22

L

When my cell rings Saturday afternoon, I already know who's calling before I've even pulled my phone out of my gym bag. The tingling heat crawling over my skin tells me it's Edie. I should have known she couldn't leave me alone. The girl doesn't know what's good for her.

It's been four days since I stormed out of her place in a stupid huff, all riled up because she dared to suggest I might enjoy the crazy shit I do for Coop.

Screw her for saying that. I never talk about my past. In a moment of weakness, I opened up to Edie, and what did I get? Judgment. Like always.

I've been ignoring her messages for days—I *only want to talk to you about Coop, L*—she says, and then bangs on and on about wanting to get my license back to me. Rinse, wring, repeat.

Right now, post-sparring, I'm tired, sweaty, starving, and definitely not in the mood to talk to her.

"Hey," I say, accepting the call anyway. All those workout endorphins are messing with my brain.

"Hi, L,"

Huh. She sounds cheerful, like she's forgotten I've recently been a prize prick to her.

"What are you up to?" she asks.

"Nothing much. Just standing in the parking lot behind Stevensons' Gym, staring at my truck."

"Are you on your way in or out?"

"What's it to you?" I say, keeping my edge sharp on purpose. Her naturally sunny nature makes that harder than it should be.

"Well, since you don't sound busy. And it's a pretty warm day. And I'm bored. I was thinking you should meet me down at K Beach for a swim." She laughs sweetly, sounding like some giggling fucking pixie, which should be annoying as hell. It's not. It's... dangerously cute.

Cute? Jesus. I can't believe I'm even thinking that word.

"Well, according to the address on your license, you could easily walk to the beach from your place."

"Yeah, about the license. Sorry I haven't returned your calls. I've been snowboarding. You know. For work. I had a shoot overseas."

And more importantly, I've been too chickenshit to call her back.

"Thanks for the invite," I say, "but I think I'll pass. It's probably not a great idea for us to see each other."

"Oh. Really?" She sounds disappointed. Or sarcastic. Hard to tell. "Listen, I've been developing a theory, L. I think you and I should be friends. Personally, I could use a few more. And if you come grab some rays with me at the beach, you can get your license back. I promise I won't ask why there's a convenient splotch of black paint covering most of your name... even though that probably invalidates it and is wildly illegal. What do you say?"

A gull squawks overhead. Bull-necked Mikey exits the gym and climbs into his rusted Buick, nodding at me. In my humble opinion, he loves that car more than his kids—but not as much as vodka. My boot scuffs the concrete, grinding over tiny black stones.

"L? You still there? I bet you've spent many a sleepless night wondering whether I wear a bikini or a one-piece, right? Well, this is a never-to-be-repeated two-for-one deal. The license *and* the bathers. Breasts like mine are inconvenient at the best of times, but they really shine in a swimsuit."

She wouldn't be wrong. Fuck.

"What time?"

It's dumb to let my dick decide, but Edie's curves—smooth, wet, straining against Lycra—are irresistible.

One day, Coop and I are going to rain hell down on each other, and I plan to win. I have to. I just need to be sure that when it happens, Edie is nowhere near the fallout.

The smart move would be to avoid her. But what a surprise—my dick is a village idiot, and the idea of a wet Edie is too good to pass up. I tell myself it's a practical decision. The perfect chance to collect hot visuals for when it all goes to shit and I'm in hiding. Or in jail, if it comes to that, and it's just me and my hand, clinging to the memory of her.

"How soon can you be there?" she asks.

"In about an hour." That's how long I'll need to shower and demolish three slices of leftover pizza. Preferably not at the same time. Then again, multitasking might get me there faster.

"Great! I'll be waiting down by the pier with two coffees. One sugar in yours. None in mine because I'm superior like that."

"Wearing bikinis, right?" I ask.

The laugh she gives me before hanging up is pure magic.

Fifty-seven minutes later I'm sitting on a stone wall next to the pier, the back of my head frying in the sun. I'm also wishing for temporary X-ray vision to help me see through her lavender shirt.

Today she's rocking a pure boho-beach-babe outfit. Copper Celtic knots hang from a leather necklace, tiny, embroidered flowers scattered across her top. To complete the look, a short gypsy-style skirt whispers around her tanned thighs. I badly want to touch her.

It's best if I don't, though. Just looking at her causes problems in my swim trunks. Not ideal when hanging at a public beach. Jaw tight, I wrench my gaze away.

The pier to our left is busy. People stroll and jog and drip ice cream down their wrists. Seagulls circle, screaming over a nearby family picnic. It's hot, inside and out, and I could really do with a swim.

"I needed that," she says, sighing as she takes my empty coffee cup. She nests it inside hers and shoves both into her canvas bag. "I stayed up way too late studying."

"You need to prioritize sleep," I say, like I'm some kind of health guru. "I believe you've got something that belongs to me."

"Oh. Your license. I completely forgot." She digs inside her bag. "Here. Very cute photo by the way. Shall we take a dip?"

The bay gleams like polished glass. "If that means you're about to take off some clothes, Edie, then I'm in." I slip the my license into my wallet. And if I don't get into the water soon, she's going to notice exactly *how* in I am.

Wobbling on the soft sand, she unbuttons her top, steps out of her skirt, and kicks off her sandals. I dig my nails into the stone wall beneath me, mouth going slack as I watch.

Fuck. Right now, I can't remember why I've spent my entire life hiding from women.

My vision narrows. "A one-piece," I mutter, sounding like a stunned idiot.

Her smile is all light and sunshine. The swimsuit is the opposite. The neckline plunges in a deep V to her sternum. Geometric mesh panels slice through the black fabric. And the mesh itself is sheer, and definitely out to ruin my resolve to keep this a strictly friends-only outing.

Before Edie, sex meant only nightmares of too-heavy limbs, rough voices, and shame pressed into my skin. But when I look at this girl, a fire burns inside me, annihilating the darkness. The nightmare of my past feels like a bad movie I once watched. Unconnected to me. Not my problem anymore.

Maybe she's cured me. Or maybe I should test her theory about other girls. See if I can manage to get hard for someone else. Diversify, the way she suggested I should.

"Are you even listening to me?" She bends over to rearrange her towel, and my eyes snag on her ass.

"Jesus Christ." This girl is killing me. "Sorry. What'd you say?" I ask.

"I asked if you were ready to get wet."

"Damn straight I am." Thinking about an entirely different kind of wet, I push off the wall, grab her hand, and tow her toward the glittering water.

Laughing, she digs her heels into the sand. "You might want to take your T-shirt off first."

Huh? I glance down. Right. My T-shirt. "Yeah. Good call. Although wearing it might reduce sun exposure." I tip my head back, squinting at the sky like a moron. "After reassessing the situation, I agree it's unnecessary."

She lets out that magical laugh again as I peel off my old band shirt and fling it toward our towels.

Her smile deepens as she nods at it. "I wouldn't have picked you for a nineties alt-rock guy who's into riot girl bands."

"Why not?" I shrug. "Powerful women are hot."

Swiping hair off her face, she says, "You know, L, I have a feeling you're not as much of an asshole as you pretend to be."

Before I can shut that theory down, she takes off, feet spraying sand as she runs.

Fuck. That girl has the wrong idea about me.

I sprint to catch up, and then dive through a frothy wave three seconds behind her.

The water is icy, which sorts out the problem in my pants. When I break the surface, I scan the water. No Edie.

Then in a burst of white spray, she surfaces, droplets clinging to her skin and eyelashes. She looks unreal. Like some kind of sea goddess. But she's too real. Too authentic. Too normal for a guy like me. I used to want that. Crave it more than anything. But this girl makes my stomach ache, my chest burn, and I don't like it. I feel weak when I look at her. Something close to fear slides down my throat and settles heavy in my gut.

I should do her a favor and get away from her without delay, because my life is a horror movie still rolling. One where the final credits haven't hit yet.

My head replays the same scenes on a slow-motion loop—vengeance, blood, and not much else. In this shit movie in my brain, there's no love interest. It's just a bare-bones revenge story with two starring roles: me and that asshole Coop. The ending's sure to be bad, a tragic final shot waiting for one of us. Him or me. Fuck, I really hope it's Coop. I hate it when the bad guy wins.

And what this girl is making me feel right now? It's not in the script. It doesn't fit with what's coming—the violence and the blood.

I don't have a future. I mean, technically I do. But it's capped. Which makes caring about anything reckless. Caring about anyone stupid and selfish.

She pants softly, slicking wet hair from her face. Her chest hovers inches from mine, her smile pulling me even closer. "How does a homeless boy get an education?" she asks. "Learn about the things you seem to know."

I struggle to keep my breathing steady, and even though I'm shivering from the cold water lapping at my waist, my face feels hot. "I did actually attend high school before I landed on the streets, you know." Most days, anyway.

"And...?" she says, tilting her head, giving me an encouraging smile.

A swirl of gray clouds smears the horizon. Great. A storm's blowing in. When I look back at her, she's still smiling. Still waiting. I run a finger slowly down her chest, between her breasts. My mouth waters. My hand settles against the fabric over her stomach, fingers brushing the edge of her pubic bone. I lean in and give her a slow, salty kiss, aiming to derail her train of thought.

When I pull back, her breathing is uneven, but her eyes are still eager. Expectant.

I sigh. "Do I really have to talk about this stuff?"

She nods.

My muscles tense. "Well, from the minute Ariana's agency got me working, I was making good money. A lot of it. And I had heaps of free time between jobs and on shoots." I scowl over at a skinny kid on a surfboard nearby. He paddles faster, like he's decided heading out to sea beats drifting too close to me, the guy with obvious anger issues. Smart move. "So I studied and... I finished high school online."

I wait for her to laugh, but she doesn't.

"That's great, L. Seriously... good on you."

I'm on a roll now, talking fast as if a pressure valve has been released. "And I read a lot, too. I'm kinda fascinated by physics and, yeah, sociology, because it's such a weird fucking world, isn't it? I'm interested in... most things."

Her expression softens. I shouldn't have told her that. In her eyes, it probably makes me seem like a safer person to be around. Why is it so damn hard to lie to this girl?

When she places her cool palm on my chest, right over my pounding heart, my skin prickles, the knot in my gut cinching tighter.

Chapter 23

L

Her hand slides down my body, brushing my persistent hard-on. "So what do you think? Shall we go back to your place or mine?"

Trying to keep a straight face, I say, "Are you asking my dick's opinion, or do you want mine?"

She punches my arm.

"Oh, so *mine*, right? You want my thoughts? Definitely your place, then."

"Right," she says. "Sounds to me like you're afraid to let me see where you live. It must be a shocking den of iniquity, then." She gives a cute little shrug. "But whatever. My place it is. But after one quick stop." She points at the hulking amusement park on the other side of the boardwalk. "Let's get some ice cream first."

My gut sinks. I mean, really, do we have to? I'm keen to get horizontal with her, and she's thinking about licking ice cream cones instead of me.

"Wait. You know this would only be a friends-with-benefits situation, right? Nothing more. You still wanna hook up?" I say, bracing myself in case we're on completely different pages.

She nods, and cool relief flows through me.

"Okay, great," I say, my voice huskier than I meant it to be. "I'm into that." Big fucking time. Starved for positive affection, I've done a complete one-eighty on getting away from her. Not encouraging whatever the fuck this is brewing between us.

While we towel off and get dressed, I grin at her, making zero effort to hide where my thoughts are headed. With Edie, this 'friends' only business is impossible to stick to.

Heat radiates from the pavement as we amble along the esplanade. "This will be interesting," I say. "I've never had ice cream in a cone before."

Her head flicks up. "How is that possible?"

"Well, my... mom was a health nut. And when I was homeless, if I had any money, I made sure I spent it on real food. The kind that would keep the hunger pains away for as long as possible."

"Remind me how old you were when you got off the streets and started modeling."

I shift her tote bag, bursting with all our beach stuff, to my other shoulder. "Eighteen. Nearly nineteen."

"And how old are you now, about twenty-five?"

I laugh. "No. Try twenty-two. Life on the streets has a way of etching extra years into you."

"Your skin is as smooth as a... well, as a GQ cover model's. It's your build that made me think you were older. Your height and muscles. Very manly. Hey—we're the same age."

Shaking my head, I just look at her. This girl is trying to kill me with her sweetness.

The choice of flavors at the candy-colored ice cream parlor is truly mind-boggling. Banana fudge. Raspberry sorbet. Even fucking bubblegum.

She tugs me away from the fruity section. "No, L. Absolutely not," she yells over Lana Del Rey singing about feeling crazy. "You're way too inexperienced to understand the mistake you're making there. Go for the macadamia nut. I promise you won't regret it."

Wanting to impress, I duly order two. I'm frowning as the guy behind the counter hands the cones over and I realize Lana's going on about being young and in love. What a stupid song.

But Edie's right. The macadamia nut is fucking good. I watch her lick and bite the creamy deliciousness. That's even better.

We sit at a bright pink bench, entertained by the families and teenagers wandering past, and stare at each other. When I start making out with my ice cream, basically giving her a preview of what to expect back at her place, she slaps my shoulder. Even that lands hot.

"So, which ride shall we go on first, the scenic railway or the dodgems?"

"What?" I splutter, choking on a macadamia nut. "I don't do kids' rides. Never have. Never will."

"I understand. It's a new experience and you're afraid," she teases.

I sigh, rolling my eyes at how easily she can manipulate me. "Fine. Looks like the lame-ass railway thing it is, then."

Fifteen minutes later, I'm certain it's the end of the fucking world. At least that's what it sounds like. And feels like, too.

The screeches, rattles, and roars of steel on steel are deafening, not to mention the bloodcurdling screams.

"Are you sure this thing's safe?" I yell, my head nearly wrenching off my shoulders as we whip around another corner and we come close to flying off the tracks to our grisly deaths. This ride is about as fun as a war zone.

Gripping my arm tightly, she screams, laughing like a wild thing. "Absolutely. On average, only about four people a year die from amusement park rides in the US." She laughs again. "Oh, L. You're completely white."

We hurtle downward, heading straight for the concrete below. "Ah, fuck," I say bravely through clenched teeth. "This isn't my idea of scenic."

"See that rickety old thing over there? *That's* the scenic railway. This is the Dragon's Tail. Way more fun."

"Yeah, real fun."

Earlier, when we were lined up for this hellish ride, instead of gluing my eyes to her lips and hot curves, I should have kept a broader focus on my environment. Because I'm pretty sure, before I even get a shot at dealing with Coop, this girl is going to get me killed.

"Hold on tight," she says.

"What—" And then we're upside down, riding a metal wave that twists, jerks, and shudders like it's on a mission to shake us off.

"Fuck," I say when we're back the right way up.

Tears stream down her face from laughing too hard. "You didn't make a sound during that."

"I couldn't. I was busy watching all the lowlights of my life flash by."

After a few more hills and dips, it's finally over, and on trembling legs, we make our way over to the dodgem cars.

"You know," I say as we creep to the front of the line, "that was kind of fun."

"Yep, it's amazing how much better roller coasters seem when you're not trapped on them anymore." She tilts her head. "Shall we get a car each or share? I'm pretty bad at driving."

"I'd love to be your chauffeur, my lady." I kiss her hand like a total sap. Jesus Christ. Never before has anything so fully sickening come out of my mouth. What's happening to me?

She gives me a gratifying giggle, and we hop into a purple car. It's a nice tight fit.

There are six other dodgems on the circuit, all filled with teenagers baying for blood. It turns out to be great fun, bumping, bashing and yelping. Angelo would love this. I make a note to abduct him from the couch one day soon and dump his protesting body in a theme park.

When we land in the middle of a six-car pileup, kids beeping and cursing out each other's mothers, I keep one hand on the wheel, cup Edie's jaw with the other, and kiss her until my head feels like it's going to rocket off my shoulders.

Well, actually, I keep kissing her until the guy behind the mic engages the speaker system and announces, "Attention, could the couple in the purple car stop eating each other's faces and get a move on? I repeat—face suckers in the purple car, quit turning each other on and reenter the fray."

The teenagers whoop and cheer, and even under the seedy lights, I can see Edie's crimson blush. That's when I lose it and laugh until I nearly split my healing stomach wound open.

We stand blinking in the daylight out front of the dodgems, me running my mouth about my driving skills and bragging about my sexual powers and how I could easily have had her right there in the tiny, purple car if I'd wanted to.

"Shut up," she says, smacking me hard, but still smiling. "You don't need to convince me of your prowess. Preaching to the converted here."

"Ow. Hey, you're really getting into beating me up today. I thought I was meant to be the one who got off on that." I wince inwardly. Shut up. Shut up.

She hooks her arm through mine and pulls me toward the park's exit. "Did you walk here?"

"Yeah."

"Good. My car's just around the corner."

The esplanade is busy. Skaters, cyclists, dog walkers, you name it, everyone seems to be out rambling along the beachside path. Despite the dark clouds in the distance, it's still warm, and I guess everyone's enjoying the good weather before the looming storm finally breaks.

"Do you really like to hurt people, L? Is it true that it turns you on?"

I feel my cheeks heat. "No, can't say I do get turned on by it." Fuck. I don't want to talk about this shit. "It's just... like I was telling you the other day, before I met you, sex equaled bad stuff. Pain and... fear. Being forced is no fun, but your body kind of reacts anyway, you know? It becomes this automatic response."

You loved it, you little shit, says the monster's voice in my head. *Those were tears of fucking joy.*

I grit my teeth against the lies, draw a slow breath, and force myself back to this sunny day. Her smile. This girl's dimples.

"I hated sex and getting off. I hated myself when I got turned on just looking at a girl. Because those feelings always came with horrible memories. Flashbacks, I guess, of being helpless."

"Oh, L. If I could take some of what you went through away, if it was possible, I'd do anything."

I bite the inside of my mouth until I taste blood, hoping it will stop the watery heat burning behind my eyes.

I cough to clear my throat and force myself to keep talking. Telling someone—telling Edie—actually feels good, so I keep talking.

"When I started earning legit money and lived in a proper apartment, I avoided sex entirely. But then Coop found me again—"

"Again? What do you mean again?" she asks.

"Listen, I might tell you the whole shitty story one day. But just not right now. And with Coop's stuff, man..." I shake my head. "I hate that guy so bad, and all his lowlife friends. He gave me no choice. But the only way I can manage to do what he wants, *physically*, is to see, and hear, those pricks suffer. I'm not proud of it. But it's just how it is."

Edie rubs my back, and I have to stop myself from reaching around and keeping her hand there forever.

"That's horrible," she says. "You have to get away from Coop. Go overseas as soon as you can. Like you planned. And you should get some counseling to work through that stuff, too. I can help you find someone good."

"But aren't you my counselor?" I joke.

"Sure, talk to me about the dark stuff anytime," she says. "I want to help, but it's a hell of a back story you've got, and I don't know..." She shivers like it's not ninety-five degrees in the shade.

"A professional can give you the tools to help you heal fully. But I think us being friends is a good development. We can have fun in bed, and you can prove to yourself that you have no problem being gentle. It's selfless of me to offer myself up like that, I know!" Her dimples flash at me again.

I should keep quiet. But the way she speaks, warm and like everything in the world is simple and there's a solution for every problem, makes it hard to keep my mouth shut. "I've never had that before I met you," I say. "Any softness."

Moisture shimmers in her eyes.

"Dammit. Don't cry. This is why you're bad for me," I continue. "You make me want stuff that in my life. It's weak. I can't risk that. Not even a little bit."

"You can, L. It's fine. Soft is good."

"But you don't understand the Coop thing," I counter.

"Help me understand it, then."

Words twist their way into my mouth. Ones that tell the whole tale of how fucked up I am. I can't say them out loud. But I owe her a wake-up call—a warning. "The truth is you should run. You're a good person, Edie. Nice... and kind, too. And I'm just... wrong."

That's right, the voice in my head snarls. *You tell her, you dumb fuck.*

Locks beep as Edie points a key at a sad-looking car on the curb. It's a gross green color, like a jar of old pickles or something, and it's dinged up pretty bad.

"You're not what they've tried to make you, L. You're just not."

She's wrong. I'm nothing but the product of every filthy imagination that has ever used and abused me. Through an ocean of tears and shame, they fashioned me into who I am today—one perfectly sick fuck.

"Nice ride," I say, ducking into the old Honda. It really isn't.

Wriggling to get comfortable behind the wheel, she gives me a sour look. "Careful. If you're mean to Olive, I'll have to get rough with you. Kick your ass around a bit."

"Huh. I'd like to see you try. It'd be entertaining, to say the least. And funny."

She flicks my cheekbone with her finger and starts the engine.

"So your car is called Olive? What a great name," I say flatly.

"Watch your mouth," she replies as she backs out into traffic, nearly killing us.

She wasn't wrong about her driving skills. Hopefully, she won't notice my sneaker hitting the phantom brake pedal all the way to her place. I have a feeling it's gonna be a harrowing ride and much worse than the Dragon's Tail.

Chapter 24

EDEN

"**Y**ou hit like a girl," L says.

"That's because I am one, you sexist loser."

"Didn't you mention earlier that you take some kinda self-defense class?"

I block my face with clenched fists, circling around L as if I know what I'm doing. "Yep. Kickboxing."

The flashy footwork stops, and his hands drop to his muscular thighs. This guy is a total showoff.

"You're kidding," he says. "What are they teaching you? How to dance?"

"You're the one who's prancing around my living room."

Through the arched window, black clouds hang in the sky, looming ominously over the apartments on the other side of the courtyard. The afternoon light is growing dim, but I don't rush to turn on any lamps.

Instead, puffing and trying to look mean, I take in the sight of him in for a few glorious seconds. His jeans hang low on narrow hips, abs ripple under smooth skin, and ink swirls around impressive biceps. Then there's the hard jaw and shockingly handsome angel-devil face. Forget about play fighting. He only needs to stand there radiating hotness to finish me off.

"I only train once a week at the moment, with school and work being so busy," I say. "That's why my skills are a bit lacking. One day soon, though, I'll be able to kick your butt. Then you won't be smiling at me like that, L."

The smug smile spreads. "Hit me again. Hard as you can this time. I can take it."

He drops both fists and waits, staring at me like he wants to eat me up. Slowly, I step forward.

"Aim for my stomach. Go."

"Your knife wound isn't fully healed."

"So try higher up."

I shift into position and pop two hard jabs into his upper stomach. He doesn't even flinch.

"Don't lift your hips up, Edie. Exhale when you let that fist rip. Try it again."

I do. And end up shaking my hand in pain.

"Jesus." He ducks and weaves around my pathetic swings, then says, "Tell me the name of this fine establishment you're attending, and I'll make a note not to recommend them to anyone."

"You think you're a real tough guy, don't you? Like you're some kind of amazing fighter?"

"I *know* I'm an amazing fighter. How else do you think I managed not to get myself killed sleeping in doorways and under bridges all that time?"

The thought of him living rough out there, being treated like garbage, makes my brain ache and my heart bleed. I smile like it's no big deal. Like this is a normal conversation. As if all my friends are ex-street kids.

Lifting an eyebrow at his package, I say, "And do you always get turned on when you spar?"

One side of his mouth quirks up, and he stalks forward, staring at my lips. With his body not quite touching mine, he kisses me softly. The room spins wildly around us.

"I know what your problem is," he whispers.

"Oh, yeah. What's that?"

"You're too constricted by your clothes. Those kicks you were showing me earlier? They would have been a lot more effective if you didn't have that skirt on. And the shirt."

"Uh, huh. So, you think if I change into exercise gear, then I might be able to give you a proper beating?"

He smiles slowly, biting his lip. "Ah, no. I wouldn't go that far. And if I were you, I wouldn't bother changing at all." He runs his finger down my shirt buttons, his voice dropping low as he says, "Just take this off." The material of my skirt rasps between his fingers. "And this too," he adds, smirk hot and unapologetic.

I smile. "You think I should spar in my swimsuit?" I nod at my wall in pretend contemplation. "I suppose it's less constricting. It could work."

"It'll definitely work for me," he agrees.

"Even if you lose this fight?" I ask.

"Especially if I do."

"Okay, then," I say. "Step back. Give me some room."

The air crackles, growing hotter against my skin as I take my time stripping down. Remaining silent, his eyes fix on mine while I complete the task. Even in the low light, they're electric blue, almost glowing.

Down to my swimsuit, I sweep my hands dramatically over my body, smiling like I'm trying to sell him something.

He purses his lips and blows out a long breath. "Nice swimsuit, Edie."

"Right?" I say, "You can do almost anything in it. Is it okay to admit I bought it two days ago already planning on inviting you to the beach?"

Looking thrilled, he laughs. "Really? So you bought it with me in mind?"

Unable to keep back a smile, I nod.

"Fuck. No one's ever done that before. Even if I'd been in the store with you, I don't think I could have selected a better one." His expression darkens. "But you probably shouldn't have told me that."

Like I'm prey, he paces slowly around me. "Well, Edie, what are you waiting for? Show me what you've got."

"Sure. I'll try a few of those sidekicks again."

He grins. "Great idea. Go for it."

My hands stay stuck to my sides. "Wait. It's hardly fair, is it? Me dressed like this and you still—"

"Stop right there. I'm already on it." He shucks his jeans quickly and then stands tall, his chest pumping and an awe-inspiring shape pressing against his tight black boxers. I bite back a groan and thwack three hard kicks into his left side.

He rubs his ribs. "Not too shabby. And you've got the face right. Very badass."

"Thank you," I say, bowing low. "Concentrating wasn't easy with that tent in your pants."

Huffing a laugh, he looks down at himself, rubs the heel of his palm over the tantalizing shape, then advances. "Now it's my turn to show off some moves. Specifically ones you've taught me."

He keeps coming at me, and I walk backward until my shoulders hit the wall.

Then he's up against me, fingers tracing the mesh cutouts on my swimsuit, breath gusting over my face. My neck.

"Edie," he murmurs, brow furrowed in concentration.

"So... was my fighting style as funny as you imagined?" I ask.

"No, not funny at all. Nearly fucking killed me." He drops his face to the side of my neck and inhales deeply. I tilt my head back, breathe him in too. His hair smells of the beach, his skin tangy, with a whisper of musk. It's intoxicating.

He kisses my neck, sucks, bites.

Electricity shoots through me as his fingertips trace patterns, palms molding over my breasts, thumb and forefinger teasing my nipples.

This man. How has he become the center of everything in just a couple of weeks? All I think about. All I want.

"I reckon we should keep the kink quota low tonight, Edie." His voice is deep and husky. "This time, how about we're both in charge?"

I nod.

Lungs working hard, he watches his hand glide over my stomach until it cups my mound, moving with perfect, shifting pressure. He pulls back briefly, using his fingers to tease through the soaked material. His gaze flickers between what he's doing and my face, biting his lip with my every dramatic reaction.

"Shit," he says after a particularly loud moan escapes me. Sweeping the swimsuit out of the away, he pushes inside.

It's obvious he's turned on by watching—seeing his fingers move, slick with my desire. I can tell how badly it affects him as his body begins to shake.

"God," I gasp, already so close. His trembling increases, hand working faster. The wet noises, our heavy breathing, make a perfect soundtrack for our mutual undoing.

"L, please... wait. I want you inside me."

Shoving his boxers down, the material catches on his erection. "Shit." He fumbles for a moment before freeing himself.

He lifts me against the wall and plunges in with one stroke. Then freezes.

"Fuck, Edie. Feels too good. Don't move. Give me a second…"

I wrap my legs around his waist. He groans.

"Jesus. Why can't you do what I ask for once?" Hips wedged tight, limbs motionless, his cock pulses inside me.

"Why does anyone bother going to work?" he murmurs, wonder in his voice. "Or go on holiday? We should all just stay home and fuck."

Dropping my head against his shoulder, I laugh, nipping him gently.

"Please don't laugh," he warns. "Or this will be over in a hot second."

Between gasps, I say, "We'd starve if we never went to work."

He pulls the deep V of my neckline aside, exposing one breast to his hungry gaze, his fingers rough.

"Who needs food? This is heaven."

I tug his head up, fisting his thick hair, and kiss him slowly.

"Time to move, L."

He gives me a worried look. "I won't last long. This thing you're wearing—"

"I know," I say, smiling. "It's obvious how much you like it. Maybe you should take it home with you."

His lips quirk. "Maybe I should take *you* home with me instead. Tie you to my bed. Cook for you. Bring you food." His voice drops. "Then I'd fuck you. Over and over."

I know the fantasy shouldn't appeal, but the way he says it, the need in his voice, pushes me closer to the edge.

He turns his attention to my breasts, one bare and the other still covered. "I wish I could fuck you and have my mouth on these at the same time." He exhales, frustrated. "I'm too tall."

"Tragic," I say dryly. "First world problems." I roll my hips against his, pinned between the wall and all that strength. "What you should be thinking about right now is coming, L... I want to hear you lose it. No holding back. Do it for me."

The instinct to resist the command flashes across his face. I wait.

When he finally gives in, his eyes narrow, something feral taking hold. Then he takes me with long, punishing strokes, fighting for control. Trying to savor it. But every time he looks down, watching himself drive into me, it gets harder. The sight of it is his undoing.

My hands sweep over his back, then I grip his face. "Let go," I whisper. "Don't hold on, L. Come."

He grunts, teeth gritted, and picks up speed. The second he loses it, his hips pumping fast and erratically, the storm rolls in.

The room flashes silver.

I count as my body slams into the wall, each impact punching the breath from me.

One.

Two.

Three.

Then thunder cracks like rifle fire. The storm clouds must be close.

One.

Two.

The sky splits open again.

L cries out like he's been hit, grips my hips hard, straining, still holding back, right on the edge as he tries to stroke me to the very end.

"Yes, L... Oh, God... yes. That's it. Just... just a couple more..."

Shaking, he keeps thrusting, his fingers working pure magic at my clit. Moaning loudly, I fly over the cliff and shatter into a billion tiny pieces.

Chapter 25

EDEN

It takes a long time for our breathing to settle. He kisses me softly while we wait, the thunder a gentle rumble moving past.

Pulling out carefully, he guides my weak legs until my feet hit the floor. "I love having sex with you, Edie."

My brain freezes, because for a stupid second there, I thought he might say something else.

"I think it's my favorite thing."

I pat his cheek. "It helps when you're doing it with someone you don't hate. Which is a pretty bleak revelation for you. You should try it with another girl. I bet you'd like that too."

Why the hell did I say that?

If I had duct tape, I'd gag my self-sabotaging mouth. Am I trying to break my own heart?

A frown appears, and he shakes his head. "No. I don't want to." A big hand smooths over my front, running over my ribs, my stomach, down to the mess between my legs. Then it comes back up, and both palms frame my face. "I like you a lot," he says quietly, and bends to collect his boxers from the floor.

He likes me. It's such a small, almost childish complement, and I can't work out if I should be happy about it or not.

Tipping his chin at my lower body, he says, "Want me to grab you something from the bathroom to clean up with?"

"I need to go, too. I'll wait. But thanks."

When it's my turn, I call out from the toilet, "L, are you hungry? Should we make something? Or we could walk to the dumpling place around the corner."

I tense, waiting for him to say he needs to leave, has something important to do, somewhere better to be.

Cupboard doors bang. Then he yells, "I'm checking if you've got bread. Let's just have toast and get back into bed."

"I've got sourdough in the bread tin. Next to the toaster."

My ringtone blares from the kitchen. The fridge is bare, and I'm waiting on Jess to call about another box of vegetables. "Can you check who's calling," I ask. "It's near the fridge."

I hear him pad across the tiles.

Voice flat, he says, "It's the devil. Apparently."

Shit. That's Coop's caller I.D. "Quick. Bring it here."

Bare-chested, wearing low-slung jeans and a hard frown, he passes the phone to me while I pull a pair of cutoff shorts up my hips with one hand. Leaving messy piles of clothes in every room can actually be quite convenient. "Thanks," I whisper as I take the call.

Throwing an extra-intense scowl over his shoulder, L shuts the door.

"What do you want?" I ask Coop.

"Why are you whispering? Got company?"

"Yes. Jess is here," I lie.

He chuckles. "Ah, our delicious fiery redhead. Say hello from me. Listen up. Next Saturday, I need you at a house party. The same guys as last time. Be ready at one p.m. Wear the red outfit again."

"But it's too soon, too close to the last one. You promised it wouldn't be like this."

"Edie, this one's special. It's worth one hundred grand off your mortgage."

One hundred grand? "Are you serious? Wait a second. Is it with L again?"

"No. Someone different. He's a gentleman. No need to worry. Just say yes."

"Damn you, Coop." I take a piece of green sea glass from a ceramic dish and roll it around my palm, stalling. "Okay, fine. Where is it?"

I'll say yes now, I decide. And I can always change my mind if something crops up—like L declaring his undying love for me, for example. But I know better than to hold my breath. L probably wouldn't care if I had sex with an entire troupe of circus performers. Edie does Cirque du Soleil and he'd be slouched in the third row, eating popcorn, clapping along with the band.

"Don't worry your pretty little head about the location," Cooper says. "A driver will pick you up. You'll find out when you get there."

"I hate you."

"I know," he says, ending the call.

Coop claims he'd never force me to do these parties. That it's always my choice. It's only if I ever show signs of wanting to back out after I've arrived at one of his functions that he lets his inner gangster out, goes apeshit, and bandies threats around. Normally, all he does is dangle the juicy carrot of my dad's farm under my nose and I fall in line. It's pure blackmail, and I've never said no before. Never had a reason to.

But L—he's beginning to feel like a very good reason.

I throw the phone next to the sink and wash my hands, studiously avoiding my eyes in the mirror.

When I walk into the kitchen, L is slumped at the wooden table, head in his hands.

"What did he want?" he mumbles to the butter knife.

The bread pops out of the toaster. I swipe the knife from L and start buttering. "Who? Nico?" I ask.

I feel L lift his head and pin my back with his stare. "Don't bullshit me. Tell me what that prick Cooper wanted."

I stay quiet while I take the lid off the honey and slather some over the bread.

"Eat," I say, sitting opposite him as I set the plate between us. I get busy chewing and avoiding L's glare. He's an expert at the stony silent treatment, and I crack within seconds. "Okay! So it was Coop. He wanted to know when he could book someone to come by and fix the bath faucet."

L blows a hard breath through his nose. "What's wrong with it?"

"It's leaking," I squeak.

For three seconds L stares into my eyes, his mouth grim. Then he walks into the bathroom. I hear water gush out from the faucet.

When he returns, he takes his seat without uttering a word and eats more toast. He waits a few moments before saying, "I can fix that leak for you. Call Coop back now and tell him not to bother booking anyone."

My mouth hangs open. L keeps crunching toast.

"It's not just a washer. It's more complicated."

"I said I can fix it, didn't I?"

"How would you know how to do it properly?"

"I can do a lot of things you don't know about," he says. "Call Coop now. I want to hear you do it."

Shit. I watch the stretch of tendons in L's hand as he reaches for his glass of water, and then drains it in one go.

I can't tell him about next Saturday, about what Coop has planned for me. It won't do either of us any good if he knows.

Except for the odd hookup, L's been clear that he wants to keep his distance from me. But, right now, he's bristling at the thought of Coop anywhere near my life, the tension palpable in the air between us. He must really despise the guy, and I can certainly empathize.

I need to distract him. And Lightning is so sexy when he's angry.

I take three more bites, chewing quickly before finishing my water. Then I say casually, "I'll call him later. Right now, I'm thinking about something more important."

L's eyes narrow, fluorescent blue under the harsh overhead light. "Oh, yeah? What about?"

I saunter around the table, plant a hand on his chest, shove him back, and straddle his lap. With my hands in his hair, I let my gaze rove over his exquisite face.

Making sure the pressure over the bulge in his jeans is just right, I say, "I remembered what you told me today back there on the dodgems. That you've never gone down on a woman before. Is that true?"

His turquoise eyes flare wide, and he nods.

"I think it's time for another friendly lesson, then."

His eyebrows twist into a hard frown.

"Don't worry, you'll be a natural."

He drops his forehead to my shoulder. "Shit, Edie."

And, just like that... he's forgotten all about Cooper's phone call.

Chapter 26

EDEN

"Would you like more goulash, girls?" Nico's mom, Zsofia, asks in her lovely Hungarian accent.

She's hovering over Jess and me, poised to whisk our bowls back to the stove if we show the slightest interest, a flare of nostrils, a flicker of eyes, anything that might indicate we'll yield and allow her to stuff us with more food.

In her early fifties with honey-blond hair, high cheekbones, and large almond-shaped eyes, Zsofia is a classic beauty. Her only child, and the sole beneficiary of her excellent genetics, scowls at her across the dining table.

"And what am I, invisible?"

"No, Nico, what I see in front of me is a big malac. Girls, that means pig in Hungarian." She laughs loudly. "Ha! Just one look at him over there slouching over his third helping tells the story, yes?" she says in her lilting accent that I could listen to all night long.

Jess and I nod vigorously.

Pointing a fork-skewered potato at us, Nico says, "Hey, I've been watching you two demolish your elephant-sized second servings. None of us are holding back tonight. So shut up."

Ignoring him, I pat my belly. "No thanks. No more for me, Zsof. I'm done. As usual, it was delicious, but if I eat any more, I'll probably lose the whole lot, and that'd be a shocking waste of your divine cooking."

"Oh, gross!" Jess pushes her meal away. "I can't eat another thing. Thanks to Edie."

"Sorry. That was a disgusting thing to say. What's wrong with me? I'm not thinking straight tonight."

"Yes, you are," Jess counters. "You're just not thinking about anything that's contained within these four walls."

I cock my head at her. "What's that supposed to mean?"

Everyone except me snickers.

"What are you lot laughing at?" I ask, getting up to rinse my plate and stack it in the dishwasher.

I love Nico's mom's kitchen. It's cozy, warm, and cluttered. Sweet Hungarian porcelain covers most of the flat surfaces—tiny figurines of carnival workers and animals, beautiful coffee cups patterned with birds and leaves, and bright red and blue embroideries crowd the walls. It's relentlessly cheerful.

Covering up the casserole pot, Zsofia says, "Well, Edie, Nico and I believe you are obsessed with that boy. Now, let me remember... What is he called? Z or X?"

"His name is L," Nico says helpfully. "And he's so tough that he only needs a capital letter to go by, like he thinks he's a superhero."

"Oh, I beg your pardon. L. Yes! What funny names you Americans have."

My face burns hot as I weave around the table collecting plates. Nico's is licked clean and clearly doesn't require further washing.

Thinking fast, I attempt to redirect the conversation. "And, Nico darling, how is that blue-haired beauty you left your gig with on Monday night? Are you officially dating?"

Zsofia spins on her heels and stares at her son. "Do you have a girlfriend now, Nico? You must show me a photo!"

Lips twisted into a tragically cute pout, Nico slumps in his seat. "Thanks a lot," he says to me. "No, she's not exactly my girlfriend, Ma. She was kinda... more like a friend for the night—"

"But still... how old is she? Younger than you?" Eyes sparkling, Zsofia wrings her hands together.

"No. Same age as me. Eighteen."

"Then she is not the one." She flicks a tea towel at Nico's shoulder. "You can forget her."

"Oh, shit. Do your best to block your ears girls. Mom's gonna whip out the ridiculous fated-mate prophecy. I'm sorry you have to fucking hear it again."

"Language," Zsofia snaps.

Jess pats Nico's hand. "Oh, yes, that's right. How could I forget? According to the creepy Hungarian oracle, your true love will be an older woman, won't she?"

Nico smirks. "Yeah. I'm on the lookout for a sexy cougar. Who knows, it could be you, Edie. You *are* four whole years older than me."

"No," Zsofia says, scraping back a chair and sitting next to her son. "Four years is not enough. Baba Vash said it will be a very big age difference. Many years! And this woman from my village—she is never wrong. People come from overseas to hear how their lives will untangle."

Nico laughs. "I think you mean unravel."

"Untangle or unravel. Same thing."

"Well, then, I'm sorry to disappoint you, Edie." Nico bites his lip piercing and picks up my hand. It's warm and rough. "You'll just have to stick with your brute of a pin-up boy. To keep my mom happy, I'm planning to make a move on the grandma who lives in the apartment across the hall."

Patting his hand, Jess says, "I've seen her. You'll make a lovely couple. You won't mind, Zsof, that Nico's bride will be twenty-five years older than you?"

"If my boy is happy, then I am happy too." Zsofia's brilliant green gaze, so like her son's, pins me in place. "Tell me about this L person, Edie. You love him, yes? But does he love you also?"

My mouth drops open. "I don't love him!" I say. "Who told you that? *Nico.* Some friend you are."

Three sets of eyes stare, patiently waiting for me to stop lying to them.

"I've only known him...what..." I count on my fingers. "Two weeks and four days."

Jess directs an annoying smile at me. "And approximately how many hours and minutes?"

"Jessica! Love doesn't care for ticks on clocks," scolds Zsofia. "Or for how many times the sun rises and sets. Love keeps time by quiet looks, feather-light touches, pulses of the blood. Tell us, Edie, when did you last see this L?"

"Last night. And I'm a mess," I finally confess. "I don't know what to do. He tells me how dangerous he is, how bad he is for me. That we should just be friends. But then he keeps showing up for—"

"Your incredible Vietnamese noodles?" suggests Jess.

"Something like that. He's so confusing. And gorgeous. And hazardous yet vulnerable at the same time. It's a very addictive mix." Before I can stop myself, I extract my phone from my black denim jacket. "Look, Zsof. Check out this picture."

She peers at my cell and then grips her throat. "His eyes are blue like the ocean! Hard and yet soft and deep. A warrior prince."

It's the picture I took in bed yesterday, immediately after my lesson on oral sex. I was answering a text from Jess when he tore my cell away, snapped a photo of me as I fought to get it back, and then quickly texted it to himself.

Pretending to even up the score, but really just desperate for something to drool over later, I took a perfect close-up of him.

One side of his lickable lips kicked up in unrepentant amusement and his eyes glowing that special electric shade of blue.

Jess stretches across the table and grabs my phone. She shakes her head. "Really? On your lock screen? You are totally gone, girl."

I snatch my phone back.

"But, Edie," says Nico's mom. "Maybe this man is not for you. He looks like that, and I think, oh boy! He is big trouble. And he says he doesn't want you, but still, he wants to sleep with you... Oh boy, again. You must look elsewhere for happiness. It cannot be easy to love one such as him."

Zsofia isn't a big fan of romantic love. Or gorgeous guys other than her son. That might have something to do with her husband, a German actor who dragged her as a teenager from the bosom of her Hungarian family to a new life in America. And then four years later, he went back to Berlin with his new girlfriend, leaving Zsof to manage a toddler and three backbreaking cleaning jobs on her own. Zsofia swears that if her husband had been ugly and Hungarian, she'd still be happily married. And Nico wouldn't be bitter and twisted because of his father's desertion.

I guess he wouldn't be Nico, either.

Nico pushes back in his chair, tipping the front legs off the floor. "But maybe he keeps coming back because he can't stay away. Maybe it's because he's in love too. I guess even good-looking assholes can have feelings."

I smile at Nico. Maybe he's not so bitter after all.

"It's clear what you need to do," he continues. "Confront him. Give him an ultimatum. Say the friends-with-benefits shit isn't working for you anymore. Tell him the truth and see if he respects you enough to do the same."

There's no way L loves me. He's tried to tell me one hundred different ways that he's not that kind of guy. But still, he was so affectionate the other day—after he finished sucking so sweetly on my clit.

I pluck my backpack from behind the kitchen door, unhook Jess's tote bag as well, and then dump it in her lap. "Come on. I've got school and a long shift at work tomorrow. We need to split. Thanks so much for dinner, Zsof. It was incredible." I bend and kiss her cheek.

"You listen to my Nico. He is wise for one so young," she says, putting her hands on her hips proudly.

Heading for the door, I say to Nico, "I'll be watching to see how sensible *you* are when you fall hard for the grandma."

Nico entertains us in the elevator with Game of Thrones character impressions, and then walks us into the crisp night air, giving us warm bear hugs when we reach the car. He smells like goulash. We all probably do.

The sky is overcast, blocking out the stars.

With his fists stuffed into the pockets of his black jeans and leaning on the passenger door, he says, "Go and see Mr. Muscles, Edie. And if he doesn't tell you what you need to hear, run."

He sounds like a school principal.

"Yes, sir. How old are you again?" I ask, rolling my eyes at Jess as I try not to think of my dad's warning, so creepily close to Nico's words just now.

Jess squeezes my shoulder, then punches Nico's, busting out a few kickboxing moves I've shown her.

When Nico stops laughing at her, he says, "And, hey! Another thing, Edie, whatever that Coop dude wants you to do on the weekend… just don't do it. Okay?"

Now he sounds like L.

"He's so sexy when he gets bossy, isn't he, Edie? See you and your gorgeous dimples soon," Jess says as she hops into the car.

Slam goes the door.

I kiss one of Nico's sweet face-craters. "Okay, Niccy. Whatever you want. See you at work."

And I'm not a complete liar, because I plan to follow through on at least one of his bossy directives. Straight after my shift tomorrow afternoon, I'm going to find L.

Nico sticks his head through the open car window. "Please don't call me that. I'm not a child."

"We'll try our hardest, but no promises," Jess says. "Sleep tight, Niccy."

Laughing, we blow kisses at his scowl as we pull off the curb and head for home.

Chapter 27

L

On Thursday afternoon, loud thumping interrupts my phone call with my agent.

"Sorry, Ariana, I'll have to call you back. There's an idiot at my door. It'll be Angelo, for sure."

"Of course, darling," she purrs. "Will you give him a kiss from me?"

"Nope," I say, and hang up.

Angelo's apartment is directly opposite mine, and sometimes I wish it wasn't. Like now, for example, because as we open our doors at the exact same moment, his smug grin is one hundred percent annoying.

"Oh, sorry," he says, mocking. "I thought it was my door rattling." Then his eyes widen at the girl standing in the hallway. Mine do too.

Because it's Edie.

Fuck.

"Well, hello there, lovely lady." Angelo raises an eyebrow and flares his nostrils at me before turning back to her. "You must be Edie." He wears a towel around his waist, a shit-eating grin, and not much else.

Unfortunately, Edie is wearing a lot more. A tight gray T-shirt with a retro cherry, a denim skirt cut off at mid-thigh, and chunky flat boots. And let's not forget the ever-present mouth-watering curves. Chocolate-colored hair hangs in waves over her tanned shoulders, and her dark eyes look huge and innocent. As a package, it sends mixed signals—tough, sexy, and sweet all at once.

She blinks twice and then checks Angelo out from his boots to his smirking face. The man gets paid a lot of money to have his photo taken for a good reason. And doesn't he know it? He flutters his lashes like he's auditioning for a leading role in a rom-com.

"Hi, Edie," I say in a voice so surly it surprises even me. "How did you find out where I live?"

She laughs. "Your license, remember? In what I like to think of as a very non-stalkerish move, I photographed it before I gave it back to you."

Instead of feeling pissed, I'm flattered and then pissed at myself for the warmth flooding my chest. "Oh yeah, right. My license," I say, my traitor eyes stuck on her dimples.

Offset against the gold and silver tones of the hallway, she looks like a girl in a painting. A girl I want to touch, fuck, and then erase, because I don't do niceness or happy dimples. I'm King Midas in reverse. Anything I touch turns to shit.

Angelo clears his throat, dragging me back to the curvaceous problem at hand. Now—how to get rid of her? "Hey, speaking of stalkers," I say, "this is Angelo. He models too."

Smiting Angelo with a sweet smile, she shakes his hand. "Well, that makes sense. You certainly look like you do."

Angelo preens, squeezing her fingers, and not letting go. Prickly heat crawls over the back of my neck. He better not be getting any crazy ideas.

I step closer to him and growl, "Go away, Angelo." Shit. Hadn't meant to say that out loud. A silent chest thrust would have done the job just fine.

"Whoa. Overreacting much, Goldilocks?" Angelo puts his hands up in defense. "I was just contemplating leaning in for a peck on the cheek. Nothing with tongue, I promise. What, did you think I was gonna try to park in your pre-booked car spot or something?"

I stare at him. "You never make any sense."

He laughs like a jerk.

Yeah. Hysterical.

When Angelo finally manages to stop snickering, he says, "Do you like gaming, Edie?"

The dimples sparkle again. "Well, I—"

I grip her arm and yank her into my apartment before she can finish the sentence.

Even through the closed door, Angelo's laugh booms. I'd be happy to never hear that sound again.

Also, I don't want her inside my place where I actually live. How did this happen? Angelo. Goading me. Distracting me. Making me lose sight of my only objective, which is to get her out of here. Fast.

I plan to ship her off promptly with a brilliant excuse, but I can't think of a single thing to say.

Shit. I'm losing it. Edie in my space. Surreal doesn't cover it.

Her mouth hangs open as she turns slowly, head swinging from side to side like she's possessed, taking in my apartment.

I cross my arms. "By the way, don't get over-excited by Angelo. He tries his luck with everyone. The guy's a regular sex fiend. You know what I mean?"

Fuck. Shut up. I sound like a jealous boyfriend.

A crease forms between Edie's eyes, her sweet lips twisting.

And, still, my mouth keeps going. "I can't imagine him being anyone's boyfriend. And he likes guys as much as girls, so whoever makes the mistake of trying to tame him will have twice as many people to worry about him coming on to. You know—both genders and..." She's staring at me like I've lost the plot.

That makes two of us wondering what the fuck I'm saying.

"Okay," she says, stepping away from me and moving into the center of the living room. "Thanks for the tip. I'll try not to fall in love with Angelo."

What? She better fucking not.

While my brain buzzes with no useful thoughts, Edie takes in my industrial, open-plan apartment. Honey-colored eyes roam over the massive leather couches, the retro kitchen opposite the living room, the black staircase curling up to the mezzanine bedroom. Her lips twitch at the red-brick walls, blond wood floors, and the orange-and-blue paintings that echo the Persian rug beneath her feet.

Her frown deepens.

"Hey, don't look so shocked," I say as she gapes at the two bamboo palms flanking the enormous, arched windows. Beyond them, rooftop gardens glow under a crimson sun slowly sinking into the sea. Light pours in, turning her hair to molten gold.

Finally, she turns back to me. "Wow. This isn't what I expected at all."

"That's a deeply offensive comment," I reply, masking a grin.

Laughing, she wanders into the kitchen and hops on one of the metal stools lined up against the island bench. The buckles of her courier bag clack against the countertop as her fingers skim the polished concrete.

One side of the bench curves down in a long, smooth wave to the floor, slick enough to skateboard on. Angelo and I do. Frequently. It's probably unhygienic, but it's also unbeatable entertainment when you're bored after a few beers on a Saturday afternoon.

"But look," she says. "You've got plants. And they're alive. And such a nice kitchen. Good heavens, does this mean you can cook, L?"

I slide onto the stool beside her and lean in close. "Of course I can fucking cook. What do you think I've been eating for the last four years?"

"Pizza?" She spins toward me and loops her arms around my neck.

Just like that, my plan to get her out of here evaporates. Instead, I picture carrying her up those stairs, pressing her into my bed. A terrible idea. And absolutely not happening.

But say if I did weaken, I'm reasonably confident my room is tidy. After spending over a year homeless, packing up my wet piece of cardboard and rotting blanket every morning, I gained one skill that transferred well into apartment living. I'm a neatness freak.

Lips soft, she kisses me, and I pull her closer. The heat of her skin is unreal as my hands slide down to her knees, lifting her legs over mine so she half-straddles me, her ass still perched on her own barstool. My arms wrap around her waist, and I hold her tight.

Why was it a shitty idea for her to be here again? I honestly can't remember.

This is exactly where she should be—pressed hard against me, warm, sweet smelling, and real.

Instead of watching a Star Wars marathon with Angelo and demolishing a six-pack, I've got my arms full of a scorching-hot girl. A girl who sets me on fire and keeps every one of my demons at bay. So if tonight requires a choice, the option that includes Edie is suddenly a no-brainer. Also, I've recently discovered that sex with an actual human being beats abstinence or porn any day or night. By a landslide.

With my hands buried in silky hair, I tip her head back and deepen the kiss. I like the way my blood feels right now, hot and slow, with my whole body coiled tight and aching in the best possible way.

"Hey." She presses her palms to my chest and gently pushes me back.

"Huh?" I say, a true master of the English language.

"I need to talk to you about something."

"What's that?" I ask, doubling down on my eloquence. "Sounds serious. You're not, like... with child or anything are you?" I have no idea why I said that. Absolute idiot.

She laughs. "No child on board as far as I know. Are you going to offer me something to drink?"

I drop my head into my palms. "Oh. Yeah, of course. Sorry... I got distracted. Do you want a beer or... whatever? I'm sure I've probably got......" I trail off. Christ.

I leap from the stool, circle the bench, and try again. "I make a great whiskey sour. Want one?"

"No, a beer sounds perfect. Thanks."

When I open the fridge, cold air blasts my skin. Good. Maybe it'll help my brain reboot.

I wrestle two pale ales from a six-pack, pop the tops, and pass her one before settling back on the stool, making sure our knees touch.

"Cheers." I clink our bottles and take a long pull of icy goodness.

Grinning, I rest my beer on the bench and lay my palms over her bare thighs. The corners of her mouth turn down as she watches my thumbs stroke her skin. Not the reaction I want. I'd much prefer she put her hands on me, too. Anywhere will do.

She gives me a small, nervous smile. "L, I have to tell you something, and it's a bit... well. It's kind of difficult to say out loud." She stares past the couches at the pink-tinged sunset, rubbing her neck. "Actually, it's embarrassing."

My ears prick. "Sounds interesting. Start talking."

I study her eyes, the shape of her nose, slightly too big for her face, but somehow perfect. I like it. I like everything about her.

After picking at frayed threads on her skirt, she says, "Okay. Here goes nothing. Firstly, I want you to know I've tried hard not to have them, but—"

I frown. "Tried not to have what?"

"Shh. This is hard enough without you interrupting. I can't kid myself anymore, and I need to tell you this in case you... in case you..." She trails off again. "L, I've got these feelings for you."

And just like that, my smile dies.

Her eyes search mine. "And I know they're unwise. And foolish. But I can't stop thinking about you. All the time, L. It's awful."

I slide my hands off her thighs.

"And, worse," she says quietly. "I think I'm in love with you."

Fuck.

While my thoughts scatter, her gaze cuts straight through me. How the hell do I respond?

"Say something, L."

I stare at the floor, but I can't even see it properly. Everything's blurred. "Shit, Edie. You've blown me away. I'm just... I don't know what to say to you."

"Just tell me the truth. Can you picture us together? In some official way?"

I know exactly what she wants. And exactly why I can't give it to her. But she asked for the truth. "Look," I say carefully, "I like you. A lot. You know that. But you can't love a guy like me. It's crazy. I'm fucked up. I don't deserve someone like you. You're good. Kind. Uncomplicated."

She laughs. "L! I'm not perfect. I'm just a normal girl who got tangled up with a bad person. *Coop* is the problem, not you or me. I feel lucky that I met you."

Normal. That word hits like a punch to the gut. The one thing I've always wanted. The one thing I'll never be.

"And if you could hear the shit in my head," I say hoarsely. "you wouldn't say that. It's bad—"

"I don't care," she says fiercely. "I want you as you are. Broken. Angry. Whatever. We don't choose who we love. It just happens. And I've never felt like this before. I think we could be better together. Happier. And then—"

"Stop." My chest locks up. Electricity skitters through every nerve. I'm spiraling fast. "What you want is impossible. I don't do love. I never will." I thump my chest. "This is all there is. Hate. That's it." I swallow hard. "You want to know what I dream about, Edie? Revenge on the people who made me like this. Every. Single. Night."

Her eyes soften, and my stomach knots tighter. Pity is the last thing I want.

"Don't look at me like that. Like I'm some sad lost dog." My voice sharpens. "One day soon I'm gonna make those pricks pay. Coop is at the top of the list. Or maybe he gets to me first. Either way, it ends ugly. And you don't want to be here when it does."

Her soft hands cup my face. Tears cling to her lashes. No one has ever looked at me like this. Like I matter. Except my mom. And that was another lifetime ago.

"L," she whispers, "let me help you. Let us help each other. You're worth the risk."

Worth the risk. Bullshit I'm not worth spitting on.

My vision tunnels. The room slips sideways, and suddenly I'm not here anymore. I'm back there.

In the white room.

I shrink, coil in on myself, until I'm nothing. And then his voice slithers in, thick and slurred. And I'm back in hell. Alone with *him*.

"*You're worthless,*" he says. "*You piece of shit. No one gives a fuck about you, kid.*"

I shake my head. My mouth stretches like I might scream, but no sound comes out. Usually, I don't hear him when Edie is near. Sometimes there's a whisper. Mostly... he's off the air.

Not now. Now, he's coming through loud and clear.

You sniveling, useless shit, the voice says. *Stop asking why this happens. You already know.*

Go away.

Stop crying and look at yourself.

A handheld mirror slams into my face. Cracked. Broken. I try not to look. But he grips my hair, shakes me, forces me... and I see it. My reflection, bruised and wide-eyed. Terrified. Which only proves him right. I *am* a coward. A crybaby. Worthless. Nothing.

Look, the voice screams.

Chapter 28

L

I n the mirror, my hair is long, stringy and unwashed.

What do you look like? he asks. *Like a weakling, right? Like a girl?*

I don't know. I don't know, I say in a loop.

Look again. Tell me.

I'm a boy, I say. Not a girl. Just a boy.

Look again.

No. My throat burns. I won't do it.

You don't want to see the truth, do you? How this is your fault. Your sinner's eyes. Look and ask why your body betrays you, calls to me, reacts. Ask.

No, please. Not now.

Ask, says the monster.

I don't think it's my fault.

It's not my fault, I whisper.

Ask *why I do this, you piece of shit!*

"It's not my fault," I shout, the sound reverberating in my head.

"L." A soft voice cuts through the noise. Warm hands on my skin. "I know. You're right. It isn't."

What? Where am I? Edie... I'm here with Edie. Not back there. Not with him.

"You didn't ask me to feel this way about you," she says. "It's not your fault."

I shove her hands away, heat stinging behind my eyes. "Don't touch me. I'm disgusting."

"Why would you say something like that?"

"Inside me..." My chest tightens. "I make it all happen. Everything. It's my fault."

That's right, boy, the voice whispers.

"There's just blackness in me. It makes people do things. And they make *me* do things... And I don't want to, but—"

"L. Hey." She reaches for me again. "Shh. It's okay. Where have you gone? Come back. I'm sorry. I shouldn't have said anything."

But it's too late. There's blood on the floor, and it's pooling beneath my boots. I know it isn't *now*-blood. It's blood from before. Six years ago. Still, I shove off the stool and pace away, my toes curling so they don't stick to the mess. Which is stupid. I'm wearing boots.

"Wait here," she says softly. "I'll get Angelo."

"What?" I drag my eyes from the floor, from the spreading red, and stare at the figure backing toward my door. Thank fuck. It's Edie. She's still here.

The blood thickens, tangling in black hair. Greasy. Puke-inducing. A thin red line trickles beneath the bedroom door. A door that terrifies me. The metallic smell clings to my clothes, my nose, my lungs. Will it ever leave me?

It's not real. It's not real. It's not real.

"L," she says, panicked now. "Should I get Angelo? Can he help?"

"No. Just go home. I'm fine. I just..."

"You don't look fine. Sit down for a—"

I grab her T-shirt, pushing her back against the bench.

With my face close enough to kiss her, I whisper, "This thing... people around me end up dead."

She tugs my wrists, trying to loosen my grip on her shirt.

"I do bad things," I say, my voice sounding unrecognizable, like a stranger's. "I get inside people's heads. Change them, like cancer."

Fear flickers across her face. I don't blame her. I'm a real life monster. "Please," she says. "You're okay, L. Just breathe."

Easy for her to say. She can't see him. Can't hear his foul words.

"I have an idea of what you've been through. Not all of it. But... I know it's bad. You feel like your past owns you. But at some point, you're going to have to fight it. Defeat it. Do whatever it takes to get on with your life."

My breathing stutters, then slows. Edie's face sharpens into focus. The other place drains away, melting into the dark corners of my living room.

"Right now, you won't let yourself get help. But, L, you need it. Stop giving the past power."

Fuck this. She doesn't know anything about me, and it would be best if it stayed that way. I stumble back, knocking into a chair.

She follows, her steps careful and quiet. "But do you even realize how strong you are? You survived the streets alone. Do you know how amazing that is?"

I laugh. "I survived because I look like this. A *thing* that attracts sick fucks. That's just dumb luck."

"The perfect revenge against all those who hurt you would be conquering your anger. And if you master it... then you can let it go. Imagine what that would feel like."

She's close now, her palm pressed over my heart. "Nothing good ever came from holding on to anger. Nothing, L. But what happens next is up to you. You've got people who'll stick by you. Care about you. Me included."

She has no fucking idea what she's talking about.

"You don't get it," I snap. "You don't know what I've done. And this anger? This is the only thing keeping me alive. One day those fuckers will pay—"

"Who?" she says. "Coop obviously. But who else?"

I fold inward, retreating fast. I don't remember all their names. Don't want them in my head. The only thing that matters is learning everything I can about Coop. All the dirt on him. I need all of it.

"You need to run, Edie," I say. "Go somewhere. Just get as far away from me and that prick Cooper as you can." My throat tightens. "And if one day I show up at your door, if I come begging, do not let me in. Unless you want to end up dead too. Because that's what happens around me. People die."

Blood surges behind my eyes. Too much of it. Always too much.

Her hands cradle my face. It feels so good, and for a moment, I lean into her touch.

I'm not thinking about her body anymore, like I was when she turned up on my doorstep. All I want is a shower and to scrub the nightmares from my skin.

"Go," I say, wrenching her hands away. She stumbles back into the coffee table. "Get out. I'll be a corpse before I'm twenty-five. I've got nothing for you."

Sucking air through her teeth, she bends to rub her shin.

I've hurt her. "Edie—shit. I'm sorry." I guide her to the couch.

She collapses into the cushions and cries like a child. I sit there, useless, waiting for her to pull herself together so she can leave and I can pretend tonight never happened. But after a minute, I can't stand watching her suffer, so I draw her against my chest and hold her tight.

Her tears wash the blood from my mind. The monster's voice fades. "Shh. It's okay. Don't be scared. I didn't mean to lose it. I just want you safe."

Her head snaps up, and she laughs. "I'm not scared of *you*, L. I'm crying because my heart is breaking. You're messed up, and I love you. You're hurting, and I want to help you. And more than anything... I want you to love me back."

Love.

Fuck love.

If my heart wasn't already dried up and useless, it would be cracking right along with hers. I was eleven the last time my mom said that word to me. Back when it meant safety. Then she died and left me with him. After that, there were no soft words, only approval when I did what he wanted. And as I got older, what he wanted got worse.

Then I was beautiful. Such a good, beautiful boy. Afterward, the words always changed.

Your fault.

Your fault.

Your fault.

Evil little shit.

I don't think I was evil at fifteen. But sometimes... Sometimes I believe him anyway.

"Edie," I whisper, gripping her shoulders. Even knowing what I am, this girl loves me. Or thinks she does. I'm drowning in her warm eyes. And right now, the voice is gone.

Unable to stop myself, I brush my lips against hers. "I'll never be able to feel what you want me to," I murmur. "Fuck, I can't even say the word. But if I could, if I could feel that way about someone, I'd want it to be you. I'd choose you, Edie. Every single time."

She takes a shaky breath and kisses me back. Soft, gentle, like a gift. Or a goodbye. Heat surges through me, burning everything away but her orange and caramel scent. I pull her closer, deepen the kiss, desperate to lose myself. But she stiffens and resists.

"Hey." Her hands press against my chest, holding me back. "What are you doing, L?"

"What does it feel like I'm doing?"

She shakes her head. "No. You're not in the right head space for this."

"I am," I insist, words tripping over themselves in my brain. "Edie—listen. If we just... if I could just—" I swallow. "You make the noise stop. You make it all go quiet." I kiss her again, gentle this time, taking care.

For a few heartbeats, she lets me. Her mouth is warm, her tongue soft against mine, and relief floods me as her arms tighten around my neck. Yes. *This*. This is all I need.

Then she pulls back.

"Make what go away?" she asks.

"Everything." I lean toward her, aching for her warmth, needing to drown in her sweetness.

"No. I'm going home."

"Wait." My voice breaks. "What happened before—it won't happen again. Not if you stay."

And I know my words are true. It won't happen again because I feel calm... well, as calm as I ever get with lust boiling through my blood. I love this feeling. It's the best drug there is. It makes everything else disappear.

"I have to go, L. You know I do."

Her sweet voice, her wrong words, they shatter my peace. My feeling of rightness.

"I'll stay if you want company," she continues, "but I can't do the friends-with-benefits thing with you anymore."

Panic slams into me. She can't leave. I crowd closer, breath rough. "What do you mean? We could... just tonight. You said you wanted to help me." The words taste wrong even as I say them. But I can't stop myself from trying to use her to make the pain stop. There's no denying I'm an asshole.

She stiffens, the warm light leaving her eyes. "Five minutes ago, I was about to call the mobile crisis team because you were in the middle of a psychotic episode. You don't need sex, L. You need help." She pauses. "I'm going to get Angelo."

"Don't do that. Please."

"I have to." Her voice is gentle but unshakable. "I want to help you... just not like this. This situation only hurts us both."

She goes to the kitchen, picks up her bag, and slings it over her shoulder.

I want to ask when I'll see her again, which is insane considering I've spent the last hour telling her to run, and then trying to fuck her. What the hell is wrong with me?

She's right. I probably do need professional help. And now that she's seen exactly how fucked up I am, she's doing the smart thing and cutting me loose. I should be relieved. It's what I said I wanted.

As we reach the door, something clicks into place.

"Hey, that thing Coop called you about the other day... you're not doing it. Right?"

She holds the door open. Her gaze drops to my boots, then lifts to my mouth instead of my eyes. "Like I said, it was landlord stuff."

"Sure. And my breakdown was a performance piece. I moonlight as a stand-up comedian."

She doesn't smile.

"Just promise me you're not doing those parties anymore," I push. "It's not worth it. I'll loan you money. Hell, I'll just give you money. Whatever it takes to keep you away from Cooper."

She shakes her head slowly. "It's not about money. Coop has something of mine. Something I want back more than anything else." She hesitates. "More than I want you."

That lands hard.

"For a chance to get it back," she continues, "I do what he wants. And thankfully he doesn't ask very often."

My blood turns molten hot. "Tell me what he's got, Edie. I'll get it back for you. I promise. Whatever it takes."

She laughs. "Why would I? You've already told me you'll never feel anything for me. Are you going to open up about *your* deal with Coop? Or explain what was happening in your head earlier?"

I don't answer.

"No?" she says quietly. Her fingernails dig into the soft flesh of her forearm as she seems to think something over. "Okay. You want my sob story. You got it."

My chest tightens.

"My dad died of cancer when I was sixteen," she says. "The bank foreclosed on our lavender farm. Guess who bought out the mortgage."

Rage snaps through me. "That fucking vulture."

Edie nods. "Exactly." Then she gives me a small, sad wave, like this is goodbye forever. "Take care of yourself, Lightning."

The door closes with a soft thud.

I wrench it open. "But you're not doing Coop's thing, right?" I call after her.

Haloed by the lights in the hallway, she turns back, looking defiant and heartbreakingly beautiful.

"It's none of your business," she says. "If you were brave enough to take a risk on us, that might be different."

She knocks on Angelo's door. It opens, and she disappears inside.

And that's it. She's gone. She made the right choice.

Nothing good ever stays in my life. I don't deserve it and never fail to ruin everything.

And even if I were brave enough to try to keep her, I'd never be worthy. One day she'd see me clearly and leave anyway.

Four years ago on Jackson Street, Edie was just a dream. For her own good, I have to make sure that—*to me*—she remains one.

Chapter 29

EDEN

"Hey, Edie," Nico yells. "There's a scary-looking lady out front who wants to see you."

"Shit."

Two pots of basil seedlings hit the concrete as I spin toward him, hoping he doesn't notice the tears I've just wiped away.

After yesterday's soul-crushing visit to L's apartment, I've accepted something important: there's no point grieving a relationship I was never going to have. That doesn't mean it doesn't hurt. Unrequited love feels like an open, festering wound. One that may never properly heal.

I need to move on and accept that L is a mess. A mess who doesn't want my help. And who wants *me* about as much as he'd crave a bout of stomach flu.

Sunlight pours into the open-roofed section of the warehouse, illuminating rows of vegetables and walls thick with living plants. Nico's eyes glow emerald as he looks me over.

"You've got dirt on your face," he says, smirking.

Good. He thinks I'm a messy klutz rather than a gushing cry-baby.

"Thanks," I mutter, scrubbing my cheek with my sleeve and probably making it worse. "Is this scary person a customer?"

"I don't think so. Her vibe doesn't exactly scream *biodynamic beekeeping enthusiast*." He bites his lip ring. "Come here."

I paste on a smile and trudge over. Nico cups my face, thumbs brushing beneath my eyes.

"There," he says softly. "Perfectly presentable again."

My throat tightens. "What does she want?"

"Didn't say. She's waiting at the café. She cleared it with the boss and everything."

Hearing that makes my temples throb. Cleared it with the boss means official. Important. And possibly something bad.

A long-lost relative, maybe. That'd be weird but survivable. A detective? Less fun. A friend of Coop's who has somehow found out where I work?

That could ruin my life.

"Right." I wipe my hands on my overalls and force my shoulders back. "Guess I'd better go see what she wants."

When I reach the massive warehouse doors leading to the fire escape stairs, I swing back to Nico. "So what's so scary about her anyway?"

He shoves fertilizer bags into place on a trolley, flicks hair off his face, and gives me a sly grin. "You'll see. Hey, fancy hitting the beach after work for a quick swim?"

I wipe sweat from the back of my neck. The heat is stifling. "If this woman doesn't kidnap me first, then yeah. Count me in."

By the time I puff my way up the spiral staircase, my lungs are burning. I really need to attend that kickboxing class more than once a week.

The woman waiting for me sits in the shaded section of the rooftop café. It's designed to resemble an old hothouse and protected from the sun's glare by a row of stained glass windows on either side of the room. Hanging plants and Turkish lanterns sway gently above her. The whole space feels earthy and relaxed, but she looks like she's stepped straight off the cover of a glossy magazine.

I'd put her age around fifty. Her face is handsome rather than pretty, and her metallic-colored clothes drape around her body with asymmetric precision. One side of her silver bob is cut sharp against her jaw; the other grazes her ear, exposing a bold spiral earring. Her arms are thin and elegant, every movement deliberate and controlled.

When our eyes meet, she sets aside the tablet she's been scrolling and rises smoothly to her feet.

"Eden," she says warmly. "I'm so pleased to meet you. I'm Ariana." She clasps my hand and shakes it with brisk confidence. "Please sit. Your coffee's just arrived. The barista told me your favorite. It should still be hot."

"Oh. Thanks." I fumble around the wrought-iron table, knocking it slightly and making the sky-blue mugs rattle. "Sorry."

Still smiling, she settles back and studies me. After a beat, she releases a satisfied little sigh.

"You're not what I was expecting at all."

My smile falters as my defenses snap into place.

"And who exactly did you say you were again?" I blow on my coffee and take a careful sip, pretending I'm unfazed.

"I didn't," she says lightly. "I'm a friend of L's."

I cough, coffee splashing down my front. "Ow. Yep. Still very hot."

She hands me a napkin, and I blot at my shirt, heat flooding my face.

"A friend of L's?" I repeat.

"Yes. His agent." Her smile wavers for a moment. "You do know he models?"

"Of course." I stir my coffee a little too vigorously, avoiding her gaze so my eyes don't betray how *recent* that knowledge is.

"I hear things went badly yesterday. I'm so sorry," she says, her forehead hardly creasing as her brow lifts. Must be the Botox.

"What? How could you know about that?"

"Angelo informed me. I believe you made the mistake of telling L that you'd developed feelings for him, and in an unfortunate turn of events, he had an episode. A flashback to a traumatic incident."

"What incident? Do you mean there's something *more* on top of the sexual and emotional abuse the poor guy suffered when he was young? Why don't you tell me all about it, since you seem to know everything about him, Ariana?" Tears build behind my eyes, my chest tightening as hysteria threatens. "I don't understand anything anymore and—"

"Shh, darling." She pats my hand, multiple jewels glinting on ringed fingers. "Please don't upset yourself."

There's something genuinely comforting about her. Her voice is lovely, smooth and crisp, and somehow it calms me.

She smiles kindly. "I don't know everything about L. There's quite a lot he doesn't tell me, I promise you. Emotionally, he's a closed book. And I suspect he's caught up in some very nasty business. But, of course, he refuses to speak of it. I had hoped you might enlighten me."

She means the Coop thing. I'm not getting into that with her. No way.

"So the flashbacks... if they're about something other than the abuse, what do you think they're from?"

Wearing a sad expression, she fiddles with her earring. "I'm not sure. But not long after I met him, he accompanied me to an industry event. As you can imagine, everyone wanted a piece of him. From living on the streets, it was another world entirely, and he was so young. But I was prideful. I couldn't wait to show him off. Of course he wasn't ready. I should have known better."

She clears her throat and blinks rapidly.

"What happened?"

"He tried to keep up. Made light of the attention and the flirting. He was his usual adorable self. People were charmed by his unique combination of beauty and roughness. Toward the end of the evening, one gentleman, very pushy, very enamored, said something that upset him. It was innocent, really. Meant as a compliment."

My stomach knots.

"He said: have you looked in the mirror lately? Do you have any idea what you're worth, kid?" She exhales softly. "L turned white. Twenty minutes later, I was called to the men's restroom to retrieve him. He was not well."

My mouth goes dry. "He was having a flashback?"

"Yes. And it was... frightening. He spoke, but nothing made sense. I heard the word *blood* more times than I care to remember." Her hands curl into fists. "I tried to stop him from scrubbing his hands and face raw—to remove blood only he could see. Whatever caused those flashbacks must have involved a great deal of it. Because when he loses himself, like he did yesterday, that's what he's seeing. Blood."

My pulse roars in my ears. "So it must have been something horrific."

"Yes." She drags a fingernail through the sugar crystals on the table. "He's had a terrible life. And yet, despite everything, his heart is good, his loyalty genuine. Incredibly, he's a kind person."

"You sound like you know him well," I admit, clacking the spoon against my teeth inelegantly. Ariana in her silver tunic, me in my work clothes—we look like opposites. Thrift store versus runway glamor. I might as well lean into it.

She sips her drink. "Edie... do you mind if I call you that? It's how L refers to you. I've grown rather used to it."

My eyes widen. "He talks about me?"

"Yes." She leans forward. "Constantly. He insists on calling you *my friend Edie*—as if that gives him permission to speak about you endlessly without giving himself away. But Angelo and I aren't fooled."

I stare at her, stunned.

"Do you see why I had to meet you?" she continues softly. "Oh, if only I could show you L the night I found him. This beautiful street urchin with something marvelous shining from within. A one-in-a-million quality. You know what I mean, don't you?"

I do. I really do.

The mirrored tiles of a wind chime clink together as the pieces of the Ariana-puzzle fall into place. "You're the one who got him off the streets."

"Yes. I'll always be grateful my friend Sergio chose that particular restaurant that evening."

At the same time, we lean toward each other over the tiny cactus pots on the table and say, "He'd be dead by now if—"

We break off laughing, startled by the synchronicity, even though there's nothing remotely funny about our words.

"It's true," she says quietly. "I believe I found L just in time."

I smile at her, warmth blooming unexpectedly in my chest. He isn't just a product or a commodity to her. He matters.

"So how can I help, Ariana?"

"I needed to meet the girl he's so taken with. And here you are, not the evil enchantress who I imagined had enslaved my Lightning after all."

I make shapes in the air, miming a spell. "I do like to think of myself sometimes as a dark sorceress."

She smiles. "You'd be a terrible one. In fact, I think you and L are very well matched. Your humor, your warmth, your openness. You're exactly what he needs."

I scoff. "I wish. He's been very clear. Casual is all he wants. And he said—"

"I can imagine what the foolish boy said." Her voice sharpens just a fraction. "And I'm here to ask you not to give up on him. To be patient."

My heart hammers. If she'd heard him yesterday, heard him tell me he could never love me, she wouldn't be asking me this. I know it.

Brushing imaginary crumbs from my clothes, I stand up. "I should get back to work. Thank you for the coffee. It was lovely to meet you. I'm so glad L has you in his life. Truly. And I'm grateful you found him that night. Please... take good care of him."

I turn for the exit.

"Eden," she calls softly. "Please think about what I've told you. Don't give up on him."

I don't turn back.

I hate to disappoint her, but letting him go is the only thing that makes sense. I wish I wasn't so sure of it.

Chapter 30

EDEN

Jess says I don't need much to be happy. And she's right. All I require is a couple of friends to hang out with, regular immersions in nature, a solid eight hours of sleep most nights, and to hear from Coop no more than twice a year. With those boxes ticked, I'm golden.

Right now, I've got two of the things that make me feel good—Nico and the beach. Unfortunately, with Coop's party looming tomorrow and only three hours of sleep under my belt, I'm feeling grouchy and mildly terrified.

Last night, lying in bed brokenhearted and sick to my stomach, I'd obsessed over what L said about how I shouldn't allow Cooper to degrade and control me. That it wasn't worth the money. And of course he's right. No amount of cash justifies that kind of humiliation.

But getting Sam's farm back?

That's worth almost anything.

Besides, Coop's disgusting gatherings are infrequent and, mercifully, brief. An hour or two at most. Twice a year, maximum, since I was eighteen.

Still, only three weeks have passed since L zapped my neurons at that city party. Only twenty days since he rearranged my brain and my entire cellular structure. So it's more than weird that Coop has booked me again so soon. It doesn't fit his pattern. The vile pest has plenty of girls under his thumb. Other girls he can drain dry.

So why me? Why now?

Unfortunately, the money is too good to turn down. A hundred grand off the farm's mortgage. Obscene really. The men Coop pimps for have stupid levels of wealth. And unless Coop is taking a personal loss, I'm almost certain he never does, whatever scene they have planned for tomorrow is going to be particularly sick.

I am not looking forward to it.

Sand splatters my shins, stinging me back to the present.

"Nico! Don't be so juvenile."

"But you're not even listening to me."

"Kicking sand at girls is a schoolboy tactic. What would your foxy grandma think if she saw you doing that?"

"She'd probably think about how hot I am." Laughing, he pushes me off the wall. Luckily, it's only about three feet high.

"So," I say, brushing sand from my legs, "what do you really make of all this Baba Vash business?"

"Oh, yeah. My so-called fated mate." Nico snorts, jiggling the skull chain hanging from his black jeans. It's a scorcher today, and I've already gone for three dips. Not my emo-boy, though. Probably for the best. Half the beach would flee screaming at the sight of all that pale skin.

"Your mom seems convinced you're about to be abducted by a hot cougar any day now. And you don't waste much effort correcting her."

"Yeah, well, I love my mom, so I humor her. It's a stupid concept. Fate, prophecies... total bullshit." He pauses. "Well. Except Baba Vash *was* right about my dad being a top-notch prick and a deserter." He shrugs. "Love is for losers, Edie. The sooner you accept that and—oh, fuck."

His gaze sharpens, locking onto something behind me.

"Speaking of losers," he mutters, "whatever you do, don't turn around. That Lightning asshole is heading this way."

"What?" I yelp.

"Just keep looking adoringly at me," Nico murmurs. "He's behind you and coming down about as hard as a freight train with its brakes malfunctioning."

Shit. Maybe he's had an epiphany overnight. Maybe he realized he can't live without me and this is about to turn into one of those epic movie scenes, like where the guy chases the girl to the airport to stop her from boarding the plane.

Except I'm at the beach.

And Nico's here.

And this feels... ominous and not in the least romantic.

Don't turn around, I tell myself. Don't turn around.

Bouncing on my toes, I whisper, "Okay, but what's his expression like? Happy? Hopeful? Anything remotely romantic?"

Nico shakes his head slowly.

"How about tortured and yearning?"

His nose wrinkles. "At a stretch, it could be considered romantic if he were Vlad the Impaler." He squints past me, then tips his chin toward a squawking seagull overhead. "Hey," he says casually.

"Hey, Nico," comes a voice from close behind, sexy and familiar.

L has arrived.

Going for casual and deeply unimpressed, I turn around with a smile. "Oh, hi, L. I thought you were a seagull."

"Hey, Edie." His gaze sweeps over me before flicking to Nico with a sneer. "Is there a goth-band video shoot happening here today? You auditioning to be an extra?"

"That's right," Nico says pleasantly. "Stick around. They might need underwear models to suck each other off in the background."

L stares at him, stunned.

"Hey, I didn't say anything about your dark past," I jump in. "Have you come down for an afternoon swim?" I let my eyes roam over his body—cut-off Levi's, inked biceps, a Stooges T-shirt. Chunks of tawny hair fall into eyes bluer than the water, and I swallow a sigh of appreciation.

He folds his arms. "Nope. I'm here to see you."

Oh. My heart ricochets around my ribcage, but my face stays calm and serene. I absolutely should not get my hopes up.

"You weren't home." His eyes make a slow, deliberate pass over my shorts, my lavender shirt. He remembers it. I can tell by the way his pupils dilate, by the way he bites his lip. He's probably replaying our play fight and everything that came after. "It's hot," he adds. "So I figured you might be here."

"What do you want?" I ask.

"What are you doing tomorrow?"

"Not much."

"So if I invited you somewhere, you'd be free?"

"No." I smile sweetly. "I wouldn't be free to do anything with *you*. Remember yesterday? When you rejected me and told me to run for the hills?"

He blinks. "Okay. Fair." Then, "But if Nico asked you out tomorrow, would you be available?"

My temper snaps. "Oh, cut the shit, L. Just say what you want to say."

"Fine." His jaw tightens. "Are you doing Coop's thing tomorrow?"

"None of your business."

He grabs my arm.

"That means yes, doesn't it?" His grip tightens. "Didn't you listen to a word I said yesterday?"

"Let go of me." I wrench free, stumbling in the sand. "What do you care anyway? It's none of your business."

Nico paces, raking his hair out of his face and looking worried too. "Edie. You told me you weren't gonna do it."

Fantastic. Now *he's* pissed.

I spin on him. "No. *You* said I wasn't going to do it, Nico. I didn't say anything."

He turns to L. "So you know about this Coop guy, right? You're involved too."

L stays silent, staring out at the waves like they've got all the answers.

"You tell me what she does for him," Nico presses. "What kind of shit she's tangled up in."

"Why don't you ask her yourself?" L says coolly. "You're meant to be her best friend. I think you already know what goes on."

Something in me snaps. I fling my arm toward Nico. "Fine. You want to know what I'm doing tomorrow? Brace yourself, because you won't like it. I'll be having sex with one of Coop's obscenely rich friends while a bunch of them watch. I'll feel scared, degraded, and sick the entire time. But afterward? I'll be one hundred grand closer to getting my dad's farm back."

Nico's jaw drops.

L looks murderous, and I instinctively step back. He lunges, grabbing my shoulders and barely restraining himself from shaking me. "You fucking idiot. Don't do it."

"You're a hypocrite, L," I say between gritted teeth.

Nico shoves him off me. L stumbles, recovers, and then barrels right back toward Nico.

A mother nearby scoops up her toddlers and beach gear in record time and hustles away.

I throw myself between the guys, palms flat against their chests. "Stop. Nico, please. Give me a minute alone with L. I'll explain everything later. I swear."

"If you hurt her," Nico says to L, his voice dead calm, "I'll kill you."

L nods once. "Likewise."

Nico grabs his things and storms off. Hopefully not forever. I need that boy in my life.

I point at the sand. "Sit."

"Edie—"

"You don't get to show up, put your hands on me, and yell like an asshole," I cut in. "So sit down and behave, or I'm leaving."

He sits.

"Look, I'm sorry—"

"Not yet. I need a second." I inhale and exhale slowly until my pulse settles. "Okay. Now you can talk."

"I don't want to cause trouble with your friends," he says. "I just need to know you'll stop with the Coop stuff. Like... completely. Never do it again."

I drop down beside him, so close that our legs bump. I scoot away and immediately get sand in my shorts.

"But why?" I ask. "You say you don't want me, and yet here you are acting like you care." I bite my lip. Red flushes over his high cheekbones. "Honestly, your best move would be to leave me alone. Unless you're enjoying the unrequited-love thing. Power-tripping on making me keep wanting you."

"I'm not *power tripping*." His voice cracks. "I just don't want you hurt. Not by Coop. And not by me. Is that so hard to understand?" He brushes my hair back, fingers grazing my cheek, and my skin erupts in chills. "Promise me you'll at least think about not going."

I knock his hand away. "Why are you touching me?"

For four brutal beats, our eyes are locked together, tension thick in the air between us. Then he looks down.

Seagulls squawk. Waves roll languorously to the shore. And I stare at the sand until it hits me. L wants something from me, which *means*, I have bargaining power.

"Okay," I say carefully. "If I promise to think about what you asked… will you tell me something real about yourself? One thing. Small is fine as long as it's hard for you to share."

"Why?" He scoffs. "Forget that. The only thing you need to know is this—Coop is never going to give you what you want. Take that seriously, and you'll save yourself a lifetime of misery."

"Tell me something you've never told anyone else, and I really will think hard about not going tomorrow. Cross my heart."

He chews on his lip. "Like what?"

"How about your real name? And don't give me any of that Lightning shit. I want the name your mother gave you."

He rubs his chin against his shoulder and mutters into his T-shirt.

"Sorry, I couldn't understand that."

"I said I've forgotten it."

"Bullshit."

"What if I don't *want* to remember it?"

I wring water from my hair and catch his gaze drop to my chest, then lift slowly back to my face.

Today I'm wearing red and purple bikinis under my clothes because I can't look at my black one‑piece anymore without remembering what he did to me while I wore it. The way he fucks like it's life or death. How he lit me up, electrocuted every nerve ending, and rearranged who I was from the inside out.

Before him, I was just a girl who wanted one thing—my dad's farm back. Nothing more. Nothing less.

And now... who am I and what do I want?

Silence stretches, and as usual, I break it. "Back to playing silent games, Lightning?"

"Shit, all right." He exhales hard. "My name is Leon."

For a moment, my heart stops beating. "Leon?"

"Yeah. My mom was French." He scoops up a fistful of sand, lets it spill between his fingers. "I can still hear the way she said it. Before she died and left me with— Forget it."

I nudge his ribs. "Left you with who?"

His mouth tightens. "My stepdad."

A chill shudders through me.

That's the monster for sure. The source of all of L's problems.

He smiles absently, like he's somewhere else, no longer here with me. "Her accent was strong. When she talked, it sounded like she was singing." A pause. "That's why I don't mind being called L now. It still fits with Leon."

"Do you remember much French?"

He stares at the horizon, hair blown across his mouth. I resist the urge to brush it away.

"Some. Mostly about food." A wider smile. "Gougères, pain au chocolate, and clafoutis."

"Of course." I snort. "What are *gooshairs* and the chocolate thing?"

"Cheese puffs. Chocolate bread." He chuckles at my pronunciation. Then his smile fades. "If I hear French by accident, even in a movie, it hurts like hell. But something immediately opens up in my head. I understand the words before the subtitles catch up."

His mouth turns down as he blows out a slow breath.

Without thinking, I rub small circles over his back. Right now, picking shells from the sand, shoulders hunched, he looks so young. And like a boy who misses his mother more than he'll ever admit.

My chest tightens. I see my dad in a hospital bed, cancer hollowing him out. Images of lavender flood my mind, rolling purple hills, an old white farmhouse covered in climbing roses, bread baking in the kitchen.

Home. The home Cooper stole from me.

"Edie?" he says quietly. "Can I ask you something?"

"I guess so."

"Did Ariana come see you today?"

"Yes."

He tilts his head back, stares at the sky. "What did she want?"

"She's worried about you. She thinks you're into something bad. I think she suspects the Coop stuff."

"That's all?"

"Yeah."

"Huh. Angelo said the same."

"I didn't tell her anything you wouldn't want me to," I add. "But we did speak about... yesterday. About the blood episode."

His jaw tightens. "I'm not talking about that. So don't waste your time asking."

"Fine." I stand, brushing sand from my clothes and stepping into my sandals. "Push everyone who cares about you away. Seems to be working great for you so far."

He watches me with a hard scowl. Ariana is wrong. He doesn't have a thing for me.

"Where are you going?" he asks.

"Home. I've got an assignment to finish."

"Need a ride? I've got my truck here."

"No. I'm good." I start walking, then turn back to face him. "See you around, Leo."

His mouth curves faintly. "It's Leon."

"Okay." The scent of lavender fills my nose as I head down the beach, not looking back.

"You're not going to Coop's thing, right?" he calls after me.

"I'll think about it, Leo," I shout, refusing to turn around and do something catastrophically stupid. Like running back. Like kissing him. Like telling him I'd do anything he asked.

I don't.

I'm not completely stupid.

Then again, considering what I'll be doing tomorrow, I guess I probably am.

Chapter 31

L

Fuck my job. I'd rather stab myself in the eye with a fork than do another underwear shoot anytime soon.

I'm wrecked. Since Edie stormed off the beach this afternoon, all I've done is stand around in obscenely tight boxers on the parapet wall of a historic fort while people took pictures of me.

And this gig? Not a walk in the park.

By dusk it was freezing. I'd been balancing for two solid hours on a crumbling wall above an old gun mount, blinded by lights, one wrong step away from a very poetic death. I genuinely thought the last words I'd ever hear would be the lead photographer rasping—

Yes... lean over a little more... work with me... that's hot... hang a little farther over the edge...

Somehow, I survived.

Now it's me, my splitting headache, and the fiery Spanish photographer out on the town, and I can't believe what I'm even considering.

After the shoot, Ines dragged me to her favorite seafood place and kept me laughing over dinner. She's sexy in a way that feels forceful. Almost weaponized.

Now it's past midnight, and we're jammed into a claustrophobic dance club full of sweaty, half-naked bodies. The bass rattles my skull. Strobe lights punch behind my eyes. And the DJ has committed the unforgivable sin of playing way too much Euro-disco.

I'm an indie-rock guy, and this is hell.

"These pictures will be magnificent," Ines says, dragging a bright blue nail down my chest.

I'm in a navy T-shirt and ripped jeans, criminally underdressed compared to the peacocking fashion crowd around us.

"Nevio," she adds in her thick Castilian accent, "will come in his pants when I submit these photos."

I repress a sigh and stare past her shoulder.

"I'll post a teaser in the morning," she continues. "Purple twilight. Indigo glow. Stars. And you standing there like a naked god."

Nope. Not a god. Just a guy who hasn't slept much in the last twenty-four hours, whose head is pounding and brain is still stuck on a girl in a lavender shirt who told him she'd *think about* not selling her soul for money tomorrow.

"Hey, you're an amazing photographer. I'm sure the photos will look cool. But please don't start porn-star rumors. I did have *some* clothes on," I joke.

"Thankfully not very many," she counters. "Come on, Lightning, time to dance with me." She wraps her arms around my neck and straddles my leg. I'm reclining on a barstool, and she's practically dry humping my thigh. Her sweat smells sweet and musky.

I inspect the deep valley between her tits. They're damn fine breasts, round like juicy melons and possibly as heavy. I should be harder than the brass-topped bar I'm leaning against. Should be, but I'm not.

I picture my hands on her, imagine sliding my fingers down into the cream between her thighs. This woman is a firecracker already lit, and yet I feel... disconnected. Unmoved. Panic washes over me.

What would it feel like to put my lips on her? So far, the only girl I've done that with is... Edie. I've been trying not to think of her since she flounced off the beach today calling me Leo, her eyes flashing, making me want to fuck her and also... hug her.

My fingers splay around Ines's waist. The blue dress she's almost wearing is silky and slick under my palm. She tugs my hand, already snaking her hips.

"No way. I'm not dancing, Ines."

She gives me a slow smile and licks her lips, then palms my balls. My dick stays stubbornly dormant, like a snake sunbathing on hot concrete.

"I like to watch," I say. "So why don't you go dance while I try to think of a way to get an invite back to your hotel room."

She laughs, already turning toward the mass of bodies grinding on the dance floor. "I've been giving you invitations since we met at the fort. A guy like you doesn't need to try very hard at all."

Right. So I should relax. Focus on Ines. Watch her move out there, guys circling her like sharks, her long dark hair swinging as she rolls her shoulders…

Exactly like Edie's does when she cracks up laughing at something stupid I've said.

No. Fuck. No.

I dig my fingers into my scalp. Shit.

Tonight, all I want is to fuck a girl who wants me in the same uncomplicated way. No strings. No expectations. No messy *feelings*.

For once, I just want to feel normal. To be like everyone else.

And the worst part? Edie showed me I might actually be capable of that. Of something normal. Something good.

Trouble is, I only want it with *her*.

The scene at the dodgem cars crashes into my head. The way I kissed her and laughed into her neck while we spun and jolted. The roller coaster. Me making out with my macadamia nut ice cream like an idiot just to make her laugh. The stupid play fight afterward. The way it felt, for the first time ever, like I was with a girl who was safe, real. And mine.

Pain knives through my gut.

I'm so angry I could roar. Or cry. And the last time I did that was in another life, when the monster in my head told me I was weak, a sniveling cry baby.

I won't ever be that vulnerable again. I just can't.

An old Motown song kicks in, some guy crooning about the tracks of his tears.

Perfect.

Ines is slow dancing now with some slick-haired asshole. His hands molding her curves doesn't bother me at all, which tells me everything I need to know about why I thought tonight, with her, was what I wanted.

Sipping my beer, I watch her grind against him. Every few seconds, her eyes flick back to me, lips curving in a sultry come-hither smile.

And I feel absolutely nothing.

Ines has chestnut hair as thick and long as Edie's. Her eyes are large and dark, too, just like Edie's. Ines is the same height, same shape, and in the dark, if I could shut out her voice, she'd probably feel just like Edie.

This is bad. Ines deserves better, someone like that guy with the silver top open to his waist who's worshiping her like she's a goddess. Yeah. I should split and leave them to it.

The cute blond bartender, who's been serving our drinks all night, grabs my arm. "Hey. You wanna buy some coke? Come party with me after my shift?"

"Tempting," I say, already shaking my head. "But I'm on my way out. See that girl in the blue dress?"

She smirks toward Ines and her Latin lover. "Yeah. Beautiful."

"Ask her. She might want to score."

"Sure." The bartender releases me and grins. "Make sure you stop in and say hi next time you pass through."

I nod, and she goes back to wiping down the bar like she didn't just casually offer me drugs and sex.

When Ines starts taking selfies while the guy kisses her neck, I shove through the crowd and spill out onto the street.

It's nearly one a.m., peak hour in the clubbing district, so it takes about thirty seconds to snag a cab.

On the ride back to the hotel, I call Edie. My headache ratchets up with every ring.

She doesn't answer.

There's no point leaving a message. I already know what that silence means. She doesn't want to talk to me. And she's going to Coop's party tomorrow.

I make another call.

Coop answers immediately. "Lightning! What a pleasure."

"Shut up," I say. "What time is your sick-fuck thing tomorrow?"

"Two."

Perfect. I've got a two-hour flight at eight-thirty in the morning. "Book that driver you mentioned. I'll be there."

Before he can crow like the idiot he is, I hang up and pinch the bridge of my nose.

This is a first. Right now, I want tomorrow to arrive more than I want my next breath.

I need to see Edie and get her out of that place before something bad happens.

Christ.

I am completely fucked.

Chapter 32

EDEN

The night of the beach encounter with L, I was a trembling mess, fumbling around my kitchen, unable to focus on even the simplest tasks, like cooking dinner. The memory of his fingers on my cheek and the blue-fire glow of his eyes beneath that unhappy scowl haunted me as I chopped vegetables.

When the pumpkin and potatoes came out of the oven baked to perfect caramelized crisps, I ate them in front of my laptop while editing an essay on food and water security, then spent the rest of the evening arguing with Jess.

Getting her off the phone was nearly impossible. Every time I managed it, she'd call back ten minutes later, louder, drunker, demanding I get my ass down to The Amaranth to check out the alleged hot guy singing nineties grunge on the tiny stage. Then she'd pivot into another lecture about Coop, begging me to cancel the party.

At eleven, I went to bed hoping I'd drift off peacefully and never wake up to face the day.

Sadly, that wish wasn't granted.

Several hours later, I opened my eyes to daylight, blue sheets, silver walls, and a cold, heavy heart.

Today is the party, and there's absolutely no escaping it. I've checked my phone more times than is sane, hoping for a reprieve.

There's a missed call from L but no message. He wouldn't need to say much. Just a few words, like *be mine*, or *I don't want anyone else to have you*, or anything that hinted at a boyfriend☐girlfriend situation, and I'd sprain my brain in the rush to call Coop and cancel, consequences be damned.

But, of course, L was probably only planning to nag about the party and gave up when I didn't answer.

I skip breakfast, drink two brutally strong coffees, then begin the excessive grooming ritual required to satisfy Coop and his perverts. It takes a while.

Three hours later, it's just past lunchtime. The sun is out, but I'm freezing. Wrapped in a down puffer jacket, I sit in a thin ray of sunshine on my couch. Other than the coat, there isn't much covering my well☐waxed, over☐perfumed skin.

The driver is late, which makes my stomach drop. Coop is a stickler for punctuality, and every passing second will only make him angrier. And an angry Coop is a dangerous man indeed.

The bleak pressure in my chest tightens another notch. I feel sick. Mostly in the heart area.

Distant noises from the neighbors are the only sounds in my apartment. Water moving through pipes, the drone of a TV, an opera aria drifting through the walls. The Flower Duet from *Lakmé*.

I like to think of myself as a hard-working student, a future successful lavender farmer. Not a sex worker.

But for the next few hours, undeniably, that's exactly what I'll be.

My stomach flips as I stare through the curved front windows at the paved courtyard below, resisting the urge to pick the dark polish from my nails while I wait.

I imagine L down there two weeks ago, bleeding as he watched me clod past him toward the stairwell. What made him come to me that night? Wanting to get his rocks off again probably had something to do with it. Maybe a lot. But he could crook a finger at any random girl on the street and she'd likely do whatever he wanted.

So why did he have to come up here and mess my life up even more?

All I can think about are his lush lips, those brilliant blue eyes, his deliciously inked skin—and the awestruck look that crossed his face every time he came undone inside me.

Three hard knocks rattle my front door.

Oh. Great. My ride is here.

"Good afternoon, Miss," the driver says when I open it. Tall and lanky in his chauffeur's uniform, he adjusts his black cap.

"There's been an accident over on Brio Street. Mr. Martinez has been alerted. My apologies for the delay."

I smile into his serious gray eyes. The sternness doesn't suit his preppy face. No older than his mid-twenties, he could easily pass for one of Coop's party puppets—smooth, polished, and pretty. Maybe he *is* Coop's guy today, and I'll have my lips wrapped around his breeding bits within the hour.

Keys tinkle as I lock the door. I stuff them into my pocket and totter down the stairs in five-inch heels. Why does Coop insist on these freaking stilettos? They make me walk like a strung-out junkie, which last time I checked, wasn't sexy.

In my grungy neighborhood, the black limo parked at the curb looks about as wrong as a zit on a Vogue cover model. No doubt sweet Mrs. Peterson, the resident snoop, is peeking out her front window, assuming I'm a high-class call girl. That'll make our next shared garbage-day encounter extra awkward. Something to look forward to.

The handsome driver opens the limo door, and I slide onto the leather bench seat trailing a cloud of perfume. I need a drink to steady my shaking limbs. As I reach for the bar fridge, his steely gray eyes narrow in the rear-vision mirror.

"Sorry, Miss. Mr. Martinez said the bar contents are off-limits today. Under no circumstance is alcohol to be imbibed."

I resist the urge to poke my tongue out at him.

Weird. Coop usually can't wait to push powders and pills at his functions, hoping for wild, outrageous behavior. But a few shots of amber courage are usually all I need to get me through the ordeal. I do what I have to, then get out fast.

Well. Except that one time with L. When he electrocuted me and I forgot all about Coop's suits. About where we were. We must've put on quite the show.

I rub my chest, remembering every detail of that first meeting. L's vulnerability, the way he shook, his eyes burning hot and intense.

Sure, I've suffered the occasional painful crush. I once obsessed for months over a hipster farmer who delivered herbs to the garden center, but that ended abruptly when I met his charming fiancé. *Callum* should've worn his engagement ring, instead of flirting like the star of Farmer Wants a Wife every single time he met me.

But I've never felt anything like the pain that comes with wanting L.

It's savage. Unrelenting. And despite how he feels—or *doesn't* feel—about me, grows stronger every day.

If he'd given me even a flicker of hope, any sign he could love me, I wouldn't be quivering in this car right now. Because I'm pretty sure L would be enough. I could give up the farm. Let the dream of it go. Make a new life. Build something imperfect but real with him.

But reality check: my life isn't a fairy tale or a schmaltzy love song. It's shaping up to be a tragedy. Like the opera my neighbor was listening to earlier.

I stare out the tinted windows at busy Saturday traffic as we crawl through the city, pretending I'm on my way to meet Jess at an art gallery for donuts, bad coffee, and inappropriate giggles. Anything but what's actually waiting for me.

After forty minutes, we've passed through town, the suburbs stretching out flat and bland on either side. When the houses start ballooning into obscene mansions, the driver pulls over on a tree-lined avenue and swivels in his seat to face me.

"From here on, I'm going to have to blindfold you."

"Sorry… what?"

"Mr. Martinez's instructions. The party's being held at a client's home. You've met before. But it's important you don't know where he lives."

My skin prickles, fear slicking my palms.

He smiles, all fake reassurance. "It'll be fine. Twenty minutes. Thirty max. I'll put some classical music on to help you relax. No need to worry, Miss."

Easy for him to say. He's not the one about to be blindfolded and delivered to a pack of perverts.

"You'll also need to leave your phone in the car when we arrive."

Oh. Fantastic. Love that for me. This is getting better and better.

As he gets out and crunches around to my side, I tilt my head back and stare at the leaves overhead. They're green and gold in the afternoon light. I wonder if this is the last beautiful thing I'll see. So natural. And pure.

"Relax, sweetheart. I won't hurt you," he says impatiently as he slips the mask over my eyes and tightens it.

Darkness closes in, and my legs start to shake.

"I'm sorry. Too nervous," I babble. "I'll try to pretend I'm getting a Lomi Lomi massage or something. Wouldn't want to make *you* uncomfortable with the situation."

Coffee breath hits my face as he laughs. The door slams.

"Remind me to ask for your number on the drive back," he says as the engine hums to life.

"Sure," I mutter. "As long as you remind me to tell you to stick your head up your ass when you do."

Vivaldi's violins swell, drowning out his chuckle as we roll back onto the road.

I think of my dad in the last months of his life, the lung cancer hollowing him out day by day. I think of L, the anger always simmering behind his eyes. I imagine dying and wonder if later tonight my body will end up in rough-sawn pieces scattered through a nearby forest.

Well. No turning back now.

Whatever happens, no matter how bad, I decide the last thing I'll think about will be L. His body pressed to mine. The way his features soften under gentle hands. How he looks when he laughs.

Then I stop myself. Any woman he sleeps with will probably see that same softness. That same smile. I'm not special. He told me so himself.

He's lived a brutal life—Coop's cronies, the streets, his stepfather—and somehow, despite it all, he's still more angel than devil.

Will I ever see that wicked smile again? Feel his hard body move with mine, every touch reverent, his whispered words the perfect mix of sweet and dirty?

Through the black cotton mask, sunlight flickers as we wind along quiet roads. This client must live in the middle of nowhere.

The music cuts out. The car slows. Stops. Then the engine idles.

"Give me your phone," the driver says, voice suddenly flat. "I should've taken it earlier. We're about to turn up the driveway. I need it. Now."

I take a breath, fumble in my coat pocket, and hold it out. "To kill the boredom, I took some photos of where I guessed your fat head was floating above your shoulders. Very artistic."

He snorts as he takes it, and I start my usual pre-Coop chant.

Think of the farm.

Think of the farm.

Think of the—shit.

"Can't we just keep driving?" I say with more bravado than I feel. "I hear Canada's nice this time of year."

Chapter 33

L

"It is so nice of you to join us, L," says the loser in the pinstripe suit. Mr. Graham is the name the scumbag goes by. "My associates and I were very pleased to hear that you would be in attendance today."

Thinning brown hair slicks back off his high forehead, and the pale eyes of a psychopath peer down his long, beaky nose. I'm not sure it's the effect he's going for, but the whole getup screams *creepy undertaker.*

I restrain myself from punching the smirk off his face and cross my arms. "Well, Cooper didn't give me much choice in the matter."

"Relax, L," says the malevolent party planner himself. "When you get a look at our mystery guest, you'll be very glad you made that decision."

I think he means I'll be very glad to pound my fist into his jaw.

Pinstripes gestures at me. "Why don't you get undressed?"

"Why don't *you*?" I mean it sarcastically, but the two weasels lounging on the dark leather couches get excited, ripping off their designer suit jackets. They're the same dudes who were at the party the day Edie and I met. A blast of adrenaline hits me at the memory—*shit yes* and *fuck no* warring inside me, turning me on and, at the same time, making me want to rip someone's head off.

The boss-creep scans my body from head to toe, instantly dousing my hell-yes vibes. "Come, L. Let us admire you while we wait for our female entertainer to arrive. Get us in the mood."

There's no doubt I'm spoiling the elegance. My ripped jeans, band T-shirt, and motorcycle boots don't exactly match the decor. What can I say? Classy floral patterns just aren't my scene.

These guys think they're so fucking smart. But I'm a step ahead. I already know who's coming and I've guessed exactly what they want. They're hoping for a repeat performance of the *Edie Does Lightning* show.

Fuck that.

I plan to talk her out of it. No way I'm sharing her with these sick fucks. Not that she's mine to share, or not share, but still. I won't touch her again in front of them. I refuse to let them see what that girl does to me. The gravity of it.

Graham starts humming a show tune. Something old-timey, something strip-clubby.

What a smartass.

Still, it manages to fire me up, just not in the way he was hoping. "Fuck you," I growl.

Today, they can forget all about Lightning Boy. He's gone, and all that remains is burning wrath. I'm going to use my hatred to melt his heart, then pull him limb from fucking limb. How the fuck dare he think he can mess with Edie again.

"I might just let you do that today, L." He rubs his pointy chin. "Because, honestly, no one fucks like you."

Yeah, yeah. I've heard it all before. Leaning against the curtains, I lash him with a withering glare. "Dream on, idiot."

A distant bang sounds, heels clack along the slate floor, and then there's Edie, standing in the doorway, looking beautiful. Eyes wide, she pushes a cascade of dark hair over her shoulder and stares at me. I force a slow smile and only just stop myself from yelling *surprise* like a complete jerk.

"L! What are you doing here? I didn't think... Coop said it was someone else today." She sets her puffer jacket on a wooden sideboard near the door. I flick a glance at the clowns. Unbelievable. They're already getting cozy on the couches, hands drifting toward their groins.

My fists clench as I turn back to Edie and take her in. She's wearing another one of those red corset things, the same kind of outfit she had on the day I met her. The day she first touched me. Gave me my first proper kiss. My first everything good.

Looking like the sweetest, sexiest hooker alive, she frowns and shakes her head at Coop. He snickers.

"Relax, lovely girl. You're not wrong. As I told you, you've been paired with someone else. Mr. Graham here has paid for the pleasure of your company this afternoon. He's going to have you. L is only a spectator. Here to spice up the atmosphere." His smile sharpens. "But if we get bored with you, we might just fuck him too. We'll see what happens."

He grins at the guys sprawled on the couches, sipping wine from glasses the size of fishbowls like it's lunchtime at a law firm.

"Normally, he won't let us touch him," Coop says to Edie. "But with you here as our bargaining chip, who knows what we can persuade him to do."

I choke on my saliva, and for five whole seconds, I can't manage to draw a full breath in.

"Usually he just fucks one of us and he's all hands-off-the-goods, no touching. Like he's a museum piece. But we don't mind. It's always worth it, watching him make a grown man cry. Quite a spectacle. Would you like to see that today, Eden?"

It takes a moment for the garbage spilling from his mouth to compute. The words spin, refuse to land, and then snap into place. When I finally understand what they want to do to her, and to me in front of her, I feel gutted. Like my insides have blown apart and my entrails are spilling across the floor.

They want to put their hands on me like that monster did back in the white room. In my bedroom. Drag me back into a place furnished with nightmares... and force Edie to watch. To finally see how weak I am.

Over my dead body.

In five strides, my fingers are twisted into Coop's sports jacket, shaking him like a doll. "You lay a hand on her and you're dead. All of you."

His laugh is unhinged. He's loving this. "Oh, Lightning, calm down. Jesus. Be sensible." He shrugs out of my grip, ambles to the bar, and pours himself a drink like this is a business deal gone slightly sour.

"Now listen very carefully." He sips the rust-colored liquid. "If things don't play out the way we want, I make the calls I should've made a long time ago. And you get carted off in handcuffs to rot in a cell for the rest of your miserable life."

"I don't give a fuck. Do your worst. But you are not touching her."

Grinning, he nods at Mr. Graham. The man's long fingers go to the zip of his pinstriped pants.

Edie drops her gaze to the floor.

I stare at her.

This is not happening.

No fucking way.

"Get to work, Edie. Make it nice and slow. I want you to take your time and show L just how much you enjoy sucking cock. Any cock."

The scrawny dick jerks, rising high, giving two eager twitches. Edie sinks to her knees in slow motion right in front of the damn thing.

This is a horror show.

With my fists clenched, I step forward. "Stop."

Her eyes flick to mine, then slide away.

"I don't care what Coop does to me," I say. "It doesn't matter. You don't have to do this. Let's just leave. Right now."

Coop lets out that wacko laugh again. "You're right. You don't matter, L. And she doesn't give two shits about the mess you're in either. But you *do* care about the farm, Eden, don't you?"

She nods without looking at him.

What? Fuck the farm. Fuck everything. The only thing that matters is keeping her safe.

I won't let them use her just to get at me. And I don't know what will happen if they touch me, if they force me to submit. The last time someone did that, it ended in blood. And I swore it would never happen again.

Never.

Cold sweat breaks over my skin as my skull tightens around my brain. I can't think through the pain. Can't form a plan.

Silence fills the room while everyone but Edie watches me pace. Cooper smirks. My shirt sticks to my back as I try to think my way out of this nightmare.

Fuck.

There's only one option. I see no other way.

I stop in front of Edie, shifting from foot to foot, my boots scraping the slate. "Don't do it. Please. Just listen to me."

The room goes still.

"Years ago, I swore I'd never beg for anything again. But I'm begging now." My voice cracks and I don't even try to stop it. "I'll rip my heart out for you if that's what it takes. Right now. Just say the word."

Coop sucks in a sharp breath.

"Why do you care what I do, anyway?" she asks, eyes locked on the guy's hairy thigh. "If I do this, I get my dad's farm back sooner. I gain everything. You lose nothing."

"No." I shake my head. "You don't understand. Every inch you move closer to him kills me. Destroys everything good. Every scrap of happiness. Snuffs out the light you showed me and—" I stop, hearing how bad this sounds.

One of the fucktards snickers.

I don't back down. I lean into it, because the terrifying thing is that I mean every word. "Forget what I said in my apartment and on the beach. I'm asking you to give *us* a chance, Edie. I need this... what we can be together. I need *you*."

Coop unbuttons his cuffs, gray stubble catching the light. "Well, I'll be fucked." He rubs his chest, looking shellshocked. "I had no idea you were into girls, L. No idea at all. So what's with the sudden interest? You like that it's easier to hurt her?"

"Fuck off," I snarl.

"No, I'm serious." He tilts his head. "After all these years, how did I not know you swing both ways?"

"I only swing one way, fuckwit."

He considers that.

"Nah. Not possible." He snorts. "So what's so special about pussy, anyway?"

My blood roars. I can already hear the sound my fist will make when it hits bone. His cheek or nose, either works. I keep my face blank.

"I'm curious," he says lightly. "Tell me what it's like, and I might let her walk. Might even still pay her."

One of the assholes coughs from the couch, growing impatient.

Five seconds tick by, my heart slamming against my ribs. He's lying. I know that. But what if he isn't? What if there's even a sliver of a chance I can get her out of here by playing his pathetic game?

Of course it's worth it.

Anything is worth it if it keeps them from touching her.

"Okay," I say. "What do you want to know?"

Chapter 34

L

Sleaze oozes from his smile. "I don't believe for one second your dick only bends one way. So tell me the truth. I'll know if you're lying. Look at me and tell me if it was life or death, which would you choose?"

What a stupid question. I blow out a breath and tilt my chin toward Edie.

Coop's brows lifts. "Pussy? Seriously?"

"It's all I like," I say flatly. "All I've ever wanted."

"Why?" He says it like desire is a choice and I've made the wrong one.

I shrug.

"Don't be stingy with the details. What's so good about it? Give me something more."

I feel Edie's eyes on me and drop my gaze to the floor. This isn't embarrassing. No, not at all. Fuck. I look back at her. She looks scared and somehow hopeful. So I decide to stick to the truth.

Face red, Coop snaps, "What does it feel like, L? Use words. I'm not asking for a dissertation."

I chew my lip. I let my shoulders loosen. Let myself remember. I close my eyes for half a second, then look straight at Edie.

"With a girl," I say quietly. "It feels right. No effort needed, just a perfect connection. Better than anything."

"And?" Coop pushes.

"And it feels like home."

With each word I uttered, his eyebrows had climbed higher. The other pricks stare at me. No one speaks.

Edie stares too.

I step forward and grab her arm. "Come on," I say, tugging her up. "Let's get out of here."

"Hold up a moment, L." The wheedling voice of Mr. Graham turns my blood to ice. "Cooper here may be willing to cancel our little show, but I'm the bank, and I'm thinking more along the lines of no play no pay." He lifts Edie's chin. "What do you think, darling? Do you want to leave?"

I smack his hand away, and he laughs.

Scarlet covers Edie's cheeks, but she doesn't look at him. Or me.

"Holy fuck, Edie. Come on! This is screwed six ways to forever. Get off the floor."

"Oh, grow up, L," she says. "Why should you care what I do?"

My gut burns, and my hands shake.

"So you enjoy fucking girls," she says. "Big deal! If there's an actual serious reason this matters to you, then you'd better tell me quickly."

The air crackles with tension. Then out of nowhere, I have a head-on collision with the truth. The truth about what I feel. I hear words in my head, and out of habit, I resist them, as if I'm having some strange stress response that's causing delusions of sappy feelings.

I try to convince myself they can't be true, but the words keep electrifying me, and I realize I'm going to have to say them out loud. In front of these turkeys. Right now.

Okay, fine. I've lived through worse. I can do this. I grit my teeth and start talking.

"You can't do it because I'm in love with you." They all gasp like they're watching a dramatic off-Broadway play. Even Edie does. "I'm not gonna stand here and watch these freaks touch what's mine. I won't let them hurt you."

I make a mistake and glance at Coop's face. It's both triumphant and full of disgust. "Well fucking done, L. As usual, you exceed expectations. I could hardly believe my ears, hearing such touching words from so foul a mouth." He points at Graham whose pasty dick is still reared up in front of my girl's face, aimed at her scarlet lips.

Those lips are mine.

"Now, Eden, don't let the words of a fool put you off," Coop says. "Time to get back to business and get sucking."

She wraps a shaking hand around Graham's shaft. A bolt of electricity zaps through me, buzzing inside my head so loudly I'm sure everyone in the room can hear it. I roar and lunge for the suit.

"Leon," Coop yells.

The room blurs around me. Leon? Did he call me *Leon*?

Metal presses against my temple. A fucking gun.

"Stand there and watch this blowjob or I'll put a bullet through your skulls. She's first. Understand?"

Silent, I shake like a hurricane I'm so filled with fury.

"Got it?" he screeches in his arresting-cop's voice. "Answer me or I'll blow your fucking brains out, and then you'll have to spend an eternity in hell wondering what we did to her."

"Yes, you piece of shit. I fucking hear you."

He whacks my forehead with the gun. Something wet runs down my face. Fucking hell, please... not blood.

"Now, Cooper, we'd prefer if things didn't get messy here," weedy dick says. "Think of the cleaning bill. We just want to enjoy a bit of sport and watch L squirm. Can you do that for us, darling girl? Make him writhe in agony?" He puts his stinking paw on her chin again, and I can't take it. If it wasn't for the pistol kissing my temple, he'd be the one bleeding right now. "I promise it will be fun, more so if your boyfriend is the jealous kind. And I believe L falls into that category."

She keeps her eyes lowered while my brain trips out over the word boyfriend... He called me her *boyfriend*. Fuck!

"Look at his face," says the pig-snout from the couch, snorting and pointing at me.

That snaps me out of my daze.

"Edie," I whisper. "Don't worry about the farm. We'll get it back one day. Or I can buy you another one. Five fucking farms if you want. Come on, take my hand, and we'll get out of here. We can just walk out. I want to start over. So badly. But I need you if I'm going to do that. I love you. And if you care about me even a little bit, then let me take you somewhere good where I can tell you properly."

No one moves. No one breathes. My skin prickles, going cold then hot.

Edie's head lifts, and I see it in her eyes, a single tear tracking down her cheek. She still cares. Loves me even. Whatever you want to call it. I don't give a fuck what the label is as long as she keeps looking at me like that.

She wants out too. Thank Christ.

She lurches to her feet.

Coop's arm snaps up, the gun aimed at her chest—and I move faster than I've ever moved before.

My knee drives into his balls. I grip his wrist and twist, spinning the barrel and wrenching it away. I flip him onto the ground and blast lead into his shoulder without thinking. I just do it.

The fuckwits start yelling. I yell back as Coop howls.

Look at that. He's the one writhing on the floor in agony. Not me.

Edie's gone paper-white, shaking like she's coming apart.

"You shitheads don't even blink," I snarl, swinging the gun between them. They freeze. Go quiet. "Edie. We're leaving."

She doesn't move. Just stares at the blood spreading across the tiles.

I follow her gaze.

Big mistake.

Black blood. Dark crimson. Long hair. Liquid dripping through a doorway crack. Guts slicking a bedroom floor. That bed. That smell. A sound tears out of me, raw and ugly, then it snaps me back to the present.

I wrench my eyes away. I'm not sixteen anymore, and Coop's still breathing. What the fuck are we doing?

"Edie," I snap. "Move. Now. We won't get another chance."

She's locked in place. Keeping the gun trained on the room, I grab her arm, haul her with me, snatch her coat from the sideboard, back us into the hall. And then we run.

Out the door. Down the drive.

By the time we reach the limousine, she's sobbing.

"Out," I bark at the pretty-boy driver, flashing the gun.

I shove Edie into the passenger seat. The guy bolts. While he disappears around the mansion, I kiss her forehead and tug her coat around her shoulders.

"It'll be okay," I say, again and again. Trying to sell it.

I swing around the front of the car so she can see me, throw myself behind the wheel.

"It's okay. It's okay. It's okay," I chant.

The engine roars. Gravel sprays. We tear down the driveway toward freedom. Or the way I'm driving, a fiery crash.

My hands shake on the wheel, my eyes flicking to Edie as she curls in on herself, crying.

"It'll be okay," I mutter. Christ, I need a new line.

"He'll kill us, L," she whispers. "Coop will kill us."

"He won't." I swerve to miss a fox darting across the road. "I won't let him touch you. Breathe, Edie. I need you here with me. I need your help."

She drags in a shaky breath and looks at me, wide moss-green eyes waiting.

"Do you know where your passport is?"

She nods.

"Good. Find your phone. Call Nico and get him to grab it and meet us at the airport. Tell him to move fast. Then call Angelo. Same deal for me. He's home gaming. This will work. Can you do that?"

"Yes," she says. "But where will we go? Coop will—"

"Somewhere great. Don't worry. When you're done, start searching for places we don't need visas to visit."

Another nod.

"Now, Edie. Please."

"Wait..." she says, fumbling in the glove box and pulling out her phone.

I grip the wheel hard enough to crack knuckles. "For what?"

The gravel gives way to bitumen. Trees thinning. Time escaping.

"Did you mean what you said back there?" she asks. "About how you feel?"

"That I love you?" I say without hesitation. "Yeah. Truest thing I've ever said. Now make the calls."

"But it's only been three weeks since we met."

"And your point is?"

"That's nothing! You've been confusing me the whole time, constantly switching between hot and cold. And now we're running away together."

"Maybe it hasn't been long. But it's still true."

She studies me, then sighs. "I need to hear more detail on that later."

"Deal," I say. "Now make the fucking calls."

She gives me a shaky smile, then makes frantic phone calls to Nico and Angelo. When she's done, she taps at her phone like a possessed woman. Five minutes later she looks up, dimples flashing.

"Any Greek islands you like in particular?"

"Hell yes. Call Angelo back. Get him to book a flight to Athens. Now. I know the perfect place. I spent a week there after a shoot last year. The guy who runs the foreshore taverna is cool. It's a tiny island near Naxos with good food and nothing to do but swim, eat, and sleep."

I don't mention fuck.

But she'll find that out soon enough.

Chapter 35

L

"We've been here a week now," Edie purrs, disappearing behind the arch that separates the living area from the bedroom.

No matter where you stand in the villa, you can see the bed, even from the patio overlooking the glittering Aegean. At least seven thousand times a day, my gaze slides from the view to that bed, my brain busy plotting how to get Edie back into it.

Sunlight spills across the stone floor. I circle a whitewashed column and kiss the back of her neck. She yelps. I prefer her hair down, shiny gold cascading over her skin, but messy buns do have their advantages.

"Yeah," I murmur. "Heaven, right?"

She spins, laughing, hand lifting, probably to swat me, so I duck behind the sheer curtain dividing the bedroom from the kitchenette.

"Sure, L. It's stunning." She glides past, drags her palm over my face, presses the gauze into my skin. Her fingers skim my bare chest. "Blissful, in fact."

Donousa is a perfect hiding place for lovers—small, remote, and rugged. The days are all warm water and blue sky. Nights are pure heat and Edie.

I ditch the curtain as she backs against the wall by the porch, arms stretched overhead against the crumbling plaster. Dust drifts down. I crowd in, forearms bracketing her face.

"You're trapped," I whisper, smiling too wide to kiss her properly. I try anyway.

"Wait. I need to be honest with you, L. I'm not one hundred percent happy."

What?

"Something's missing." She's smiling, so it can't be terrible. She slides her fingers through my damp hair.

"I've been waiting," she says softly. "And waiting."

I frown. "For what?"

She tilts her head. "Remember the day we left that place? Coop's party. You said some things. Made me think stuff." Her eyes hold mine. "It's time you tell me if they were true. Or if you were just saying whatever it took to get me out of there."

My skin prickling, I swallow. I'd hoped she'd forgotten and wouldn't make me talk about my feelings again. It's really not my forte.

"I've been patient, and I haven't brought it up. Not once. I've been waiting and hoping. But you'd prefer to avoid this conversation forever, wouldn't you?"

If we're thinking about the same thing, then yeah, she's right. I would.

I tuck strands of hair behind her ears. "Well, come on. Spit it out. What do you wanna know?"

"Do you love me, L?"

I breathe deeply through my nose, trying in vain to steady my heartbeat. I can do this. I can. Because it's true. "Yeah. More than anything."

She bites her lip. Her hand cradles my cheek as her eyes plead for me to go further, say the words that terrify me. I can do that, too.

"I really do love you, Edie. It seems crazy because it's only been weeks but, fuck, you've changed everything. I'm nothing anymore without you. I had no idea I could feel like this. I didn't think..." Shit. Heat burns my eyes, and I stare at the purple polish on her toes.

Lifting my chin, she says, "Hey, that makes me so happy. I feel the same way. I love you, too, L. So much."

Warmth spreads through my veins. Blissful happiness.

Pulling my head down, she presses her curves against me. I moan into her mouth and nudge my hips closer.

When I nip her lip between flicks of my tongue, she breaks away. "Ready to go again? That'll be the third time today, and it's only just past lunchtime."

Breathing like a dying man, I grasp the hem of her dress, and she wriggles helpfully so I can inch it over her body in an agonizing, slow reveal.

"There's nothing better than this," I say, lifting her into my arms and heading for the bed. "You know, if I didn't need to eat or drink, this would be all I'd do."

"It pretty much *is* all you do," she says.

I drop her onto the white bedcovers. She laughs, her whole body tensing as she waits for me to pounce. But I don't. While I soak in the incredible sight of her in the black lace bra and panties, I slowly push my jeans to the floor and kick them away. She bites her lip as she watches.

Kneeling next to her, I ease the bra straps down her arms, pull the material low, and bring her tits together so my mouth can give equal attention to both nipples. The sound her nails make as her fingers claw the sheets catches my attention, but not for long.

I plan to drive her crazy, but to do that, I need tools. I sit back.

"Where are you going?" she asks as I lean toward the nightstand.

I laugh and grab a handful of wild chamomile flowers from a glass vase. "Nowhere."

Her brow creases at the flowers I'm holding across my thigh. "What are you going to do with them?"

I smile and drop the bunch on the pillow. "So many questions." The green stems look bright resting near the honeyed tones of her shoulder.

"Now what are you doing? Hoping there's a copy of the Kama Sutra in there?" she says as I creak the drawer open.

I glance over my shoulder. "No, I've got my own ideas. I'm just getting this." I thrust a black tube toward her.

Coming up onto her elbows, she quirks an eyebrow at the lipstick I'm waving around.

"Down you go," I say, pushing her backward. "Now you'd better stay still or you'll ruin my artwork."

I lean beside her and click the lid off the lipstick. It's a rich, dark-red color.

She squirms as I write slowly over the swell of her left breast. When she tries to sit up, I say, "Be good and do what you're told," pushing her down again. I start on the silky skin around her right nipple.

As I rest back on my heels and inspect my work, she gazes at the words scrawled over her heart, squinting to decipher them. "Leon... loves Eden. Aw. That's so sweet." Then she tries to read the letters circling her nipple. "Mm...."

"Mine," I say, a little too proudly.

Sitting up cross-legged, she says, "Give that here," and snatches the lipstick from my fingers. With one hand wrapped around my throat, she draws a gigantic love heart over my chest.

"Nice," I say, grinning down at it. "Now come here and sit on my lap."

She shakes her head. "I'm not finished."

Aimed at my lips, the black tube zooms closer.

I inch backward. "No way."

She laughs. "Don't be a coward. I promise it won't hurt. Now go like this," she says, making a theme park laughing-clown face with her mouth.

Sucking my lips together to hide them away, I shake my head. "No."

"Do it, L."

The pressure of her fingers increases around my throat. I make the stupid lip-face, and she gets to work.

"Now do this." This time, she smacks her lips together.

Without complaint, I follow her instructions. Probably because I'm distracted by the sight of her rouged-up nipples.

She rolls the stuff over my lips again, then with her palms covering her mouth, she sits back and stares at me. "That's not fair. You should see what that color does to your eyes."

I check out her lace-covered ass as she races to the bathroom and brings back the shaving mirror. Thrusting it at me, she says, "See? So, so pretty."

First, I smile because I don't have my usual freak-out at being forced to look at my reflection, then I scowl down at myself. In my opinion, messy hair, stubble, and tattoos don't go with that particular shade of red. "I look ridiculous," I say.

She climbs into my lap, and there goes my scowl.

"So ridiculously hot. Now give me those luscious lips of yours, L."

"You can't kiss me while I've got that shit on." I rip my pouting lips away.

"I can."

"You'll get it all over you."

"Yep." She nods cheerfully, and then sucks and bites my lips, her tongue pressing between them.

Sighing hard, I open up for her and angle my head to deepen the kiss. Impatient bastard, my cock jumps, and I pull back and drag in a quick breath.

Red blotches cover her mouth and her chin. The bra is still fastened around her ribs, and the material hangs down, leaving her gorgeous tits exposed. My gaze trails over the markings I made, lingering on the word *mine*, and my dick throbs harder.

She grins wickedly, plants her palm over the love heart she's drawn on my chest, and drags her hand along my skin, smudging the lipstick—down, down, down.

I hold my breath.

Red smears over my ribs, my stomach, then lower. "Fuck."

Kneeling over my lap, she pulls her panties to one side. "My thoughts exactly."

Gently, I tease in slow motion through her wetness. It never fails to get her panting. When I circle over her clit, she shudders, her hot moans filling the room.

"I can't wait, L."

That makes two of us.

One hand pressing my stomach, she takes a firm grip and slides the head of my cock through her folds. It's too slow. And infuriatingly good. Now my thighs are shaking, my hips moving beyond my control.

"Shh," she says against my lips.

Did I say something?

And then she's lowering her wet heat onto me and any chance of making sense disappears through the gauze curtains and out over the sea. Groaning and panting like a wild animal is all I'm capable of.

Seven times she glides up and then sinks down. I counted. It's the only way to stop myself from erupting like a volcano. The sight of her body, my dick plunging into her, it's too much. If I'm going to last, I need to take control.

On her next glide up, I lift her off me.

"What are you doing?"

"You'll see," I say as I flip her over. I grin at her frown. "Now I've got you where I want you. Pinned tight."

"Like having me at your mercy, do you?"

"I like you any old way. You can hang upside down from an olive tree branch if you want and I'll find a way to make it work." Dragging her knee up high, I push into her heat, loving the sound, the wet, juicy feel. The smell—tangy and musky.

She braces herself, probably thinking I'll pound into her. But that's not where I'm going with this at all. I mean to go slow and make us both sweat.

With my hand fisted in her hair, I hold her head exactly where I want it and kiss her deeply, sucking on her tongue while I roll my hips at a leisurely pace. When she digs her nails into my ass, pushing and pulling and urging me to go faster, I cup her breast, pinching her nipple hard, and fuck her more slowly.

I tilt her hips up and press my face against her hair, huffing hot breaths in her ear. My hands shake harder as her moans get louder.

"Please, L."

My pace falters at the sound of her broken voice.

"L..."

"What?" I pant out.

"Please..."

Our noses touch, her eyes burning into mine. "Please *what*, Edie?"

She gasps and fights against my grip. The one that keeps her hips locked still.

Just once I slam into her hard and then freeze. "Say it."

She smacks my shoulder, struggling against my hold. "I can't take it anymore. I need to come."

"What's stopping you?" I ask, wheezing like I've just gone ten rounds in a cage fight.

"Oh, you Schwein. *You're* stopping me. And on purpose too!"

I shake with laughter. "I didn't know you spoke German."

She slaps me again, and I huff out another laugh. I'm stalling so I can stay in the game. No way I'm ready for it to end yet.

I nip her bottom lip. "Just tell me what you want, Edie, and I'll do it. Simple."

Chapter 36

L

Five beats of silence pass.

Wearing a grimace, her fingers wrap around my throat and squeeze a little.

I give her a tiny pump and a grin. "Hey, I like that. Keep going."

She makes a frustrated sound and shakes me by the neck. "Listen up. I'd like you to fuck me hard and fast. Right now, please."

"Because you used your manners, sure, no problem," I say, taking hold of the iron headboard and shifting into a better position. "Why didn't you speak up earlier?" The smile I give her feels lopsided, unhinged. "Hold on tight."

The bed clunks into the wall as I pound into her perfect body.

"L," she breathes in a throaty whisper.

"Man, please, don't say it like that. You're gonna make me blow." I'm about to burst into a trillion tiny pieces, like stardust, snowflakes, ash. Don't do it. Not yet. Not yet.

And then Edie cries out.

It's so loud I wouldn't be surprised if the neighbors up the hill came running. The whole island feels like it's shaking as my body spasms hard and I come inside her.

"Hell," I moan as I collapse onto her.

She gives me a quick kiss. "I'm about to die of thirst. I need a drink."

The bed squeaks as I push off it. "Don't move. I'll get water and clean-up stuff."

The bathroom is out on the patio. A circular stone room with not much in it other than a showerhead, a toilet, a long bench, and a window that has no glass and looks straight out to sea. The view is spectacular, but it will be unbearably cold in winter. I wonder if we'll still be here then.

In the oval mirror, I'm a mess. Disheveled hair, lipstick-smeared skin, and my eyes are weirdly bright. So, this is what happiness looks like. I'm still getting used to the idea that I might deserve it. Here in Greece, it feels like I'm living someone else's perfect life.

After I take a piss, I grab wads of toilet paper, guzzle water from the kitchen faucet, and pour Edie a glass.

Gloriously naked, she sits up to drink. "Thanks." As she clunks the glass down on the nightstand, her gaze lands on the flowers tangled in the covers. "So, what was the point of the chamomile? Were you deciding between a pot of tea and sex when you grabbed them?" She uses the paper to wipe between her legs and then throws it in the trash bin beside the bed.

Tipping my chin at her, I say, "I got distracted by the lipstick and hypnotized by your body. Lay back. I'll show you what I was gonna do."

Wearing a grin, she shuffles down. I pluck petals and place them on her chest, her stomach, and over her mound.

She giggles and flinches. "That tickles!"

"Uh, huh." I take some stems and feather them over her skin. Her nipples pebble, and my dick takes notice.

Stilling my hand, she says, "Come here."

That sounds promising. I move down beside her, wrapping her tight in my arms, and she kisses me softly. I grip her hip and tug.

"Hey, wait a second. Before you get any bright ideas, do you feel like telling me a bit more about Coop?" she asks.

"Coop?" I scowl down at her. "What? Why? I don't want to talk about him. Not here."

She strokes my hair. "Here's as good a place as any. And now is a perfect time. For starters, I just want to hear how you met him. I want to know how you ended up living the way you did. Is it so bad that I'm interested in knowing everything about you?"

Yes. She has no fucking idea.

"Don't you trust me?"

I fling onto my back. "Of course I do. It's just..."

I stare at the flaky ceiling while she stares at me.

"Just what?" she presses.

"I'm a guy. You know how we roll. I'd rather forget about my past and repress the fuck out of it."

A dark eyebrow raises. Shit. I'll never hear the end of it unless I tell her.

I stare at the sky through the French doors. As much as I want to escape this conversation, deep down I know that stories need to be told. They're important. They make us who we are, and as a show of trust and love, I need to give her mine.

But where to fucking start?

Like always, I guess the beginning is a pretty good place. I heave the biggest sigh of my life, and then force the words out.

"I was eleven when my mom died in a car accident. A head-on. Instant death."

Her fingers stroke my chest, soothing and reassuring. "Oh, no." She dips her head and kisses my neck. "I'm so sorry, L. What was she like?"

I laugh. "French. As small as a bird. Always flitting around and never still. Her hair was dark, like yours, but she cut it real short. She loved me."

"What did she do for a living?"

"She was a dental nurse. But she studied drawing at art school. There were always sketches everywhere. Of me. My stepdad. Wait a second..." I get off the bed and find my wallet. "That's me... see?" I unfold my most precious possession. The drawing of me sitting by the creek, long hair almost touching my bare shoulders, a goofy grin directed at Mom. The day was sunny and warm. And I was happy.

Edie's eyes water over the creased bit of paper. "Oh, wow. She was so talented! How old were you when she drew this? You look like an angel."

"Ah, about ten I think." I crawl back next to her, lie down, and flop an arm over my eyes. I need to get the next bit over with quickly. "She came to America to be with my loser dad. He drank himself into oblivion when I was a baby. I can't even remember what he looked like or where he went. As sweet as my mother was, she had a taste for deadbeats. My stepdad was happy to take care of me when she died because he was pretty keen on me, but not in a fatherly way, so... the accident was a win-win situation for him."

"Oh, God. That's horrible, L. I had my suspicions it was him who abused you. I wish I'd been wrong because I can't imagine how terrifying it must have been for you stuck there with him, feeling like you had nowhere to go. No way out."

I swallow noisily. "Well, at least he held back on the hardcore stuff until I was fifteen. Nice of him. Sometimes he'd have a break for a while. You know like an alcoholic trying to stay on the wagon for a few months and be good. Then he'd fall off and it'd be every night. Telling me it was my fault I looked like I did. Coming on to him or some shit."

I close my eyes, and the voice is there. *Tell her why*, it says.

It was your fault, Leon. Yours.

Edie makes sounds of pity while I do my damnedest to push the past away. I can't look at her. I can only swallow, over and over.

An actual tear slides down my cheek. I had no idea I could produce those anymore. I haven't cried since I was sixteen. There was never any point.

You sniveling baby, he'd say. *Don't make those sounds. This is your fault.*

Don't even look at me. If you don't look at me with those eyes, it won't happen.

Fucking eat your dinner.

Eat.

But it did keep happening. Even when I kept my eyes on the ground. Even when I shaved my head and didn't eat and didn't wash.

"Hey, but it all turned out good. When I was sixteen, I blew his guts all over my bedroom floor with his shotgun. So that was a happy turn of events. Scared the shit out of me, but I was glad he was dead. The first cop on the scene was our mutual friend."

"Cooper?" she says.

I glance at her face. It's turned gray.

"That's what the flashbacks are—shooting your stepdad."

"Yeah. I'll never forget the stench. What he looked like. The blood and..."

"Shh," she says, drawing my head close and pressing her lips against my forehead. "And let me guess... Coop made everything worse?"

"Yeah. He didn't report the crime, just covered it all up. Blubbering idiot that I was, I told him why I'd done it. It must have given him ideas. He took me back to his city apartment. Let me live there. He waited nine months before he started messing with me, always threatening to send me to jail so I'd let him do whatever he wanted."

The skin on her cheeks is now a deep, violent burgundy.

"I got away when I was seventeen, vowing I'd never let that shit happen to me again. And I haven't since. Out on the street, I found I could get money, stay alive, because guys wanted to do stuff to me. But I never let anyone fuck me again. I fucked people if I had to, but only if I could hurt them. Mostly, I gave blowjobs. But I'd make damn sure to humiliate them, and I'd make them come so fast that it really couldn't have been much fun."

"*Lightning*," she says with disgust.

"Yep, quick as lightning, that was me."

"And then you got picked up by Ariana. I bet in your wildest dreams, you never imagined a modeling agent would save your life. I need to call her and thank her again."

"She saved me physically, but you're the one who got my soul out of hell."

She kisses me, and my insides melt.

"Remind me how Coop found you again."

"Through the modeling. He saw a billboard. And he's been blackmailing me ever since. I just wish it was only money he was after. But no, it's control that prick craves. His favorite pastime is watching me make those guys suffer, and even though I never do it as often as he wants me to, if he has his way, he'll never let me stop."

"You know he's in love with you, right?"

My gut churns.

"L," she says. "He's obsessed with you."

"Well, yeah. It's something like that, I guess."

Her muscles tense, dark eyebrows drawing together as she covers her mouth with her hand.

"What's wrong?"

"I think... I think I saw a photo of you in Coop's wallet once. Years ago. It must have been just before you got away from him the first time. I can't believe it. I'm sure it was you, sitting on his couch. You were laughing, but I'll never forget the look of pure hate on your face."

"Yeah. I know the photo. He's such a fucking creep, carrying it around like that. Makes me sick." I turn my head away. This would be the perfect time to mention that I saw her once before, too. On that rainy life-changing night four years ago when the sight of her blew my mind.

I don't know why I hesitate. Maybe it's shame that keeps my lips sealed. I'm embarrassed I didn't have the guts to speak to her that night, didn't try to track her down after it, and then fucked it all up when I finally met her.

"Shit, L. He's never going to give up looking for you."

"You're right. Like a bloodhound, he'll probably keep sniffing around for leads." I roll toward her, grip her face between my palms. In the bright light, her eyes shine more green than brown.

"Don't worry, Edie. I promise he won't find us. We just need to lay low for a few months while we work out where we want to settle. Then we can go anywhere. Do anything we want."

"Are you sure about that?"

I take a breath and force myself to keep my eyes on hers as I lie. "I'm sure."

"But isn't anything and anyone traceable these days?"

"Angelo used darknet contacts to book our tickets and to set up money transfers. It's all cool. Untraceable."

Kind of.

I don't know if that prick can find us. It's unlikely. I shouldn't promise her, but I can't help myself. I don't want her to worry, and if hell exists, I'll be heading there as soon as I die. Apparently, that's what happens to liars.

Chapter 37

EDEN

It's been four and a half weeks of bliss, and L was right. There's nothing to do here but hike, swim, eat, and laugh. Each perfect day rolls gently into the next.

And the highlights aren't just the times we spend in bed. Okay, if I'm being honest, mostly they are.

But I've never been this happy, even when my dad was alive. I'm so relaxed I barely think about the farm, let alone worry over it. All that matters is being with L. Loving him.

I marvel at him constantly. How someone who's lived such a bleak, painful life, who seems so hard and angry on the outside, can be sweeter than syrup inside.

Distant music drifts down the hillside across the tiny port where we're lounging in the afternoon sun, crisp notes plucked fast on Greek lutes pulling me from my thoughts.

"...so that's what Irena said to me this morning, Edie," L says. "She's pregnant. And she's pretty sure it's my baby."

I choke, spraying frappe across the checked tablecloth. "What?"

L smirks, stretching his chiseled torso away from the taverna's rickety table. "I knew you weren't listening."

"I daydreamed for *five seconds* and missed the thrilling tale of how you supposedly impregnated our elderly cleaning lady?"

"Well, you should pay more attention to me. Obviously," he says, then adds, "Hey, you're not going to eat those, are you?" His tanned arm darts out, stealing a handful of fries from my plate.

The taverna owner hovers nearby, wiping tables. "Help!" I yell for his benefit. "Thief!"

Christos's laugh booms as he waddles over. "Your mister is eating all your food again, Edie?"

I throw my napkin at L. "Yep, as usual."

Shamelessly, he shrugs. "For some reason, lunch always tastes better from your plate."

Christos clears the dishes from the next table, stacking them on his metal tray. "You need a man who feeds you, not steals from you. Maybe I'm a better choice. I have a restaurant, and I take good care of my woman. Edie, you will eat lots and be happy all your days."

"That sounds good." I laugh.

"Yeah, but not to me," L mutters, scowling.

"You're lucky I'm old and fat," Christos says, patting his stomach. "Fit, but fat. If I was a young Adonis, Leo, I'd steal your pretty girl away no problems."

Gulls squawk around L's bare feet. He ignores them, crossing his arms. "Very funny. And where's your wife again? Slaving in the kitchen?"

Christos cuffs L on the head with the menu. L laughs, reaching for his wallet.

"Don't worry. Pay tonight when you come for dinner. We'll have Panos for music, eat kavourma, drink raki, and dance until morning." Tray lifted high, Christos Zorba dances through the tables and disappears indoors.

His eyes on my lips, L leans close. "Let's go back for a siesta. And when I say siesta, I'm not talking about a nap."

"Better me than the cleaning lady," I tease. "Let's go."

I stand, gathering my sunglasses and straw beach bag.

We head back along the foreshore, wading in the shallows, dodging cartwheeling kids and splashing each other. Then we hike up the hill to the villa.

In the bedroom, I push open the turquoise shutters and stare at L's shirtless back. He's leaning on the patio railing, binoculars pressed against his face.

"Put those things down and get back in here."

Without turning, he waves a hand behind him. "Wait. I won't be long."

"Come on, Leo. I'm getting bored. I'll have to go play cards with French-Anna if you don't quit being a super-sleuth soon."

"The ferry's late. It's coming in right now. You know I need to see who gets off it."

Three times a week, he stands there, every muscle tense until the last passenger disembarks. I'd forgotten today is Thursday. Flopping onto the bed, I sigh and pick up my Kindle. He'll be out there for ages.

Nose buried in my book, earbuds blasting music, I get lost in Greek mythology. Dionysus, the god of fertility and wine, apparently lived here on Donousa. Figures. That's about all anyone ever does on this island, drink wine and make babies. No wonder L and I are constantly—

"Fuck! Get up, Edie. He's here."

I blink as L whirls around the bedroom, stuffing things into a backpack.

"Who's here?"

"Coop!"

My brain doesn't compute, and neither does my body. I just lie there, staring.

"Fuck, Edie, get up. Please. Pack some food."

This can't be happening. He's seeing things, hallucinating. It's just a paranoid delusion.

"Now!" L yells.

I tumble off the bed and run around the room like a headless chicken three times before he grabs my shoulders and stops me, shaking me gently. I think I might pee or vomit. Maybe screaming would help.

"Hey, look at me. Edie…" He enfolds me in his arms, warm and smelling impossibly good. "I won't let him hurt you." His lips brush my head, and then he's gone again, moving so fast he blurs at the edges.

"But where will we go? This is an island, a tiny one, and—"

"Here, take this." He shoves a small backpack into my hands and pushes me toward the kitchen. "Food," he says, then thrusts his hand under the mattress and draws out a handgun.

I stare, jaw hanging open. "When did you get that?"

"Never mind. Food!" he snaps.

After a startled jump, I scramble for the fridge and cupboards, tossing random items into the bag. A cucumber? Sure. Toilet paper? Why not. Something to drink. Check.

"Come on, Edie. Go, go, go!" L herds me out the back door like a drill sergeant with a hapless recruit.

We clamber onto the sunbaked motorbike. L hands me a helmet, and I dig my nails into his ribs, squeezing tight enough to make him groan.

"We'll head to the goat guy's hut up the mountain. Don't worry. I've thought this through a million times. I know what to do. We'll get there and wait."

That doesn't sound like much of a plan to me.

As the engine roars and we speed away, I wonder what exactly we're waiting for. I mean there will be us, Coop, and a gun. And nowhere to run. Every option for how this might end is terrifying.

Twenty minutes later, we hunker down in a tiny stone hut, perched on the dusty covers of an old camp bed. A wobbly table, a sink, and an ancient wood stove are the only other furniture.

The rear of the shack abuts the hillside, which makes it sound secure, but there are still two doors for an enemy to enter through. Our attention is fixed on the entrance that faces the sea, but it's the rear one I'm worried about. It leads to a mudroom and then outside.

Unwrapping his arm from my shoulders, L kisses my cheek. "Hey, it'll be all right. Pass me some of that water, will you? I'm dry as a flame."

I reach into my pack and withdraw a bottle of sweet rozaki.

His eyebrows knot. "What the fuck... I hope you brought something other than wine. There's no running water in here."

I twist the hem of my cotton dress. "I didn't exactly have time to think logically."

"Shit, Edie. I really don't need to get buzzed right now." He yanks the cork free and takes a long pull, then wipes his mouth and passes the bottle back before pushing off the bed and taking a position at the window.

With the gun shoved into the waistband of his ripped jeans, he looks like a sexy cowboy. One who might die in a shootout any minute. This is my worst nightmare come to life.

I join him, peering through the glassless windows. We're lucky it's summer, otherwise we'd be freezing. I tip the bottle up and drink.

"Give that here." Without looking at me, he takes it back and drinks again.

"Is that wise?"

"Turns out it's actually not bad. It's steadying me." He blows out a breath, holding up his shaking hand. "Don't worry. I've been ready for this prick since I was seventeen. If it's the last thing I do, I won't let him hurt you. I promise."

That *last thing I do* part is exactly the problem.

He grips my shoulders and moves me aside. "Get away from the window. He'll find us. It'll just take time. He knows how to ask the right questions to the locals. And I need to know you're out of sight and safe so I can think straight."

Safe. With a psycho ex-cop hunting us, that feels stupidly optimistic.

I huddle back onto the bed. "L… if this ends badly, I need you to know how much I love you. I wouldn't wish away a second of the time we've had. Not one. No matter what happens."

He turns, eyes soft. "I know. Me too. I didn't think I could feel like this about anyone. You're the love I was born to find, Edie. It was always you."

Those words make everything okay. Even if I die here today.

"How long have we got?"

"At best, until dusk. Three hours." He closes the shutters and comes toward me. "At worst, an hour."

He crawls onto the bed. "Plenty of time to fill. How about we make out for a bit?"

"No. Are you crazy?" I snort. "That's like asking me to dance while we're standing in front of a firing squad."

His nose scrapes along my jaw, then he presses his forehead to mine. "It'll take our minds off this mess we're in."

"I doubt that," I huff. "Anyway, it might be your last kiss ever!"

"Fuck." He rocks back. "Don't say that."

"But it's true." I tug him closer. "So maybe you're right. Come here."

The gun clatters onto the shelf above the bed as he curls beside me. His hands frame my face, and I kiss him until my chest tightens and my breath stutters. Honestly, if I were comatose, this man could still turn me on.

Nearly an hour slips by in slow touches and whispered promises meant to last a lifetime. Cicadas sing. Goat bells chime. His arousal presses against me, but he doesn't push it further. It's intense and restrained, like we're in a house with parents lurking downstairs, knowing any second they might bang on the door. Except parents don't usually want to shoot you.

Suddenly, L freezes.

"Listen."

A motor rumbles nearby, then cuts out.

He's on his feet instantly, gun in hand. "It's him. Parked downhill. He'll walk up."

"Oh my God. Will he have one of those?" I nod at the gun

"Yeah. A guy like him would have no trouble getting one anywhere. He has the contacts."

Fantastic.

I curl in on myself, teeth chattering. L gives me a devastating look, equal parts love and agony. "Turn the bed on its side. Get behind it."

I scramble, babbling. "Shit. Shit. Shit. What are you going to do? You're not going to shoot him are you? You can't just—"

"Edie. Quiet." His voice is deadly calm. "I don't know what's going to happen. But I'll do whatever it takes."

I hide behind the bed frame and try not to whimper.

We wait.

And wait.

"Maybe it wasn't him," I whisper.

The hut creaks.

Wood groans.

Then the back door scrapes open.

L swings around, gun raised.

Cooper fills the doorway, sweaty and smiling like a horror movie villain, with his gun aimed straight at me.

No one speaks. Our breathing saws through the air.

"Well, hello friends," Coop says mildly, his gaze devouring L. "It's been a while."

L's gun is trained on Coop's chest. Coop's is trained on mine.

I wonder who can shoot faster.

"Don't be stupid, L. I'll put a bullet in her the second I see your finger twitch. You might kill me, sure, but she'll be dead and you'll spend the rest of your life replaying the moment you failed her. If you want to get her out of this alive, you'll need to be smart."

Bravely, or more likely foolishly, L glances over Coop's shoulder, out the window. "Has hell frozen over? Nope. Doesn't look like it. Guess it hasn't been long enough since I last saw you, Coop. What about you, Edie? Think you could've gone a bit longer without seeing this dickhead?"

Coop's face darkens.

I swallow. "Yes. Definitely."

Coop laughs, but he doesn't sound amused. In a blink, he steps in and jams the gun beneath my chin. L inhales sharply.

"Careful, Lightning Boy. I wouldn't run my mouth if I were you. Want me to put a bullet straight down her throat?"

"Hey—no. Coop, look at me. Please."

He does. "Throw the gun over here."

L tosses it. Coop kicks it into the hallway without looking. How did this go so wrong so fast?

"What do you want?" L grinds out. "You want money?"

"I could say it's about money. Compensation for the deal with Graham you fucked beyond repair." He sneers. "But that'd be a lie."

Chest heaving like bellows, L waits. Cicadas continue to sing outside, the sound obscenely cheerful.

"Don't play dumb," Coop snaps. "You already know what I want."

"Nope. No idea."

"I want you," Coop says. "You, in exchange for her safety."

L shakes his head.

"If you come with me, do what I want from now until the end of time, I'll let her go." Coop jerks his chin at me. "She gets to live out her boring little life. Farm. Husband. Bratty kids. Maybe she thinks of you once in a while, maybe not. What do you say, Leon?"

"Don't call me that," L whispers, sounding so young. Then his voice hardens. "Lightning. That's all I ever was to you. Don't even think the name my mother gave me."

"Don't give me orders, Leon. Give me your answer. Then Eden here can go and find a brawny Greek fisherman to wipe away her tears."

L presses his lips together. Says nothing.

Seconds crawl past.

Then he grins.

His shoulders loosen, his pose casual as he scratches his chin. "Okay. Fair enough." He turns slightly, gazing at the blue sky. "Me for her. Fine. We can do that. But honestly? I'm disappointed. This is pretty boring. For a bad guy, you're kind of a letdown."

Coop scoffs.

"I mean," L continues, eyebrows lifting, "you love a gamble. Why not make this interesting? Let us run. Chase us. Sounds like the perfect game for you."

Coop lowers the gun from my face and aims it lazily at L. "You think I'm stupid? Crazy?"

Right now, I'm pretty sure L is the unhinged one.

"I'm serious. Give us a head start. Twenty minutes. Then come after us. If you catch us, I go with you, and she goes home. You can't lose."

"What's the point?" Coop says. "There's nowhere to go on this island."

"Exactly. It'll be funny, watching us run like rabbits."

Coop studies him, then laughs. "Unbelievable. You've always been an optimist." He tilts his head. "Fine. Run as fast as you can. Five minutes. Toss me the bike keys."

L pulls them from his pocket and drops them at Coop's feet.

Coop grabs my hair and shoves me into L. Then he flips the bed on its side and perches on it with a loud creak. "I'll sit right here, counting down and imagining how pathetic you're gonna look scurrying away like terrified rats. Now *go*."

L shoves me through the door, and we run like the devil is after us.

Because in five minutes, he most definitely will be.

Chapter 38

L

By my count, we've got three minutes before that prick comes after us, slobbering at our heels like a bloodhound with distemper.

"Is he going to kill us?" Edie screeches as I drag her along the stone path winding around the arid hillside.

"Pipe down. Do you want to get shot?"

She plants her feet, hands on her hips, eyes wild. "Yes, please!"

I scowl hard enough to break my face. This is not the time for jokes. "Move." I yank her arm and we stagger a few paces before I stop. She's too slow.

I crouch in front of her and then cup my hands behind me. "Get on. Now."

She jumps onto my back. I bounce her once to settle her weight, then take off, running like we're in a low-budget horror film.

"So what's the plan?" she asks, panting in my ear. "Cooper shoots me off your back and chains you up as his sex slave for the rest of your life?"

No, not the plan, but unfortunately the most likely outcome.

The sun dips lower, the light growing dull. Sweat burns my eyes, stinging like hell, but I don't slow down. Any second now, Coop will burst through the door of that hut and come tearing after us.

And then we're fucked.

"Listen, there's a ledge up ahead in the cliff face... in a part that's not so steep. It's got a kind of mini cave set into the wall. Theo showed it to me. He hangs out there while his goats climb around on the rock shelves and try to sex each other up."

Edie's arms wrap tighter around my neck. "No, please. Not a cave! We'll be like mussels stuck to rocks just waiting to be scraped off and cooked."

"At the moment, we're on forks about to be chewed to bits. Believe me, the cave will be better. He'll have to climb down to get to us."

"Oh, no. Just... no. Please, L. Don't make me go down there."

Too late. This is the spot. I skid to a halt.

Theo's marker, a metal spike surrounded by loose stones, pokes out by the lip of the cliff.

I dump Edie on the ground and pull her close. "Grab the spike, swing over, and slide down. It's easy."

I whip my head over my shoulder and see a vision from a nightmare. Behind us, a black-clad figure lopes up the hill. "He's coming, Edie. In a minute he'll be in range to shoot me. I can't get out of sight until you do first. So move it!"

Terror and rage pump my heart fast. I'm fucking furious. I want her to survive this more than any damn thing I've ever wanted.

"This is it," she says, staring into the distance like she's conversing with a ghost.

"What? Don't talk in riddles. Just move. Now!"

"Sam was right. My dad—he warned me... I should have run away from you, not run with you."

"You can complain about me all you want later. Right now, you just need to move!" I push her forward.

Tears stream down her cheeks as she lowers herself over the side, her hand shaking on the spike and her mouth lamenting all the way.

When I hurl myself after her, I hear a sharp yelp. Shit. What has she done? Rocks scrape my chest and stomach as I slither over them. Once gravity stops helping, I have to push myself over another lip of rock to make the final drop onto the near-flat ledge.

Edie is sprawled on the ground with a sneaker lying beside her. I crawl over to her. "What happened?"

"I sprained it when I landed. It really hurts."

"How did you manage to do that? It's hardly rock climbing." I press and prod her foot. "The bones feel okay. I don't think it's broken."

"Well, Doctor Leon, it hardly matters if it is. We're probably never gonna get off this cliff." Panic written all over her face, she takes in the meager comforts of our shelter.

An uneven slab of bone-colored rock stretches four meters wide and juts a further two meters toward the sea. To the left, the drop off isn't as steep, and there are a bunch of connecting shelves and ridges where Theo's goats usually play. Fuck knows how they get down here.

A cool breeze picks up, coming in with the dusk. The water below is turning a flat, dark indigo color.

Pushing her toward the cave behind us, I say, "Get in there. Stop fucking around."

Coop watched me go down the cliff. He knows exactly where we are, and I need her to be safe... well, relatively speaking.

He'll be here any moment.

She ducks her head into the musty space. "No way. It's the size of a coffin! I'm not going in there."

"You'll be able to sit up fine. Get moving."

She scuttles in like a crab.

With my body pressed flat against the rock and my heart trying to bash its way out of my chest, I wait.

And wait.

Gulls circle over the water, looking for their last feed before nighttime. The sun sinks lower, shades of orange and pink softening the sky behind the port of Stavros town.

Then a laugh saws above us, and Coop says in a low, guttural voice, "There you are, little rabbits."

It takes every bit of willpower I have and then some to stay silent.

A loud whimper echoes from the cave. *Edie.*

"I hear you down there. I saw you climb over, L, so no point cowering. Just come on up."

Like hell I will.

"You're the coward who likes to hurt anyone weaker than you, Martinez. Why don't you come down here and get me?"

"No... L... please," Edie begs.

Coop laughs again. "Oh, hello, Eden. I hope you're comfortable down there. If not, why don't you climb on up? You do that for me, and I promise I won't hurt him. Well, I won't if he does what he's told. It'll go easier on you both if he behaves himself."

"Stay there," I hiss in Edie's direction. "Hey, you're the one with the gun, Cooper. You've got nothing to be afraid of. I wonder if you can make me suck your minuscule dick with that hunk of metal pressed to my forehead. That sounds exactly like your kinda sick thrill. Am I right?"

Yep, I'm spot on. Because, immediately, I'm showered in dirt and stone. The guy couldn't resist a fucked-up sex opportunity if his life depended on it. And today it does.

I step out from the overhanging rock and watch him slide down the steep part of the cliff, his gun pointed at my head. My heart is throbbing so hard it feels like a bomb about to detonate.

His biceps flex as he pushes off for the free-fall section. A hulking shadow in the gray light, he drops down. Adrenaline shoots through me, and I leap as he lands, slamming him into the stone wall.

Now fury pumps the blood through my veins, and I feel bigger than a mountain and at the same time as small as a roach.

And scared. I'm so scared for Edie.

I need to split this bag of bile and guts open. Smash it and destroy it before it gets to my girl.

She screams as Coop and I tumble into a heap together. He smashes the gun butt into my temple, and I black out for a moment, then see stars. While I lie there reeling and wiping blood from my eyes, he stomps on my ribs. The white-hot pain of bones breaking sears through me.

I kick out and connect with his wrist. The gun skitters along the ledge beyond his reach. Here's my chance.

While I'm still on the ground, I swing over him, my fists pummeling his gut, his face. The pain of my ribs crunching together weakens my punches, but then I picture him touching Edie and rage boosts my strength. He struggles to get out from under the holy hell I rain down on him, landing a couple of blows to my head. They don't have much effect. Despite my broken ribs and my dizziness, I'm stronger. Angrier.

I use dirty MMA tactics, groin strikes and throat punches. He yells and curses. Apparently, I'm a gutter-whore. A fuckboy. Useless and worthless.

I've heard it all before.

Edie's screams get louder.

Coop pushes onto his knees. He's a tough old fucker. I lunge, propelling him backward.

"I'll fucking kill her, L," he says as I straddle him.

He's using her to distract me, and it works, too. "Shut up," I grunt as I look over my shoulder to check where she is. Big mistake. I cop an elbow right in my head wound. I rock backward from the force, and he puts everything he's got into the world's best shoulder tackle. I'm hurled sideways, my head smashing against stone.

Before I've even landed properly, I throw my fist out blindly and feel the satisfying crunch of bone. But like a Night of the Living Dead zombie, Coop refuses to stay down.

Chapter 39

L

Each desperate strike lands on my numb body like a wet thud. I barely feel it. I can do this all night long.

"Gun! Gun," I bellow in Edie's direction. She has no clue how to use it, but if we can get rid of the damn thing, she'll be safer.

She scrambles forward on her belly, yelling like a banshee as she reaches the gun, hefts it through the air and watches it sail over the precipice.

Thank fuck. I'm so relieved I could cry. Now I've just gotta knock this prick out. Here's my opportunity to finish him off—it's what I've waited six long years for, but all I can think about is Edie, getting her out of this alive. And how she wouldn't want to be with someone who killed to fulfill a vendetta.

So, with blood and possibly brain damage blurring my vision, I realize that my intention isn't to end Coop unless I have to. It's a surreal, life-changing moment.

Time warps slowly as I stagger to my feet and pull Coop up with me, wondering if it'll be a fight to the death regardless of what I want. Thankfully, he's out of condition, but I'm not. I'm used to suffering and have learnt how to just keep going, push through untold horror, no matter what.

And right now, if I must, I'm fully prepared to fight to the end. *My end.*

For her. For us. And for something it took me far too long to believe in… *love.*

So even with busted ribs and a pistol-whipped skull, I prepare to crush Coop with my last breath if it's the only way to keep him away from Edie.

This prick, his fists knotting my T‑shirt, his rotten breath panting over my face, embodies every horrible memory from my stepdad to every bastard who has ever used me. It won't be too hard to hurt him like he hurt me. Like they all did.

"L," Cooper wheedles, voice high and thin. He's struggling to breathe. He knows he's fucked.

I steer us toward the ledge where the ground drops away straight into the Aegean. He scrabbles uselessly, shoes skidding in the dirt.

I shake him close to the edge, knock his hands away, and crack my palm against his skull. "Give it up, you dumb fuck. You psychopaths never know when to stop. Let me knock you the fuck out. Then you can scuttle away and leave us alone forever."

He laughs and swings. "Never." I duck, and he misses. "I'll kill you, Leon, and then I'll ruin her life just to fuck with you!"

Red floods my vision. Rage is the only thing holding me upright. A sound claws up from my chest, a growl turning feral.

Coop freezes. "You gonna kill me, Lightning Boy? Add me to your body count?" He lands a punch on my busted ribs. "You're a murderer—"

"He's a trillion times a better man than you could ever hope to be," Edie screams.

Coop glances back at her, and I take my shot.

Crunch. "Leave us the fuck alone."

He fist collides with my temple. Stars explode. I grab him and shake him hard. "You can't win. I'm about to beat the shit out of you. How do you not see that? Stay fucking down."

Edie's sobs cut through the loud wheezing noise coming from Coop's chest. Our foreheads nearly touch as we stagger in a punch-drunk embrace.

"Leon," he gasps. "I saved you. You were nothing before you met me. I fed you, protected you. You liked everything I did to you. You know you did."

"I fucking *hated* it." Why do abusers always want a medal for the torture? The delusion would be impressive if it wasn't so sickening.

My fist smashes his nose. Bone cracks. He collapses near the edge of the cliff.

I try to haul him up by his collar, but he kicks my legs out and drags me down with him. My ribs crunch as I hit the ground.

Using his body to claw onto my knees, I seize his shirt, and with the last of my strength, I tug, shove, and kick.

I can't believe it when he rolls over the edge.

As I stagger upright, Edie rushes to me, wrapping her arm around my waist. We peer down. Coop hangs ten feet below, fingers jammed into rock seams, boots scraping air.

"Help me, L."

I can't see his eyes, but I bet they're bugging out with terror. His voice sounds exactly like mine did at seventeen, begging him to stop. Too stupid to realize he loved my fear. Thrived on it.

"Please," he whines. "Don't let me fall. Whatever you want…"

He's out of time. And I'm out of mercy. He only has seconds left to live.

Memories swarm through my head.

Ten. His hand on my throat. Me gagging on his whisky breath.

Nine. The sounds he made when he came.

Eight. His pathetic tears when I told him I'd rather scour my own skin off than have him touch me again.

Seven. That first party. The first groan of pain I caused that wasn't mine.

Six. The fire that burned inside me after. The sense of restored power. The fury and shame.

Five—

Edie's palm smooths over my back.

Coop screams as his hands give way and he falls, the sound carrying across the water toward the horizon, growing softer and softer.

Then silence.

I sag into Edie's arms. "Leo," she whispers, using the name no guy in a filthy restroom ever called me.

I break, sobbing into her hair, raw like I'm hacking up my soul.

It's over.

It's really over.

I haven't cried since my stepdad died. Now I can't fucking stop.

Somehow we're on the ground together. The rocks don't hurt. Nothing does. I grip her face. "Edie, I have to tell you... I saw you. That night—"

"It's okay," she murmurs.

"No. Listen. That night I got off the streets you were there. Outside that burger joint on Jackson, with Coop, shivering in a black dress. I was eighteen and broken, and you were the saddest, most beautiful thing I'd ever seen."

"That's not possible."

"I swear it's true. You were the first girl I ever let myself dream about. And when I saw you again at the suits' party, I couldn't believe it."

Now she's crying, too. "Why didn't you talk to me then? I could've helped you."

"Because of him." My vision darkens. "I felt unworthy, dirty. Didn't know what he might unleash on you. I hope that fucker burns in hell."

"He's gone," she says, pulling me close. "No one can hurt us ever again."

She kisses me, and I kiss her back like I'm drowning, shaking. Losing my mind. Losing control.

"Careful." She pulls back gently. "You're a little scary right now."

I try to smile in a way that says I'm fine but fail hopelessly.

She peers at the dark sky. "Can we get up that cliff tonight?"

"No. We'll leave at first light."

Pain finally crashes in, the numbness turning to agony.

"Are you okay?" she asks, feeling my face, my ribs.

"I'll live."

"We'll have to go to the police," she says softly. "You'll have to tell them everything. People from your past will remember, come forward, and verify your story. You won't be alone. If you do this, L, you'll be free."

"Or in prison forever."

But freedom... Even the word tastes so good on my tongue. I want it so bad. For both of us.

She curls against me, careful of my injuries, and I hold her like she's the only thing keeping me alive.

My eyes close, my breathing finally slowing.

I'm so lucky I found this girl—not once but twice.

Now I'll never let her go.

Chapter 40

EDEN

L doesn't spend the rest of his life in prison. If he had, we wouldn't be traipsing around Europe like the entire continent is our playground. From ancient Turkish ruins to the ridiculously clean streets of Vienna, the last four months have been idyllic—the best of my life. Even better than our time in Donousa because Coop is gone forever.

Yes, pushing Coop off a cliff meant the ghosts from L's past finally caught up with him. But some of those ghosts turned out to be friendly. Supportive. Even helpful. He hadn't known that people would demand retribution for a boy who'd lived through unspeakable horrors. They clamored for justice. And at last, Leon got it.

There was a trial and, for a while, our faces decorated newspapers and cluttered up social media feeds. L was a sensation, a beautiful, damaged boy saved, and our story a nightmare with a fairytale ending. People couldn't get enough of it.

When it was over, we bolted, desperate to be free.

We backpacked through lavender farms in Provence, perused Parisian galleries, immersed ourselves in the hustle of Rome, and traveled wherever the warm breeze blew us, nearly always choosing trains, buses, and small guesthouses over hire cars and five-star accommodation.

Today, we're in the forest on a hike, near the German town of Baden-Baden, and should be puffing up and down mountains, enjoying nature's beauty, while keeping fit.

Instead, the only place I'm trekking is along L's body as I push him against a fir tree and pant into his mouth. The smell of crushed pine leaves in the air around us is heavenly. But L's moans and kisses are even better.

Longing for relief, I grind against his thigh, my roughness making his denim jacket rasp against the bark.

"Hey, don't do that. I've got dendrophobia," he says biting my neck.

I laugh. "What does that mean?"

"It means I hate trees."

I press my nose to his. "No, you don't. You don't hate anything anymore, L."

He gives me a sexy smile. "You're right. I love everything, but you most of all, Edie."

A wild wind picks up, whipping hair over his face, his eyes gleaming brightly in the silvery light of the forest. A storm is on its way.

Thunder booms, the treetops flashing white. Bang goes a second crash. It's so close.

The sky splits open, rain splashing my upturned face.

L pulls me closer, his hands burrowing under my sweater and warming my skin. "If we don't want to get fried by lightning, we'd better get out of here."

Grinning, I squeeze his cheeks between my palms. This boy has been electrocuting me from the moment I first laid eyes on him, and I don't want him to ever stop.

My dad's words pulse like a faulty neon sign in my mind, his warning to run fast if my heart ever ached from loving someone too much.

As I finish kissing L, I think to myself, *if you can hear me, Sam, I'm so sorry. I know you warned me to go. You asked me to flee, but if I ever run anywhere again, I'll be holding this boy's hand tight and taking him with me. I hope you understand.*

Using his boot, L shoves away from the tree. "Come on, Edie." Turning around, he says. "Hop on quick. If we don't want to drown, we need to make a run for it."

Fine with me.

Pine needles crunching underfoot, I pace backward then accelerate forward, hurling myself through the air.

He grunts when I land on his back. "Do you trust me to get you down there safely? Because I'm gonna go fast."

With my arms around his neck, I bend forward and kiss his face. "Of course."

Then he takes off, bouncing me through the trees while the rain drenches us.

The afternoon air is chilly, the wind wild, and before long I'm wet through. But L's body is warm and solid beneath my own, and in the place where we're staying tonight, a toasty fire and steaming bowls of leftover soup await us. There's a down quilt and a massive bed we can snuggle into in a cozy room tucked high under the roof of a charming old house. I can't wait to get back there.

How I feel about Leo is frightening, but he's worth every erratic heartbeat that comes with the risk of losing him. I have faith in our love and most of all in him. That he's the one. The one I was meant to find.

When we're ready, we'll go home. Dad's lavender farm will still be waiting for us. We plan to transform it into a refuge for lost kids like L was. Like we both were, really.

It will be a haven. A safe place for damaged souls and broken hearts to learn forgiveness, renew belief in themselves, and most importantly, heal.

If my dad could see us now, I know he'd be proud. Happy that I ignored his warning.

Because Leon plus Edie equals home.

Forever.

Thank you for reading L and Eden's story. If you enjoyed it, you might like to check out Ivy and Nico's story, Tempting Ivy, and join them on a visit to L and Eden's farm!

Try my spicy fantasy romance duet, Courts of the Star Fae Realms, written under my pen name Juno Heart.

I love to write about broken golden-hearted guys and gals who, after much angst, find redemption together. When I'm not obsessing over damaged heroes, I'm listening to indie music, drinking nuclear strength coffee, or writing about arrogant fae princes and kings and their human fated mates.

Check out the Damaged Souls Golden Hearts series:

<u>Loving L</u> - An ex-street boy and the girl who won't give up on him.

<u>Tempting Ivy</u> - An older woman younger man romance. You'll join Nico and Ivy on a visit L and Eden's lavender farm!

<u>Saving South</u> - An angsty, hidden-pregnancy rock romance.

Read my spicy villain-gets-the-girl duet, King of Storms and Feathers and King of Fire and Flames, written under my pen name Juno Heart. Or the swoony grumpy-sunshine series Black Blood Fae.

Acknowledgments

Thank you so much for reading Loving L.

Many years ago, in my distant back-packing days, I visited the beautiful Greek island of Donousa, where L and Edie flee to. Back then, there were no cars or roads and the friendly residents had only recently gotten electricity in their homes.

I've taken liberties with the layout of the island and the timing of the ferry arrivals—the boats used to arrive at night!

Amy,

X

www.ingramcontent.com/pod-product-compliance
Lightning Source LLC
Chambersburg PA
CBHW021955130726
47903CB00014B/1417